WE WALKED THE SKY

WE WALKED THE SKY

LISA FIEDLER

RAZORBILL

RAZORBILL

An imprint of Penguin Random House LLC, New York

First published in the United States of America by Razorbill,
an imprint of Penguin Random House LLC, 2019

Visit us online at penguinrandomhouse.com

THE LIBRARY OF CONGRESS HAS CATALOGED THE HARDCOVER EDITION AS FOLLOWS:
Names: Fiedler, Lisa, author.
Title: We walked the sky / Lisa Fiedler.
Description: New York : Razorbill, 2019. | Summary: Seventeen-year-old Victoria escapes an abusive father by joining the VanDrexel Family Circus in 1965, and fifty years later her writings guide her granddaughter, sixteen-year-old Callie, in facing the uncharted waters of public high school.
Identifiers: LCCN 2018056330 | ISBN 9780451480804 (hardback)
Subjects: | CYAC: Circus—Fiction. | Aerialists—Fiction. | Change—Fiction. |
Family life—Fiction.
Classification: LCC PZ7.F457 We 2019 | DDC [Fic]—dc23
LC record available at https://lccn.loc.gov/2018056330

Paperback ISBN 9780451480828

Printed in the United States of America

1 3 5 7 9 10 8 6 4 2

Interior design by Corina Lupp
Text set in Garamond Premier Pro

To my new little cousins, Graham Hayes and Mae Mealey—
Welcome to the loudest, craziest, and most wonderful
circus in the world . . . our family!

"The noblest art is that of making others happy."

—*P. T. Barnum*

PROLOGUE

Massachusetts, 1965

SHE SHOULD HAVE NEVER asked to go.

It had been an innocent enough request, and there was always a chance things might have gone differently—because that was how he was. She always had just as much chance of being surprised as she did of being thrown halfway across the room. (All the way across when she was younger, but she was sixteen now and almost as tall as him.) Had it been last Thursday or next Tuesday, or if she'd been wearing yellow not blue, perhaps he would have simply smoothed the pages of his Sunday Globe *and huffed a brusque, "You may." But it was today and he was him, and his fists had a way of coming out of nowhere before she could even duck.*

She had discovered recently that a whimper of pain from her mother was a guaranteed trigger for his trademark unpredictable violence. He loathed the sound of weakness, hated that she was frail, as though somehow it reflected poorly on him—on Davis Winston Hastings—to have a sickly wife. Early on, she'd tried to suppress the noise of her misery, but things were worse now and she could no longer manage it; the malignant thing had become all that there was of her, nestled there between her ribs.

And although Catherine was smart enough to know better, she could never quite shake the feeling that he had somehow placed it there, that he had conjured the tumor just to be cruel, just to exert his unyielding authority over them. "I can make you sick, then punish you for not being well." Because he was the one in charge, make no mistake about

1

that. *He was the one with the name and the money and the manhood, and so he held their whole world in his eager fists.*

He made the rules and the rules were everything. Unwritten, unspoken, undeniably understood: remain at the dinner table until given permission to leave; earn excellent grades, but never appear smarter than the boys; appreciate what is given to you and ask for nothing more.

She should have never asked to go.

But sometimes the smack did not come; sometimes the insult went unspoken; sometimes her meals would not be withheld in the wake of some perceived misbehavior or shortcoming. On some days he could be utterly indifferent. Some days he'd return home from work, his trademark pocket square still folded flawlessly even after a long day at the office, acting as if he were surprised to find Catherine and Meredith there in his house—like two forgotten knickknacks, or things caught in a cobweb. He was never gentle, never kind, never good, but praise the Lord in heaven for indifference. Catherine's best days were the ones when he just ignored her.

Today, as it turned out, would not be one of those days.

"I was invited to stay at Emily Davenport's tonight," she said. "I was hoping I could—"

His hand had lashed toward her like lightning, his fingers wrapping around her long dark ponytail, yanking it hard. "You don't tell me what you're hoping for. You ask if I will allow it."

Swallowing the degradation, she quickly rephrased the question. "Please, Father, may I stay at Emily's house tonight?"

His answer was lost to the sound of a sudden commotion outside. Not an ugly din, like the kind generated by the riots she'd heard about in Harlem last year and Birmingham the year before. No—this was a beautiful upset, a ruckus of unadulterated joy.

"What in holy hell is that?" he demanded, as if it were her job to know, as if the noisy interruption could somehow be blamed on her.

"The circus," she muttered in disgust, because she was sure that was how he would want her to feel about such a garish display. She'd

heard that it was in town, but had forgotten until just now, as the parade came unfurling along the perfect Brooksvale avenue on which their perfect brick house stood among other perfect brick houses (though theirs was the most perfect by far—because it was his).

Perhaps it was the gleeful intrusion of the circus parade that compelled him to increase the duration of his torment. He was usually appeased (or perhaps bored) sooner. But today he held tight until her scalp stung and her face was streaked with tears.

Without releasing his hold on her hair, he dragged her toward the open front door. Squinting through the spring shadows that fell across the covered porch, Catherine saw her mother, hardly more than a shadow herself, bundled under woolen blankets on a wicker chaise. She was watching the circus performers file past in the late-day sunshine—a roaring, dancing, tumbling rainbow.

The music was as irresistible as if they'd hired the Pied Piper himself to lead the band. Catherine wished it would stop. She wished it would never stop. It was at once too lovely and too strange, and it did not belong here, dancing and cartwheeling through her humiliation.

"Be back in this house by ten o'clock tomorrow morning, or I will come after you," he said, punctuating his consent with a shove that sent Catherine stumbling through the front door. She went skidding across the porch on her hands and knees to land at her mother's feet. "Have I made myself understood?"

Her knees throbbed; her palms burned. Damn right she understood. Eyes on the porch floor, she nodded.

He hovered there long enough to remove his pocket square and use it to mop his brow. It wasn't until his footsteps had clomped up the stairs and faded to silence that her mother spoke.

"Go, Catherine."

It was a wisp of a voice at best, words almost without sound, but they had Catherine snapping her gaze up to meet her mother's pale eyes in disbelief. Because while the suggestion seemed innocuous enough, there was something chilling in the delivery that made her heart race.

"Mother?"

"I'm dying, my love, my darling girl. We both know it. I'll be surprised if I live out the week."

"Mother, no—"

"Catherine." Meredith Quinn Hastings held up a shaky hand to silence her child; the exertion of even that showed in her gaunt face, but she did not let her trembling fingertips fall back into her lap. Instead they went to the satin lapel of her bathrobe, to the Cartier brooch her sadistic son-of-a-bitch husband insisted she wear, despite the fact that the weight of it was now too much for her to carry. "There's always a chance a friend or neighbor might stop in to ask after your health," he'd snarled more than once, so if she couldn't honor him by looking healthy, she could at least look wealthy—she owed him that much, didn't she? The jewel-encrusted brooch had been weighing her down for months.

Until now.

With the fire-eaters crackling past and the plumed horses trotting like something from a dream, Meredith fumbled with the clasp, then held the pin out to her daughter. Because another thing they both knew was that this brooch was virtually priceless.

"Go. Now."

"To Emily's, you mean?" Catherine's throat was tight.

Meredith's chin trembled, but she lifted it defiantly and lied, "Where else?"

For the space of a heartbeat her eyes shone with determination, with hope. Over the vanishing strains of circus music, she used what little strength she had to jerk her chin in the direction of the last grinning clown as he skipped out of sight. Then came the last words she would ever speak to her child.

"Go, Catherine," she urged.

So Catherine did.

ONE

~

CALLIE STOPPED AT THE end of the buckling brick walk and frowned. "What is this place?"

"It's a carriage house," Quinn pronounced brightly.

"It's a *garage*."

"Oh, come on—it's adorable. Look at that tile roof. And those arched windows! I think it's charming."

"I think it's a *garage*."

Quinn cocked her hip. "Guest suite?"

"Servants' quarters."

"Fine, Calliope." Quinn sighed and yanked a jangling keychain from her jeans pocket. "It's a miserable little garage apartment. But you know what else it is? It's where we live now. The Sanctuary is home."

Well, that was *wrong*. Dead wrong. Home was *not* this crumbling, peeling outbuilding on the grounds of an animal rescue facility in Lake St. Julian, Florida. Home was everywhere *else*—a train speeding through a twilight filled with promise, a field on the outskirts of some small town Callie had never heard of, a sprawling meadow in the European countryside, or an arena in any bustling American city. Home was motion, change, adventure.

Home was the circus.

Or at least it was, until Mom decided to destroy my life.

Callie eyed the second floor of the so-called charming carriage house, where two curved balconies stuck out from the façade like a pair of buckteeth. Their iron railings were rusted and broken, giving the impression of braces applied by a substandard orthodontist. "I'd say it's a pretty fair gauge of how much a place sucks when the banisters commit suicide."

"Mr. Marston's already promised to have them repaired," said Quinn, battling with the ancient lock. "In a few weeks those railings will be back to their original splendor and dripping with bougainvillea." Jerking the door open, she leaned against it, holding it wide for Callie to enter.

"Just so you know, Mom, people run away *to* the circus. It's, like, a *thing*. Nobody runs away *from* the circus." Brushing past her mother, Callie climbed the stairs to the apartment, where several packing boxes, suitcases, and duffel bags lined the walls. CALLIE BEDROOM STUFF; SUMMER CLOTHES/TOASTER; QUINN MISC. OFFICE SUPPLIES.

Three days ago, the boxes had been loaded into a moving van and sent ahead from Providence, where Callie still had one show left to perform. Her final walk across the high wire—billed dramatically on posters and in online advertising as "Calliope's Crescendo"—had dazzled the Rhode Island crowds. Callie had signed autographs for hours afterward, and the next morning she and her mother had said their goodbyes. Quinn's were lengthy and emotional, but Callie's hadn't taken long at all. The farewells she'd received were cordial, of course—she was the star attraction of VanDrexel's Family Circus, so naturally her fellow performers were disappointed to see her go. But it had occurred to her as she was accepting a perfunctory group hug from the Bertière triplets (who'd interrupted their trapeze rehearsal just to see her off) that although she'd spent years in the same schoolroom with these girls, she'd never really managed to learn which one was Bianca, which was Beatrice, and which was Brittany. She did vaguely recall some rumors about Brittany dating one of the Chinese acrobats—Liang, she thought his name was. Brittany always seemed to be talking about him, but Callie had a way of tuning things out. She was never overly interested in gossip, which was probably why people rarely bothered to share it with her.

Returning her attention to the boxes, Callie felt a surge of panic. "This can't be all of it. Where are my costumes? Where's the practice wire?"

"Your costumes are downstairs," said Quinn, tearing into a carton marked BEDDING. "We've got use of this whole carriage-house-slash-servants'-quarters, so I figured there was no point cluttering up the closets with stuff you aren't going to need."

"And the wire?"

Quinn looked up from the box to her glowering daughter, hesitated, then tossed her head toward a bay window overlooking the back lawn.

Callie went to the window, wiped away a layer of grime, and looked out. There in the small shady patch that constituted the backyard was a three-foot-high tightrope, all set up and ready to go.

"I called ahead," said Quinn, taking a quilt out of the box.

Callie stared down at the line and said nothing. She knew some expression of gratitude was in order, but the only sensation stronger than the ache to feel that tightrope beneath her feet was the anger she was harboring toward her mother. Quinn could have had three rings and a Big Top set up out there, and Callie still wouldn't have given her the satisfaction of saying thank you.

And why should she? Callie was never supposed to leave. The plan was always for her mother to resign from VanDrexel's Family Circus as soon as Callie turned fifteen and was old enough to travel under the guardianship of her grandmother. In fact, Quinn had been on the verge of leaving a little over a year ago, when the circus's parent company made the dramatic decision to stop using most of its exotic animals in the show. This had left Quinn—the show's animal specialist—essentially without a function to perform, so she'd promptly arranged a Skype interview with Brad Marston, the owner of the same rescue facility to which her beloved elephants and big cats would be retiring. It was a newly established preserve called the Sanctuary, whose philosophy and mission had been enthusiastically heralded by all the proper animal welfare federations and authorities. Knowing that many American circuses were on the verge of making similar changes to their performing animal policies, Marston had listened to Quinn's qualifications and personal beliefs and offered her the executive director position on the spot. The job came with what he'd called "a full relocation package," including transportation costs and moving expenses, as well as a rent-free home right on the Sanctuary grounds.

Quinn, of course, had accepted.

Then, a week later, out of absolutely nowhere and to Callie's complete astonishment, Quinn had called her new boss back to say she'd changed her mind.

At the time, Callie couldn't understand why. Though Quinn had been born and raised in VanDrexel's Circus (indeed, she *was* a VanDrexel) running an animal sanctuary had always been her dream.

Callie hadn't learned her mother's real reason for staying until three weeks ago. And she'd learned it the hard way.

Spinning away from the window, Callie bolted back across the room.

"Where are you going?"

"To make sure my costumes aren't being devoured by cockroaches," Callie said, as she made her way down the stairs.

More boxes: TAX INFO/BANK RECORDS; WINTER COATS (DONATE); TUPPERWARE (MISSING LIDS). The one marked CALLIE'S COSTUMES was the largest by far, bulging at the sides.

Dragging the box to the center of the garage, she ripped off the clear packing tape, revealing the perfect plum-colored sheen of her first performance dress. A shaft of sunlight made gray by the dusty garage windows caught one of the five hundred Swarovski crystals that dotted the purple bodice. She'd been only seven when she first walked the wire for a crowd, and she'd begged for a purple dress with cascades of pink ruffles and a tutu that could only be described as an exercise in hyperbole.

Was I ever really this tiny? she wondered, holding the dress up to the meager light. *Or this gauche?* Apparently yes, and there was a matching purple parasol to prove it.

Laying the dress aside, Callie gingerly removed the next costume—a svelte unitard she'd worn the year she turned twelve. Because it had been designed during her Harry Potter fangirl phase, the fabric was a deep shade of scarlet, accented with shimmering gold stripes. It was in this costume that she'd learned to do a backward somersault while lying on the wire, and she smiled now, remembering how she'd secretly imagined that if she were to fall while executing it, it wouldn't have been into the bouncy embrace of the safety net her grandmother insisted on, but into the waiting arms of a young Daniel Radcliffe.

Next in the pile was a mod little minidress her grandmother had designed for her to wear at a charity benefit performance. In it, she had delighted an audience of wealthy baby boomers by performing a dance called the Watusi on the wire. Her grandmother's idea, which Callie had found both campy and fun. And while she might not have been world famous in the strictest Lady Gaga sense of the term, in the circus industry she was hailed as a swiftly rising star, the darling of the tightrope.

Just as her grandmother, Victoria VanDrexel, had been when she was a girl.

Callie's eyes were suddenly drawn to a battered carton in the farthest corner of the garage—not one of the crisp, pristine boxes the moving company had supplied but an old, worn one, with dented corners and paper tape peeling upward at the ends. Written on the side of the box in faded block letters was the name VICTORIA.

It was as if by thinking her grandmother's name, Callie had somehow conjured her spirit. Why hadn't her mother told her she had kept some of Gram's belongings?

Maneuvering through the cardboard labyrinth, Callie lugged the unwieldy carton to a roomier spot. Her fingers caught one of the upturned corners of the tape, and when she tore it away, the sound filled the garage like the drumroll that had always preceded Victoria's act. Callie opened the flaps, and a magnificently familiar scent assaulted her: sawdust and old suede and Chanel N°5.

"Callie?"

She didn't answer; she was engrossed in a new routine she was choreographing for opening night in Tulsa.

"Callie . . . come down."

"I'm kind of busy, Mom."

It didn't occur to her how unusual it was for Quinn to interrupt her during a practice session. It was always just Callie and Gram in the tent at rehearsal, speaking the almost-secret language that only they and the wire understood.

"I have to talk to you, honey," Quinn called up. "Please come down."

"Can it wait? And where's Gram? She was supposed to meet me here at seven. She never sleeps in."

"Callie . . . please."

Callie climbed down from the platform and presented herself, scowling, to her mother.

"Baby . . . I'm so sorry."

Callie didn't understand. The full truth was still hidden in the shiver of her mother's voice, but the heaviness of the words as they fell from her tongue landed hard on Callie's heart. "Sorry for what?"

Quinn lowered her eyes. She shook her head as a sob escaped her.

Callie was suddenly seized with terror. She couldn't stand up; she couldn't move forward. The world shrank to a vicious wire, rotating violently beneath her feet. She couldn't find her balance. Balance no longer existed.

"Gram's gone, baby. She died in her sleep. It was so peaceful. Graceful, almost, just the way she would have wanted it."

And then more words from her mother, truths that felt like lies. "Cancer . . . last year . . . aggressive tumor . . . didn't want you to know."

But Callie couldn't listen anymore. Her world had just changed forever, and no amount of explanation could reverse it. Without a word, she turned away from her mother, climbed back up the ladder, and disappeared into her routine.

So Quinn had delayed her departure and stayed on at VanDrexel's to be with Gram while she was dying. Except no one had bothered to tell Callie that.

As if the shock and heartbreak of Victoria's death hadn't been enough, Quinn's first order of business following the funeral was to call Brad Marston and ask if her job was still available.

It was. And this time, the relocation package would cover two plane tickets.

Wiping her eyes with the back of her hand, Callie stared down at her grandmother's tightrope shoes, the perfect leather slippers with the suede soles. Her grandmother hadn't worn them in ages, but the uniquely molded shape of them, the worn quality of the leather, had Callie imagining Victoria taking them off just moments before.

They'd been packed into the cardboard box on top of a vinyl-covered chest—an old-fashioned jewelry box, Callie thought. Stuffed in around the box were other keepsakes: framed photos, old circus programs—even a faded VanDrexel's Family Circus T-shirt.

Setting aside the shoes, but without removing the chest from the carton, she carefully lifted the lid.

A sort of shelf was nestled into it, and on it sat a black-and-white photograph of two pretty girls. Callie had never seen the photo before, but there was no doubt that the dark-haired one was Victoria. Judging by the other girl's hairstyle, Callie guessed it was probably taken sometime in the 1960s, and Victoria and her friend appeared to be riding in the back of a pickup truck. Squinting, Callie saw that her grandmother was holding a paper bag with the word WOOLWORTH'S emblazoned across it.

Putting aside the photo, Callie lifted the velvet tray, shocked to find that, instead of jewelry, the box was filled with several strange scraps of paper. Each was a different shape, color, texture; each had a phrase or sentence written on it by her grandmother. Some of the phrases were carefully inscribed in the lovely looping script Victoria used when signing autographs; others were written in her tidy, careful print, and still others seemed to have been dashed off in a hurry, their letters all sloppy and smudged.

If the balloons can do it, so can I.

A name is a kind of enchantment.

A thing that's wild can be taught, but never tamed.

It was all too much for Callie—too close, too far away, too . . . *over*. With a shuddering breath, she closed the lid and left the garage.

"Did you find what you were looking for?" asked Quinn.

Callie gave a curt nod. Tamping down the ache in her chest, she forced herself to focus on her new living situation.

It was certainly spacious enough, spreading out across the width of three garage bays. It was also profoundly musty and dank; the oxygen felt vintage, like it was so old it had forgotten how to let itself be breathed. Cobwebs dripped from the empty curtain rods like amateur aerialists, and the floor was coated with dust. All the furniture was draped in white sheets, giving the impression of a gathering of ghosts.

Worst by far was the kitchenette with its amalgam of roaring twenties cabinetry, 1950s linoleum, and disco-era appliances.

Two rooms opened off the main living space. Callie trudged into the first, where a double bed with a wicker headboard was shoved haphazardly against the far wall. The mattress, she was relieved to see, was brand-new, still in its plastic wrapping. She supposed she had Marston to thank for that (though she wouldn't). There was an antique dresser next to the closet, and the floor was fashioned of wide bamboo planks that would probably gleam after a good sweeping. A glass door with leaded panes opened onto one of the little balconies, which, precarious condition of its banister notwithstanding, Callie didn't hate. Across the room, a large window looked out on a pair of swaying palms.

Maybe, if she *tried,* she could get used to this place.

But she had no intention of trying.

Why bother, since she had no intention of staying.

Because even if this were the cutest apartment on the planet, it would always be *standing still.* There would be no more falling asleep to a snowy mountain view outside her window, only to awaken to a balmy seaside sunrise.

Just keep moving forward. Callie's grandmother had drilled that phrase into her head from the moment she'd first mounted the practice rope at age three. It wasn't simply good advice, it was a rule, a commandment. *Directional inertia*—the means by which those who walked the wire stayed alive. Standing still for too long meant failure.

Which was why tucked into one of those suitcases in the other room was a letter addressed to Signore M. Ricci, owner and operator of Un Piccolo Circo Familiare in Perugia, Italy.

When she heard the soft squeak of her mother's sneakers behind her, Callie didn't turn around. Out of the corner of her eye she saw Quinn placing something on the dresser—a pewter urn engraved with a single *V*. As if by some unspoken agreement forged of anger and heartache, neither of them acknowledged it.

"Not a bad little room," Quinn pronounced, joining her daughter at the window.

"Sure, if you like wicker," Callie baited.

Quinn shot her daughter a look and began opening windows. "Anyway, it's just temporary. Mr. Marston's going to have the whole place remodeled for us. He's already apologized a thousand times for not having it done already, but it's not like I gave him much notice. He's promised that come summer, our home will be state-of-the-art."

Come summer, Callie thought, *I'll be gone*.

TWO

Massachusetts, 1965

THE WORDS FOR THIS parting do not exist in any language, so I bid my mother goodbye without them, kissing her lightly on her forehead.

Then I run. Because that's what you do when you're running away, isn't it? You *run*, knowing that what you're running from might at any moment discover you've escaped; you *run*, fearing that the danger will follow you for the rest of your life. But that's the bargain you've made, that's the risk inherent in all actions undertaken in desperation. If nothing else, at least I know I'm going with my mother's blessing.

I wonder briefly if I will look suspicious to anyone who might notice—a rich girl in a pair of pristine white Keds, plaid pedal pushers, and a powder-blue cotton blouse, sprinting at full tilt along the manicured lanes of Brooksvale. Perhaps on any other day I would, but today, I imagine—*I hope*—it will just seem like I'm eager to get to the circus.

I run until I can see the fairgrounds ahead, where the Big Top looks like some floppy canvas version of the Taj Mahal. *Just keep moving forward*, I tell myself, *keep moving forward*. Slowing my pace, I do just that, visually transforming myself from frightened runaway to carefree circus-goer. It's amazing how easy it is to disappear, to vanish into this crowd of eager strangers, into the colors and the music, into this place where my father would never even think to look for me—the me *he* thinks I am, at any rate; the me he has created with the back of his hand and the heel of his shoe and the unwavering gleam of ownership that both lights and darkens his eyes whenever he looks at me.

Or at her. I take cold comfort in the fact that he won't have her to look at for much longer and wrap my fingers around the diamonds, emeralds, rubies, and sapphires clustered in her brooch. It occurs to me that my mother's gift contains all the colors of the circus, and I squeeze it once, gently, before slipping it into my pocket. I'm relieved to feel the few coins and dollar bills I slipped in there earlier today. My plans with Emily for the evening, in addition to listening to records in the Davenports' rumpus room, included a walk to the soda shop, where Emily has a charge account. Not me. When you're not supposed to be someplace, you don't run a tab. You pay cash and hope your father never finds out where you've been.

The crush of the spectators envelops me, as the ruddy-faced barker, in a parody of himself, cries out, "Step right up, step right up . . ."

And so I do, and he sells me my escape for three dollars and fifty cents.

"Better hurry 'n' grab a seat, sweetheart," the ticket salesman advises. "The Spec'll be startin' in five."

"Spec?"

The barker laughs. "Our big entrance. A real grand circus parade."

The ticket in my palm is like a talisman; I will go where it takes me. The flow of the crowd sweeps me into the tent, and my heart races as I enter. I hadn't been prepared for how glittering and seductive a world made of canvas could be. Three enormous rings have been set up in the dirt, and I take my seat on the bottom bleacher. I am as close as I can be to the show, as far as I can be from my life of just minutes ago. Overhead is a vast network of ropes and wires, like the rigging of the tall ships I've seen in Boston Harbor. Vendors hawk sodas and souvenirs over the noise of a thousand eager conversations. The anticipation is palpable, the din oddly womblike.

I catch a glimpse of a woman in fishnet tights climbing a ladder toward the pinnacle of the tent. She has feathers in her hair and looks utterly calm, despite the fact that she has now risen forty . . . no, forty-five . . . fifty . . . *sixty* feet above the ground! The ladder deposits her on a small platform with a hand railing, and she stands there with her hip cocked, her toe pointed, perfectly still, like a doll placed on a high shelf out of the reach of careless children. Stretched out before her is a wire that reaches clear across the center ring.

Others have spotted her now and are pointing, gasping.

Suddenly I'm gasping too, but it has nothing to do with the girl in the sky.

Panic seizes me. *What am I doing here? This isn't a fairy tale. I can't run off to join the circus!*

I feel myself rising from the bleacher, but my legs buckle and my back pockets reconnect with the hard wood of the bench.

A voice over the loudspeaker fills the tent. It's rich with authority and promise and something else I can't quite name. "Ladies and gentlemen . . . children of all ages . . ."

No one moves; every guest in every seat is instantly breathless, wide-eyed. A spotlight ignites, and in the center ring stands a man in white jodhpurs and a red velvet blazer trimmed with gold braid. With his arms outstretched and his silk top hat tipped at a jaunty angle, he is elegance and whimsy rolled into one. He is the Ringmaster, a human miracle of entertainment mixed with absolute power. He is a secret, standing there for all to see.

His voice rolls over us like thunder. "I am proud to present for your amusement and amazement, an evening of *unimaginable* thrills, a show of *magnificent* splendiferousness, the ONE . . . the ONLY . . . VanDrexel Family Circuuuusss!"

He cracks his whip and the sound makes me jump in my seat. The band strikes up—a brassy fanfare of piano and percussion. More spotlights erupt, chasing themselves around the tent.

My panic fades, and in its place I feel something new, something like sugar melting into my soul—warm and sweet and a little bit decadent.

The tent flaps are pulled wide and six putty-colored horses charge into the Big Top. They are dressed as if this is their coming-out ball, in white tulle, silver fringe, and sequins that seem to outnumber the stars in the sky. An olive-skinned young woman rides without a saddle. Her hair bounces in time with the fluttering of six silken manes and tails. The ground shakes, the bleachers shake—we're all of us a part of this ride.

Clowns on tiny bicycles roll in; then a troupe of aerialists enters behind them—the men, bare-chested athletes in satin trousers, wave to us like old friends; the women dazzle in their shimmering leotards, their upswept hair spilling ringlets.

Two young men walk in behind the aerialists. They're surely brothers, and they couldn't be more handsome if they tried—rugged, with their shirtsleeves rolled high to show off their muscled arms. They wear khaki pants and tall unpolished leather boots. Just behind them on a float is a tiger in a cage.

Dancers.

Tumblers.

Baton twirlers.

A man juggling swords.

This is the bigger, bolder brother of the parade that passed by my house. The last thing my mother and I experienced together.

"Go, Catherine."

Another spotlight flares to life, haloing the girl on the wire.

The band plays a new song, something delicate, crystalline. I lift my face, squinting into the glare just as the girl takes her first step onto the tightrope; an awed gasp escapes my lungs, crashing into the thousands of other gasps from the crowd. The girl is so accomplished, so ethereal, that the tightrope barely dips with her weight. I've never seen such confidence, such purpose. She has perfect posture and an otherworldly sense of balance. I pull my eyes from her, scanning the area beneath the rope. *Surely there's a safety net.*

No. No net. Just her, on the wire, in the spotlight.

Just her.

Just me.

No net.

I'll change my name. I'll tell a story, put on a show. I'll march right up to the man in the red blazer and tell him I am seeking employment with his troupe. Anything to secure myself a temporary spot in this marvelous caravan that will put enough miles between me and my soon-to-be widowed father, earning a few dollars while I'm at it. Then three, perhaps four towns from now, I'll quietly disappear again. I'll lose myself in a whole new place. I'll find a job, an apartment, and I'll finally have the one thing that has always been most forbidden under my father's reign: independence.

A simple thing, but one I never could have imagined for myself before—the freedom to dress as I like, to choose my own friends, to *not* marry the sort of boy my father would have chosen for me. I will rely on no one and answer only to myself.

I'll find a way to take classes at night and finish high school. I'll save money and go to college. I'll teach myself to have what the girl on the wire has. *Confidence. Purpose.*

Sixty feet in the air, she is practically skipping now, skipping across the wire to the other side. The music swells, she spins, pliés, making it look easy. But it's *not* easy, and *that*, I realize, is what makes the circus the circus—doing what's difficult and making it look simple. It's the presence of that one thing I've never had but always needed and didn't even know I was missing.

Magic.

And suddenly, I'm no longer afraid.

I follow him at a short distance, like some deranged fan creeping in his wake past the sideshow tent and into the writhing shadows thrown by the glow of the post-performance midway—an area bustling with carnival games, snack stands, and souvenir booths. Behind us, the grounds continue to bustle; clearly I'm not the only one who can't bring herself to go home.

When he reaches the circus train, he places one black-booted foot on the vestibule's bottom step, then whirls around, startling me.

He doesn't seem annoyed, just curious when he asks, "May I help you, young lady?"

The short answer of course is *I sure as hell hope so.* But even up close, he is so imposing, so debonair and mysterious, that my voice fails me. So I just stand there, gulping and fidgeting. Not exactly the best way to start a job interview. Or a stowaway interview. Or whatever this is.

"If it's a refund you're wanting, you'll be required to take that up with the manager," he informs me, each syllable measured, musical. "I'm so sorry you didn't enjoy the show."

"Oh, I *loved* the show," I blurt out, meaning it more than he could possibly know.

"Then you're not looking for a refund?"

I shake my head, remembering the girl on the wire. "I'm looking for a job."

The Ringmaster—Cornelius VanDrexel, according to the program I'm clutching in my clammy hand—regards me with eyes that twinkle.

"Ah! Well then, please, my dear, do come in." He makes a sweeping gesture with his arm, and I, like a marionette, leap onto the metal step beside him. A quick left turn puts us in his office . . . an office *in a train car*.

What's even more surreal is the fact that I am thrilled by it, as if I were in an episode of *The Twilight Zone*. It's like I've crossed over into another dimension—and surely I have, because in *reality*, Catherine Hastings would know better than to place herself alone in a train car with a strange man, well out of earshot of anyone who might come to her rescue should she find herself screaming for help. I'm slightly comforted by the fact that Cornelius is older than he looked in the spotlight—close to sixty. *I could probably outrun him if it came to that.*

I spy an open ledger on his desk, an oversize book filled with numbers and notations. He closes it and says, "So you want to join the circus." A grin spreads across his face. "What is it you do?" I hesitate, and he thinks I've misunderstood the question. "What sort of act do you perform? Are you a tumbler?"

Three years on the pep squad have provided me with a pretty good cartwheel, but based on what I saw tonight, that hardly qualifies me to be a circus acrobat. I shake my head.

"Dancer?"

"I'm looking for something more in the area of . . . odd jobs."

"Odd jobs?" Cornelius allows himself a laugh. "This is the circus, young lady. Some would argue that all our jobs are odd."

He removes his hat and places it on the desk. His hair is lush, mahogany with brushstrokes of gray at the temples. Have I dreamed him?

"Perhaps you do an act with snakes?" he prompts.

Another head shake.

"Do you hang from your hair and spin?"

First of all: *ouch*. And second: "I'm not actually a performer,"

I explain, my cheeks flushing. "I'd very much like to be . . ." (Where did *that* come from?) "But for now, I'm not looking to ride a tiny motorcycle through a flaming hoop or anything like that."

"Well, that's fortuitous, since we already have someone who does that."

"I know. I mean, I saw." I squirm in my chair. "Ideally, I'd like to do something behind the scenes." *Way behind the scenes.*

The Ringmaster sighs thoughtfully, and I am almost surprised when his breath does not come out in a cloud of glitter. "How old are you, miss?"

He asks this casually, but I know it's a trick question. So I give him a trick answer. "Eighteen."

"Eighteen," he echoes, his right eyebrow rising ever so slightly. He's deciding whether or not to believe me. I've only rounded up two years, so I think he might. "What's your name?"

Another loaded question.

Because I know that tomorrow morning, at the stroke of ten exactly, my father will phone the Davenports' house to ask—jovially, politely—if Dr. Davenport will be driving me home or if he should "come round to collect me."

Collect me. Like a stamp, or a baseball card.

With any luck, Dr. Davenport will report that, according to Emily, "the girls were up late, and Cathy is still asleep on the rumpus room sofa, so why don't you just let her sleep in a little and join us for lunch?" (Emily's parents never visit the rumpus room when I visit, and for whatever reason, they believe everything she tells them.) At Emily's behest, I've told that same lie in reverse to Dr. Davenport more times than I can count, enabling Emily to stay out until all hours with Cliff Parker, doing who-knows-what in the back seat of his GTO.

I'm hoping my failure to arrive at her house earlier this evening will have been enough of a clue for Emily to set the rest of my plan in motion. I don't have a Cliff Parker, of course, but Emily's not the sort to worry about details. Plus, she's seen the bruises. I'm counting on her instincts and her compassion to give me a head start.

So if both Emily and my father behave true to form, I have until about noon tomorrow before my father actually understands that I am missing—before he officially reports the disappearance of *Catherine Hastings* to the proper authorities, or (more likely) comes gunning for me himself.

Cornelius is still waiting for my name. My exodus being entirely unplanned, I haven't had time to come up with a proper alias.

A name comes to me; it's the name of a housemaid I used to pretend was not a maid at all, rather my doting older sister. She was young and giggly and taught me to jitterbug to Bill Haley's "Rock Around the Clock" when I was six. A year later, she fled the house in tears after witnessing one of my father's particularly violent outbursts.

"Victoria," I christen myself. I pick the name partly because I adored her, but mostly because it sounds like *Victory*. And I need a win.

Cornelius smooths his jodhpurs and doesn't meet my eyes. "Victoria what?"

I am on the verge of choking out my mother's maiden name— Quinn—but I catch myself in time. Such sentimentality will only make it that much easier for my father to hunt me down. Instead, I choose a name that nearly burns my tongue, the one name that will never allow me to forget, even for a moment, exactly what I am running from.

I take a deep breath and stammer myself into a false identity: "My last name . . . is . . . um . . . it's Davis. Victoria Davis."

Cornelius VanDrexel strums his manicured fingertips against the handle of his whip. "So one Victoria Davis, eighteen years of age, presently absent of any ostensible circus skills, wishes to join my spectacular little mud show," he summarizes.

"Yes, I do." *For the next few weeks, at least.*

"Very well, then." He slides off the desk, struts two steps to a file cabinet, and withdraws an official-looking form, which I assume is some manner of employment paperwork. I might actually vomit.

I take the form with trembling hands. Not surprisingly, the job application wants to know who I am, where I live, when I was born. My social security number, my next of kin. The most basic, innocuous facts of my existence, which have suddenly become terrifying and unspeakable.

"Have you any identification currently upon your person, Miss Davis? A driver's license perhaps?"

For the first time since I stepped into his office I can answer him honestly. "I don't drive," I explain. My father would have never allowed such freedom.

Cornelius sighs, closes the drawer, and returns to the edge of his desk, seeing me, not seeing me . . . I can't be sure. There's something ethereal about him with his tall boots and velvet lapels and his worldly wisdom. And here I am, ordinary—or whatever comes *before* ordinary—asking him for a favor, a future, a chance.

He knows I'm lying to him. He *knows*. So why should he do me this kindness, grant me this wish? Why should he risk anything just to help me?

The answer is, he shouldn't.

But then his eyes meet mine, not just with a twinkle, but with a deeper, more portentous sort of spark. When he speaks—slowly, meaningfully—his words resonate, filling the space of the train car: "The best kind of charity is to help those who are willing to help themselves."

I immediately recognize the quote. "P. T. Barnum said that."

His eyebrows lift in surprise. Incredibly, this is not just a lucky guess on my part. My father worships anyone with a knack for earning money, and Phineas Taylor Barnum amassed fortunes in his day.

I hold Cornelius's gaze without flinching. My unspoken answer to his unspoken question is, *Yes, Mr. VanDrexel, I will help myself. I am already helping myself by hitching a ride with your circus, the world's most boisterous getaway car.*

Now Cornelius's mouth twitches at the corners, as though he's trying not to smile. "You know, some believe that Barnum also said, 'There's a sucker born every minute.' If he did, I sincerely hope that our association will in no way serve to prove Mr. Barnum right about *that*."

"It won't, sir."

Because somewhere, miles from here, I will slip out of this caravan as soundlessly as I slipped in, and Cornelius's promise of sanctuary—because we both know that is exactly what this is—will have been fulfilled. Perhaps it would be fun to stay, but I don't belong in the circus any more than Cornelius belongs in a brick mansion in Brooksvale.

He stands gracefully, then crosses the narrow car toward the door, pausing to contemplate a framed handbill on the wall. Its artwork is a dreamy ink-and-watercolor rendering, and there are words written in fussy Old English letters across the top:

VanDrexel's Family Circus: Three Rings of Fantastical Fun

"Early days," he explains. "You see, our show was the waking dream of two young Polish immigrants, my father, Oskar Vanovich, and his cousin Lukasz Drecki. They quickly discovered that a name is a kind of enchantment, and there is little to no charm in a moniker like 'Drecki,' so while folks were flocking to see the Coles, and the Coopers, and the Baileys, we poor Vanoviches were all but starving to death. So the resourceful cousins concocted the pretty portmanteau of 'VanDrexel,' and it has been magic ever since."

"VanDrexel's a lovely name," I agree, smiling. "It must have been a wonderful way to grow up."

"Oh, it was," he assures me. "When I was quite young, it was my task to set up the ring curbs. They were like tremendous puzzles, incomplete until the first piece met the last, and a perfect circle was formed. Such a paradox—by ending, they became infinite. And from this I learned a simple, but lasting truth."

Tell me.

"'Everything will eventually come full circle.' As a boy, I could not decide if that constituted an assurance or a warning, but I learned, as I grew to be a man, that like most things, it contains a bit of both."

The next thing I know, I'm being whisked through the train—like a mouse being digested by a gleaming metal boa constrictor—to what the Ringmaster calls the pie car. There I am introduced to a smallish man named Duncan, who is finishing up a late-night slice of lemon meringue pie like a diminutive king. He is freshly scrubbed of his clown makeup, but still sporting a colorful plaid suit with an oversize plastic flower in his lapel. Clearly, he is someone Cornelius trusts.

"Find her something to be good at," the Ringmaster decrees, then takes his leave of me, calling over his shoulder as if it were an afterthought, "Observation is where understanding begins."

Folding the job application, I slip it into the pocket of my pedal pushers and sit down in the booth across from Duncan, who polishes off his pie and smiles. "Welcome to the circus, Miss Victoria Davis."

Somehow, that makes it all real.

I am now and forever Victoria Davis.

And for the time being at least, I belong to this circus.

THREE

~

CAUTION:
DO NOT STRAY FROM DESIGNATED PATHWAYS.
WANDER AT YOUR OWN RISK.
THANK YOU.
THE SANCTUARY MANAGEMENT TEAM

CALLIE AND QUINN PICKED their way along the twisting maze of walkways that led from the garage to the main house. Already, Callie had seen four such warnings posted. Seemed like a waste of signage to her, since one of the few things she knew about the Sanctuary was that it was unequivocally and emphatically *not* open to the public. This was the primary reason why, a year ago, Quinn had chosen to relocate her beloved animal retirees here. It was important to her that it did not bill itself as a "zoo" or an "attraction." The owner, millionaire (possibly billionaire) philanthropist Bradford Marston, had made it his mission to create the most authentic environment possible for the elephants, big cats, and various other species of out-of-work quadrupeds he took in . . . and an authentic environment did not include toddlers gobbling Cracker Jack or teenagers toting selfie sticks.

On the flight down from Providence—before Callie had pointedly popped in her earbuds—Quinn had gotten as far as explaining that in another lifetime the Sanctuary had been a lavish estate known as Casa del Santuario. It was built by Bradford's great-grandfather Grover Marston in 1927—a mere two years before the Great Depression.

"He was a very successful bootlegger," Quinn was revealing now, scandalously delighted by the provenance of her new home. "As a wedding gift for his young bride, Agnes, he bought two hundred thirteen acres outside Lake St. Julian and built her this house. Can you guess what Agnes's wedding gift to Grover was?" Her expression was suddenly somber. "A Bengal tiger cub that she had to have *smuggled* into the United States."

"A bootlegger and a smuggler. Sounds like Grover and Aggie were made for each other."

"They named the tiger after the amendment that made Grover a millionaire—Prohibition. Hibby for short." A little crease—a lion's wrinkle—formed between Quinn's brows as she frowned her distaste. "When he got too big to keep indoors, they turned him out to roam free on the property, but one of Grover's henchmen happened upon the cat one night and shot the poor thing dead."

Does she really think any of this is going to make me feel better about living here? She's the animal freak, not me.

"Brad's grandfather lost the house and the land in the seventies," Quinn continued, "when he went broke from an excess of illegal gambling debts."

"So I guess the gene for good criminal instincts skips a generation?"

"When Brad graduated from college, he used his trust fund to buy the place back, and it sat empty for decades, until the animal rights activists brought the plight of performing animals to the world's attention. Brad remembered the story of Prohibition the tiger, and he knew what he had to do."

Callie slid a glance at her mother's giddy smile, realizing that every time Quinn referenced Bradford Marston her voice went all squeaky, as if she'd just inhaled the contents of a helium balloon.

Note to self: Mom wants to sleep with her new boss.

"Callie, listen—" Quinn began, but cut off abruptly as they came around a tall hedge into the wide-open front lawn of the main house.

Callie could only gape at the masterpiece of creamy white stucco and rippling red roof tiles that loomed before her—all curves and columns, angles and niches, verandas and stairways. She felt a little like Dorothy arriving at the Emerald City.

"Mr. Marston *lives* here?"

"The second floor is the residence. Administrative offices and other workspaces are on the ground floor. One of the wings is a fully equipped veterinary hospital."

Callie was reluctantly impressed. As they made their way toward the front terrace, she was momentarily distracted by a trickling fountain, the centerpiece of which was a massive bronze tiger, a monument to Hibby no doubt.

"What were you going to say?"

"Hmm?"

"Before you and the Scarecrow and the Tin Man and I were all struck dumb by the sight of the Wizard's palace. You said, 'Callie, listen.' I'm listening."

"Right. Well . . ." Quinn looked suddenly serious. "Mr. Marston might ask you about your plans for school."

"Yeah? So?" A curl of concern formed in the pit of Callie's stomach. "He's not gonna offer to send me to some fancy academy or something, is he? Because you promised me I could be home-schooled." The swirl of worry widened into a Kansas-sized tornado of panic. "He is, isn't he? He wants to send me to private school!"

"No!" Quinn bit her lower lip, thoughtfully. "Not that I know of, anyway. He *is* very generous, so I suppose there's always that poss—"

"*Mom!* I am *not* going to private school. I don't care how generous your billionaire boss is. I'm not."

"Callie, relax. You don't have to go to private school. But . . . I don't think homeschooling is going to work out either."

"It's *homeschool*, Mom. What is there to not work out? We have a *home*—sort of—and you already signed me up for the online courses." Callie narrowed her eyes. "You *did* sign me up, didn't you?"

"I did. But this morning . . . I canceled them." Before Callie could challenge her, Quinn barreled on, her eyes filled with a mixture of resolve and regret. "I think you should go to the public high school in town. I think you *need* to."

Callie thought she might faint. Or puke. Or both. "Give me one good reason why."

"I'll give you three," said Quinn. "The Bertière triplets."

Callie blinked at her mother in amazement. *She's lost her mind.* "That doesn't even make sense."

"It makes perfect sense, Callie. I watched you say goodbye to them. There was nothing there. No affection, no friendship, no *interest*. Nothing. You spent fifteen years living and working with those girls, but it was like you'd never even met them. And it was the same with the Cortez boys, and Patty-the-cook's daughter, Suzette, and Dabney. How many times did you say no to Dabney when he'd offer to teach you to juggle?"

"I already *knew* how to juggle!"

"I'm aware of that, Callie, and so was Dabney. The juggling was just an excuse. He wanted to spend time with you because he had a crush on you. The point is that there were plenty of kids your age living on the VanDrexel train, but—" Quinn's voice caught and she turned away.

"But *what*?" Callie demanded.

"But you didn't have one single friend."

Callie's mouth fell open. "Suzette and I were friends. We studied together all the time."

"Really?" Quinn looked skeptical. "Who is Suzette's favorite singer?"

"What?"

"Who's her favorite rock star?"

Callie shrugged and pulled a name out of the air. "Beyoncé."

"Nope."

"Taylor Swift?"

"Not even close."

"Okay, fine. I have no idea. Why does that even matter?"

"It matters because if she was your *friend*, you would know that sort of thing." Quinn shook her head. "It wasn't even a difficult question, Callie. My God, the girl listened to Shawn Mendes constantly."

"And that's the kind of thing you'd have wanted me to pay attention to? Suzette's pop music obsession? Instead of focusing on my routine?"

"Callie, you spent *all* your time on that damned tightrope."

"I spent my time with Gram," Callie fired back, tears making their way to the surface. "I was training. Practicing. That's what you do when you want to be the best at something. And I *was* the best. Everyone knew it. And then you just . . . ruined it."

Quinn glared but said nothing. Callie glared back; if she thought she had a snowball's chance in hell of finding her way back to the carriage house she might have turned and run.

"Gram knew what it meant to be a VanDrexel," Callie said, grinding the words out through her teeth.

"What in the world is that supposed to mean?"

"Never mind. The point is, you were never like us. You never cared about honoring our legacy, you never cared about becoming a star." She knew the next words rising up in her throat would be hurtful, but somehow she couldn't—or wouldn't—bring herself to choke them back. "Then again, you wouldn't have amounted to much anyway. It's not like you had any talent."

"Hey there!"

Callie whirled around to see a tall man in his midfifties coming down the broad front steps of the house. He wore faded jeans, a loose-fitting white linen shirt, and a beat-up pair of pricey tennis shoes. His intentionally shaggy brown hair was shot through with silver streaks, and his tanned face boasted the scruffy sort of almost-beard movie stars grew when they got cast in action-adventure films. His eyes were the blue of pool water.

"Bradford," said Quinn, blushing. "Hello."

So this was the Man Behind the Curtain.

"Welcome to the Sanctuary!" he said, joining them on the lawn. "So sorry I wasn't there to greet you when you arrived, Quinn. The town council called me in for an emergency meeting." He turned to Callie. "You must be Calliope. I've been looking forward to giving you the grand tour. Where would you like to start? Bears? Tigers? We've got a lion who's pretty darn handsome."

"That's okay," said Callie quickly. "Actually, I think I'm just gonna go . . ." Since she couldn't bring herself to say "home," she settled on "back."

Marston looked genuinely disappointed. "Are you sure? I just had the housekeeper brew a big pitcher of iced tea, and I was really looking forward to showing you both around. Athos, Porthos, and Aramis can't wait to meet you."

Butler, chauffer, and gardener? Callie guessed, eyeing the behemoth of a house. "I've got a lot of unpacking to do," she said, aiming a polite smile at Brad, which morphed into a barely concealed snarl when she turned it on her mom. "Ya know, before I start *school*."

"I understand completely," said Marston. Stuffing his hands into his pockets, he flashed a boyish grin, looking like the world's most earnest, not to mention well-dressed, ten-year-old. "So how about just one glass of iced tea and a quick tour of the conservatory? Then you can head home and unpack while your mom and I walk the grounds."

Quinn shot Callie an imploring look. Or was it a threat? Either way, it was clear she was *not* to say no to the hospitable landlord-slash-boss-slash-Viagra-print-ad-model.

"Sure. Great," she mumbled.

"Terrific!" Brad inclined his head, indicating that Callie should lead the way.

With a sigh, she trudged up the steps to the Mediterranean mega-mansion. Moments later, frosty tea glasses in hand, the three of them were making their way across the shining marble foyer toward an elegant iron gate. It was a miniature version of the towering one their Uber driver had driven through back at the Sanctuary's front entrance. As they drew nearer, Callie could see that the gate opened into a glass-enclosed conservatory, lavishly appointed with a small rain forest's worth of greenery. Every pane of glass, from the floor to the gently arched roof, sparkled as if it had been vigorously Windexed just seconds before.

"What was it you were saying about an emergency council meeting?" Quinn ventured, sipping her tea.

"Seems the locals aren't entirely thrilled about our ever-growing population of apex predators and thundering herds," said Marston, reaching into the pocket of his jeans to withdraw a designer keychain. "I guess when it comes to man-eating cats or nine-thousand-pound elephants, folks tend to adopt a firm NIMBY attitude."

"Nimby?" Callie echoed.

"It stands for 'not in my backyard,'" Quinn explained. "It's what people say when they object to something they perceive to be dangerous moving into their neighborhoods."

"But it's typically invoked with regard to things like toxic waste dumps and methadone clinics," Brad added.

"Are they talking about a lawsuit?" Quinn asked.

"Could be. It's been going on the whole year I've been open. But now that you and your wildly impressive credentials have arrived, I'm hoping the fine citizens of Lake St. Julian will relax. We just need to educate them about our mission." He turned his snapping blue eyes to Callie. "To that end, I was thinking you might want to take on the role of Sanctuary ambassador."

Quinn was positively beaming. "Callie, you'd be perfect for that job. What do you think?"

Stalling, Callie took a long swallow from her glass; the clinking of the ice echoed through the cavernous foyer. "Um, thanks, but I think I'm gonna pass."

"Callie!"

"What? I'm just being honest. I'm not interested."

"And that's absolutely fine," said Brad, his tone utterly reasonable. "It was just a suggestion. But may I ask why not?"

"Truthfully?" Callie shrugged. "*Nie mój cyrk, nie moje małpy.*"

"*Callie!*" Quinn covered her face with one hand, looking mortified. "I'm so sorry Brad. She's normally not this rude."

"*Was* that rude?" Brad laughed. "I wasn't sure. I don't speak— what was that, Polish?"

Callie nodded. "It's an old proverb my grandmother taught me." *Like she taught me everything else.*

"And what does it mean exactly?"

"It means 'Not my circus, not my monkeys,'" Callie translated. "Basically, it's just a way of saying, 'It's none of my business so I'm staying out of it.'"

"Not my circus, not my monkeys," Brad repeated, chuckling as he fit one of the keys into the lock of the pretty gate. "Well, here's the thing, Callie . . . This *is* my circus, and these *are* my monkeys. And my tigers, my elephants, my horses, my camels, my bears . . ."

God complex much?

"But mostly"—Brad pushed the gate open and fired off three sharp little whistles—"they're my monkeys."

From deep within the indoor jungle, a gleeful chattering erupted, followed by the urgent rustle of palm fronds, and the frantic swishing of twigs. Suddenly, there they were—a springy trio of puppet-sized primates. Their faces were creamy white, as was the fur on their shoulders, chests, and heads, except for a perfectly round marking of black on their heads, which made them look like beret-sporting street mimes.

"Athos, Porthos, and Aramis," Brad announced, as proudly as if he'd given birth to the three furry little beasts himself. "My monkeys."

"Capuchins!" Quinn cried out.

"Gesundheit," Brad joked, as Athos leapt into his arms. Porthos seemed happy just to cling to the billionaire's leg, but Aramis appeared to be a bit more needy, reaching up with both arms in a plea for Quinn to lift him.

The animal specialist was happy to oblige. "They're adorable," she said, as the little white-faced creature nuzzled her cheek.

"Callie," said Brad, "would you like to hold one?"

Callie was about to explain that she was never particularly comfortable around animals, but Athos was already climbing onto her shoulder. He posed there, pleased with himself, his tail draped around her neck like a living scarf. Callie endured this only long enough to seem polite to both monkey and owner.

"Okay there, See-No-Evil," she said, "time to go back to Daddy." As she awkwardly disengaged the capuchin from his perch and handed him over to Brad, another rustling began from the verdant depths of the conservatory.

"Another one?" Quinn gushed.

"That would be d'Artagnan, my chimp." Brad's smile flatlined. "Poor little guy's been through a lot. He's not as enamored with us humans as these three are. Quinn, I'm hoping you'll be able to get through to him."

Just beyond the gate, a pair of cautious amber eyes was peering out from behind a palm frond.

"Has he exhibited any threatening behavior?" Quinn asked, lowering her voice.

Brad looked reluctant to testify against his troubled pal. "He has been a little aggressive from time to time. Nothing overly violent. He just gets anxious when someone a little higher up the food chain comes too close. He screams, he flails, claps his hands . . . So far it's all a big show, but I don't have to tell you how strong he is."

The palm moved again, sweeping away to reveal d'Artagnan in all his swaggering glory. Callie immediately realized that Marston's use of "little guy" as an endearment was indeed just that; the ape stood nearly four feet tall and must have weighed well over a hundred pounds. "How strong *is* he?" Callie asked, feeling compelled to back away.

"Strong enough to do significant physical damage if he were so inclined," Quinn replied.

"Can he kill someone?"

"Callie—"

"Can he?"

"If he were so inclined," Quinn repeated. "But my job is going to be to prevent that inclination."

"And mine," said Brad, "is to make sure that every possible safety precaution is taken at all times, not just in here but throughout the entire Sanctuary grounds."

D'Artagnan took two tentative steps forward, as though to better assess the tableau before him—three humans and three capuchins. Callie imagined they looked like the opening credit sequence of some bizarre alternate-universe *Brady Bunch* rerun.

"He's limping," she observed.

"His right leg was broken when we rescued him," Brad explained. "Probably better I don't tell you how it got that way."

Now the chimp's expression changed. His lips pulled back, curving outward and back, showing off his gums and displaying a set of disconcertingly human-looking teeth.

"At least he's smiling," Callie remarked.

"That's the fear grin," said Quinn, the concern in her voice immediately contradicted by the fact that she was now stooping low and tiptoeing directly toward the chimp, showing him her empty, upturned palms. "Don't smile back. He'll think you mean him harm, and he might attack. If you absolutely must smile, make sure your upper lip is covering your top teeth."

Callie held her mouth closed, lowering her shoulders until she was, like her mother, in a stooping position. Now she could see the hairless places on d'Artagnan's arms and neck, badly scarred skin from where, clearly, he'd been bound. Pulling his gaze away from Quinn, he looked at Callie, tilting his head this way and that, as if trying to remember her.

Then without so much as a hoot, he ducked under the palm and disappeared.

And for the briefest of moments, Callie almost missed him.

FOUR

New Jersey, 1965

"LET'S GO, FIRST OF May. Up and at 'em!"

The voice slams into my head as if it's been shot out of a cannon. It's gruff, and completely unknown to me. So is the muted light pressing against my eyelids and the strange, flat surface of whatever it is I've been sleeping on.

Cot.

Train.

Booze.

Right . . . booze. And lots of it: a butterscotch-colored liquid slurped straight from the bottle between intervals of nervous laughter (mine). Disappointingly, the drink had tasted less like butterscotch, and more like the epicenter of the sun.

A rush of images darts into my head: *A girl with feathers in her hair . . . a diminutive clown with a crooked nose . . . a lion's roar, as loud as a jet engine; the clown—Duncan—is in love with the magician's assistant . . .*

It's a lot to take in, and on top of it all, it seems I am also in the throes of my very first hangover.

I vaguely recall that we left Massachusetts just after midnight the night before last. It was astonishing how quickly the circus could fold itself up and become portable. One minute it was a dazzling small city, the next a popcorn-scented memory lingering over a trampled field.

We'd traveled through the night. The clack and whir of the locomotive lulled me into a deep sleep—a dreamless sleep. And why

38

not? For me, the best dreams were now to be had during waking hours.

Yesterday, I wandered and watched. Almost no one spoke to me, and I didn't mind. They weren't rude, just busy. So incredibly busy! I saw stakes being pounded, tents going up, generators humming to life. The making of the show was a show in itself—orders were barked, adjustments were made. I watched dancers dusting their eyelids with shimmering powders before slipping into silken tights. I grabbed a sandwich in the pie car—my first encounter with pastrami on rye. Cornelius and I did not cross paths, but he had advised me to observe, and so I had. Dutifully, hungrily, I observed it all, until it was time to watch the show a second time, again from the bottom bleacher, and somehow I found myself loving it here in— where were we?—New Jersey!—even more than I had loved it in Massachusetts. Perhaps because I had seen the spectacle come to life, and was beginning to know its secrets.

When the show was over, Duncan had found me and told me it was time to meet my new family. I think I may have flinched at the word. Taking note of my reaction, Duncan rephrased.

"Time to have some fun," he'd said.

Much better. Bring on the alcohol, cue the small talk: *Go on, taste it—it won't kill ya! Davis, huh? Got arrested with a fella name of Davis once, in Salt Lake City. Or was it Harrisburg? You from around here, Vicki? Ha! Me neither!*

Again, the voice explodes from outside the train car. "Move it, First of May. I ain't got all day!"

"I'll be right out," I rasp, not quite getting the calendar reference, but somehow knowing it's meant for me.

Rolling off the cot, I pull on my pedal pushers and step into my sneakers, quietly so as not to wake the girl sleeping on the cot opposite mine. The feather boa and the glittery high heels strewn around the train car remind me that she's a dancer. Her form beneath the threadbare blanket is lithe and long, and her curls, splayed

39

across the pillow, are the rusty red of autumn leaves, though I suspect their shade, rather like the booze I consumed far too much of, comes straight from a bottle.

Stepping outside, I'm hit by an onslaught of strong scents—some human, some animal, fleeting whiffs of sugary things fried in old grease, but mostly piss and paraffin and hay bales baking in the sun.

A stout man in overalls stands with his hands on his hips, scowling impatiently. It seems he's the yeller. Beside him is a man in a dark suit, and my heart sinks because I'm sure someone has summoned the authorities—whatever branch of the local government is responsible for retrieving teenage runaways.

"Good morning, Miss Davis."

The "Miss Davis" throws me until I remember with a wave of nausea that I am no longer Catherine Hastings of Brooksvale, Mass. Then, another flash of memory, this one from two nights ago—*red coat, white jodhpurs, curling leather whip . . .*

"Oh! Mr. VanDrexel," I say quickly. "I'm sorry. I didn't recognize you without your . . . um . . . epaulets."

He gives me a jolly laugh befitting a man of his profession. "I hardly recognize myself without them either," he says. "Unfortunately, my presence is required at a nuisance meeting with some city officials."

My heart flips over. So he *has* come to haul me to the police station and send me back to Boston.

But Cornelius simply nods to his companion and walks away. Without me.

I turn a baffled look to the man in the overalls.

"Seems some local busybodies are up in arms about the way we might be treating our animals. VanDrexel is off to assure them we ain't never nor will we ever hurt a living creature in the name of entertainment."

"Is that the truth?" I hear myself asking. "Or just what he's going to tell them?"

"It is God's own truth," the man assures me. "Might not be the case with our competitors, I'm sorry to say, but round here, the beasts are like family. Loved and respected. Spoiled in fact. Cornelius's sons wouldn't have it any other way." He hitches up his overalls, which seem to be part of his very being. "The name's Vince. I'm the gaffer, which means I manage this mud show. Which means I'm your boss."

"I'm Cath—uh, Victoria."

"No, you're First of May," he corrects. "For the time being, any-way. Means somebody who's new to the circus, and round here, you gotta prove yourself." Then without even offering a handshake, he turns on his heel and trudges away from the tent.

For a portly guy, Vince moves fast. I have to practically run to keep up with him as we hurry across the grounds, which are littered with crumpled programs, soda cups, cigarette butts, and hundreds of slender white paper cones, some with sparkling pink filaments of cotton candy still clinging to them. It looks like a herd of unicorns passed through and chose this spot to simultaneously, perhaps cere-moniously, shed their mystical horns . . . and then eat popcorn.

I bend down to pluck one of the cones from the sprawling mess. When Vince sees what I'm doing, he stops in his tracks. "It's not your job to pick up garbage," he says brusquely. "We got people for that. We got people for everything. Circus runs smoother when everybody does the job they been given, so just do what you're meant to do, and leave the other stuff to other folks."

"Sorry," I say, crumpling the cone and stuffing it into my pocket. "I don't know all the rules here yet."

"It's not a rule," he says. "It's common sense. But if you run better on regulations, so be it."

My father's house was filled with rules—most of which were

impossible to abide by. I kind of like the idea of making my own rules for a change, so I make a mental note: *Everyone has a job to do.*

Vince starts walking again, and again I am galloping in his wake. We pass the wagons where the big cats sleep, their mobile homes garishly painted in hues of candy-apple red and sunshine yellow. I'm struck by how these wagons can be so utilitarian and fanciful at the same time—the harshness of the metal bars offset by the ornately carved architectural borders, a fancy façade masking the danger within. *Beauty on the outside, danger on the inside.* Exactly what I've run away from.

Around me, the bustle of activity is like a balm. Roustabouts in dirty dungarees lug tools and equipment I have yet to learn the names of. Star performers, free of last night's flashy garb and flamboyant makeup, are back to being merely people. A gang of little boys has snuck onto the grounds and no one bothers to chase them off. They should probably be at cello lessons or Little League practice but they've come to the circus instead, and everyone here understands that the circus is always so much better than where you're supposed to be.

In the distance, I hear strains of music, a tinny glockenspiel and the brassiest brass section ever to blow a note, rehearsing for the afternoon show. And . . . "A calliope!" I cry out, mostly because in my whole life, I've never had cause to say the word *calliope* out loud, but also because it is the most magical sound I've ever heard.

"Pretty, ain't it," grunts Vince, still walking. "Now watch out for the horseshit."

"Where are we going exactly?"

"The elephant cage."

"Really? Why?"

"Because it ain't gonna clean itself, that's why."

I don't think I like the sound of that.

But the music is making me want to march, to tumble head over heels. The band beckons, *Come with me! Something's about to happen!* I am so mesmerized by the sound I almost forget there's an elephant cage in my immediate future.

Most impressive by far are the colors. The whole place is a traveling prism that's been to more cities than I can even imagine. It's been admired and marveled at by countless spectators. How many millions of people have been lured by the poppy-red stripes of the sideshow tent and the go-light-green paint of the snack stand with signs in bold pink print, promising ice cream bars for a nickel and funnel cakes dusted with cinnamon?

Someone in pajamas rolls past on a unicycle. The unicycle is silver; the pajamas are polka dot—magenta, cobalt, chartreuse. My father would pronounce them gaudy, and technically he'd be right, but I love them anyway. A handsome roustabout passes, leading a camel on a rope. The camel is the shade of a perfect pancake and the roustabout's dungarees are indigo. So are his eyes; they hold on me as he draws nearer, and my heart skips.

"Mornin', darlin'," the roustabout drawls.

"Morning," I say, liking the semisweet scratch of my hangover voice, liking his scruffy good looks, and especially liking the sound of that "darlin'."

"What's his name?" I ask.

"His name is Forget It," Vince says unhelpfully, and I get the feeling it's not the first time he's dispensed that particular advice about this particular guy.

We breeze past the entrance to a private backstage area that appears to have been set up just for the clowns.

"That's Clown Alley," says Vince, with something close to reverence. "Admittance is by invitation only."

I spy a bouquet of purple and orange balloons tethered to a pole. The remaining few that went unsold last night, they wilt and pucker, but they're still afloat, and to me, they're beautiful just for trying.

If the balloons can do it, so can I.

At last we reach the elephant cage (really not a cage at all, but a trailer). Its enormous gray inhabitant is coming down the ramp guided by his handler, a young man who murmurs words of encouragement in a deep, kind voice. "That's it," he says. "Good boy. Few more steps, pal . . . yeah, you got it."

The handler is even cuter than Forget It the roustabout. He's got green eyes and a ready smile. It's a moment before I recognize that he's one of the handsome lion tamers I noticed the first night. During last night's performance he nuzzled the cheek of a full-grown lion as if it were a newborn kitten. Today he's wearing a snug-fitting VanDrexel's Family Circus T-shirt, clean blue jeans, and water buffalo sandals—the brown leather ones with a ring for the big toe to slide into. I really wanted a pair last summer, but my father deemed them "too bohemian," and that was the end of that.

When the boy sees me staring at his feet, he laughs. "Still don't like my sandals, huh?"

"Oh, it's not that," I say quickly, "it's just—" I stop short, tilting my head. "Still?"

"Last night you asked me if I borrowed them from Jesus. But then again"—he mimes tippling a bottle toward his lips—"I guess I shouldn't be surprised you don't remember."

Before I can ask him what he's talking about, Vince clears his throat. "Allow me to make the introductions," he says, giving the elephant an affectionate pat on the trunk. "This big guy is Rabelais. And this not-so-big guy is James."

"Rabelais," says James, "meet the new girl."

"Pleasure to meet you, Rabelais," I say with a perfectly straight face, and Rabelais makes a jolly trumpeting sound: elephant for "the pleasure's all mine."

"Wanna see him wave hi? It's his signature move." When I nod, James lowers his voice and says, "Give him some room, then shout 'hello.'"

I take two steps to the side, then call out, "Hello!"

Recognizing his cue, Rabelais happily swings his trunk in a wide arc.

At the same moment, someone shouts Vince's name from across the yard, anxiously alerting him to two of the company's day laborers in the midst of a brawl.

"Be right there!" Vince hollers back, then stomps up the ramp, muttering under his breath.

I am unnerved at the sight of such violence. "Does that happen often?" I ask.

James shrugs. "Often enough that I'm not getting involved." He gives me a lopsided grin. "Or as we say around here, 'Not my circus, not my monkeys.' Ain't that right, Rabelais?"

The animal drapes his trunk playfully around James's shoulders—an elephant's version of a hug. It's strange how utterly natural it seems.

"I thought you worked with the lions," I say.

"I *perform* with the cats. But I work with all of the animals. See, I've got this special . . . connection to them. Probably because I was born in the jungle. My parents were missionaries in Africa."

I'm immediately impressed. "That sounds exciting."

"Well, it was. Until they died." His voice catches, his muscles flinch. "Of malaria. I was just an infant at the time, totally abandoned. Luckily a family of apes took me in and raised me till I was three. Then some scientists found me and I was sent home to the States, where Cornelius put me in his sideshow. For the next five years, I was Baby Bongo, Child of the Congo." He shrugs. "That's my life story."

"Or . . ." I mutter as realization dawns, "a really bad twist on the plot of *Tarzan*."

James laughs, pleased with himself. "Okay, ya got me. But c'mon, you were buying it for a minute there."

"Do you begin all your new friendships with a bold-faced lie?"

"Maybe." His eyes twinkle, and his voice is a rugged purr, perhaps a side effect of hanging around with lions. "But who says we have to be just friends?"

Lesson learned: *The cutest guy in the circus will turn out to be just as cocky as the cutest guy anywhere else.*

Thankfully, Vince returns with a shovel, which he thrusts into my hand.

Shaking off James's flirtation, I frown. "I don't mean to be difficult, but why exactly am I cleaning the elephant cage?"

He looks at me as if I'm some kind of simpleton. "Because it's dirty."

"No, I understand *that* . . . I mean, why *me*?"

"Because James requested you."

I whirl back to face the Baby Bongo impersonator. "You requested *me*? Why?"

"Wow, you really don't remember, do you?" James chuckles, giving Rabelais a rub behind one of his kite-like ears. "When we met last night, in Duncan's trailer, you were already somewhere between real tipsy and completely plastered."

"And my punishment for that is to clean up after the elephant?"

"It's not punishment. You're here because you lost a bet."

I have no memory of making any wager.

"Well, it was more of an audition, actually. You explained—adorably, by the way—that you and Dunc were trying to figure out what job you'd be good at. He was leaning toward putting you in charge of the midway game where you guess customers' weights and ages, but I had my doubts about you being able to pull it off. Then you got all huffy and mad—also adorable—and bet me you could guess my weight and age blindfolded and with both hands tied behind your back. To which *I* said—"

The fog in my brain begins to lift. "You said, 'That could definitely be arranged,'" I recount, scowling.

"Yeah, and you didn't think it was funny *then*, either. Anyway, we decided that if you guessed right, you'd get the job. If not . . ."

"Elephant cage," I finish, considering my surroundings.

"You guessed I was a hundred and thirty-six years old, and weighed seventeen and a half pounds—"

I fold my arms indignantly. "Did it ever occur to you, seeing as I was somewhere between tipsy and plastered, that I may have accidentally inverted my answers?"

"Of course it occurred to me. Especially because I *am* seventeen, and I weigh about one forty. But you still lost the bet. And then you threw up."

Way to make a first impression, Catherine—I mean, Victoria.

"Look on the bright side," he drawls. "We're a small show—we've only got the one bull."

"Wait. I have to clean up after the cattle, too?"

He laughs. "This isn't the rodeo, sweetheart. 'Bull' is what we call an elephant."

Then, with a gallant sweep of his arm, James motions to the ramp. We march up side by side into the long dark tunnel that is Rabelais's home, and James sets about educating me in the intricacies of elephant-cage maintenance. It's a short lesson because my job is basically to shovel up the poop—of which there is plenty—then deposit it into the barrel located right outside the trailer. When he sees that the stench is making my already bleary eyes water, he looks almost sympathetic.

"Don't worry. After the first seventy or eighty pounds you don't even notice the smell."

"Seventy or eighty *pounds*? Are you crazy? I can't—" My complaint is interrupted by a voice from outside the trailer that's almost as ethereally lilting as the calliope I heard earlier.

"James? Are you in there?"

A girl about my age suddenly pokes her head into the trailer, wrinkling her nose at the odor. She's wearing one of the new Lilly Pulitzer dresses from Palm Beach that I've seen Emily wear, and a pair of lime-green Pappagallo flats embellished with oversize grosgrain bows. Her blond hair is swept up loosely to showcase an expensive choker of graduated pearls. I have a similar strand sitting in my jewelry box at home. If I had known the circus called for formal attire, I might have thought to bring them along.

"You promised to give me a tour of your circus," she reminds James, batting her eyes demurely, first at him, then at Rabelais. "I really like your elephant."

I pivot toward James. "What kind of bet did *she* lose?"

"Actually . . ." James grins. "She *won*."

Rolling my eyes, I scoop up a huge pile of elephant dung and toss it through the trailer's wide opening. I'm not sure why, but it's an effort to aim for the barrel and not the blond. She narrowly escapes the splatter and shoots me an icy look.

"You might want to step back a bit," James tells his date. "I'll be right out."

Still glaring, she of the pearl choker removes herself from the path of flying crap.

James brushes the hay off his jeans. "She's the mayor's daughter," he explains, stuffing his hands into his pockets. "It's a favor, a public relations thing. People can be mistrustful of the circus, so we like to stay on the good side of the local bigwigs."

"Well, then I wouldn't walk her through Clown Alley, if I were you. They'll probably think she stole those shoes from one of their costume trunks."

James laughs again, and again, his eyes twinkle . . . just like Mr. VanDrexel's. And that's when it hits me.

"You're Cornelius's son, aren't you?"

He rocks back on his heels, grinning. "The younger one. As well as the braver, more interesting, and much better-looking one. Also the old man's favorite. Did I mention I was better looking?"

"You did. And I'm sure the mayor's daughter would concur. But does she know you're a compulsive liar?"

He gives me a confused look. "The Congo thing? That wasn't a lie, it was a joke."

"You told me it wasn't your circus." I deepen my voice to quote him. "'Not my monkeys, not my circus.'"

His smile would be patronizing if it weren't so charming. "First of all, you got it backward. And second, *that* wasn't a lie either, it was an expression. An old Polish proverb to be exact. And the part about the monkeys happens to be true, because we don't have any monkeys. So they can't be mine, can they?"

It must be a rhetorical question because he doesn't wait for my response. He simply saunters down the ramp, snaps Rabelais a friendly salute, and walks away with the girl's slender arm tucked cozily in his.

"Maybe he *was* raised by apes," I grumble to Rabelais.

The elephant shakes his giant head and lets out an amused little roar.

After shoveling dung for the better part of the morning, I decide I deserve a break. I sit down on the edge of the trailer, letting my legs dangle, just as a woman in a pair of short-shorts and a midriff top approaches; she pauses to nuzzle Rabelais's trunk, then turns her attention to me.

"Anybody ever tell you you've got great legs?"

"Not really."

"Well, you do." She lights a cigarette and gives me a smile.

Now I recognize her. My next words come out in a squeal of excitement. "You're the tightrope walker! Your act is amazing!"

"Thanks, hon. I'm Sharon."

"Victoria." We shake hands; I'm sure I stink to high heaven, but Sharon is polite enough not to say so.

Lounging against the side of the trailer, she blows out a cloud of smoke and offers me a cigarette, which I decline.

"Okay, sister," she says, "here's the part where we get to know each other. You tell me yours, and I tell you mine."

"Beg your pardon?"

"Time to swap sob stories. I'm guessing you've got one. Why else would you be here cleaning up after old Rabelais?"

I look down at the dirty knees of my pedal pushers and swallow hard. "Maybe I just like elephants."

"And maybe I'm Ladybird Johnson." Sharon laughs and takes another long drag on her cigarette. "All right, fine, I'll go first. When I was about your age I dropped out of high school to try my luck in Hollywood. Real original, huh? Well, I got as far as Peoria, Illinois, and ran out of cash, so I was compelled to seek other means of, shall we say, *gainful employment*. One night on my way home from . . . *work* . . . I spotted a poster announcing that VanDrexel's Family Circus was opening the next day." She takes another puff and exhales with a dreamy expression. "Honestly, are there any other words in the whole damned English language quite as seductive as 'the circus is in town'?"

Right now I can think of a couple . . . *soap*, for instance, and *air freshener*. But she seems to want me to agree with her, so I smile.

"The next morning, I treated myself to a front-row ticket, and I was hooked. I thought, 'Screw Hollywood . . . This is where the real glamour is!' So I came back the next day, and the next, and when I found out Cornelius's tightrope walker had skipped out on him, I inquired about the job. Didn't matter that I didn't know the first thing about tightrope walking. I figured tiptoeing across a high wire in here had to be better than crawling around on my hands and knees"—she jerks her head toward the perimeter of the grounds—"out there."

I nod, studying her face. "So you've been with the VanDrexels since . . . ?"

"Since 1945," she says, tapping the cigarette with her index finger, dislodging a flurry of ash. "Okay, your turn. How'd you find your way to the Big Top?"

I open my mouth, fully prepared to tell her a lie—something trite and harmless like *I've always wanted to travel*, or *I'm great with animals*, but I hear myself telling her a shorthand version of the truth:

"My mother is dying. For all I know, she's already dead. And my father is a controlling brute who gets more violent every day. If I stayed in that house long enough, he'd probably kill me. So I left to join the circus."

I realize my eyes are welling up; Sharon's are too.

It seems I've learned another lesson: *They call them* sob *stories for a reason.*

But while Sharon looks deeply sad for me, she does not look overly shocked by my confession, so I guess she's heard this sort of story before. She's quiet for a long moment, then grinds out her cigarette in the dirt and places a motherly hand on my cheek.

"The thing about running away to join the circus," she says, her tone somber, "is that it's a good idea when you believe you're running *toward* something. But it can get awfully complicated when you're running *from* something."

I can almost swear I hear Rabelais rumble his agreement.

"The point is, you've found us. You've found *this*." Her hands flutter to encompass the surrounding blur and thrum of the circus. "And if you've found it, then it's meant to be."

She has no idea how *not* meant to be this is. I'm not staying; I just have to make it look like I am until I get where I'm going.

Wherever that is.

"And of course," she adds, smiling softly, "it always helps if the circus is in your blood."

I spring up abruptly and grab my shovel. "I guess I'll find out if it's in mine," I lie.

"I guess you will," says Sharon, tapping another cigarette out of the pack—the last one. "Meantime, maybe you should stick close to me."

I tilt my head. "Why?"

"Because it helps if you have someone to show you the ropes." Laughing, she crumples the empty cigarette package and tosses it toward the barrel but misses. "And in my case, I mean that literally." Wrapping her smile around the new cigarette, she lights it and takes a long drag, sucking away half of it in a single puff. "I'm taking you on," she announces.

"What do you mean?" I ask, waving away the smoke she exhales.

"I'll be your mentor. Or if you prefer, friend. Point is, we learn from those who know, it's as simple as that." She looks me up and down and grins. "Now, other than a long hot shower, what do you need?"

"Everything," I tell her, only just realizing it myself. "I left in a hurry."

Her eyes say *of course you did.* "Lucky for you, we circus folk are generous."

Then, with a wink, she turns and makes her way back across the yard.

Find someone to show you the ropes. Learn from those who know.

Sharon vanishes into the Big Top tent, just as another round of calliope music swells to a happy, spine-tingling crescendo.

I decide to take it as a good omen.

FIVE

~

"BENIGNO'S PIZZA!" A GIRL'S voice burbled into Callie's ear. "This is Shana. How can I help you?"

Callie tapped the screen of Quinn's phone to put it on speaker. "Hi, do you deliver?"

"Uh-huh, we sure do."

"I'd like a small pepperoni and mushroom pizza please."

"You got it. Address?"

"It's on Sanctuary Way. There isn't really a street number, because it's the gar— the carriage house. But you can't miss it."

Shana hesitated. "Can I put you on hold for just a bit?"

Callie's stomach growled. She was beginning to wish she'd taken Mom and Mr. Marston up on their offer to join them for an early dinner.

Shana returned, flustered. "Are you the chicken parm grinder no onions on Palmetto Boulevard?"

"No, I'm the small pepperoni and mushroom on Sanctuary Way."

"Okay, yeah . . . we're not sure we can deliver there."

"Why not?"

"Well, wouldn't it be, like . . . dangerous?"

"Only if you brought me the chicken parm instead of the pepperoni and mushroom."

"Oh, okay . . . so now you *don't* want the chicken?"

"I never did. I just want the pizza. But it's starting to feel like you don't want me to have it."

"Oh, no, it's not that at all," Shana assured her. "It's just, well . . . because of the lions."

"Lion," Callie corrected. "We've only got the one. And it's not like he'll be sitting on the front porch when the delivery guy gets here. He's in a locked enclosure."

"Oh, okay." Another pause. "Can you hang on one more sec?"

The sec became a "min." Then two, then three. With an exasperated sigh, Callie flung herself onto the sheet-draped sofa to wait.

"Pepperoni and mushroom? You still there?"

No, the lion ate me. "Yep, still here."

"The driver says he'll bring your order as far as the main entrance, but he won't come inside, so you'll have to meet him at the gate. He's going to get out of the car, leave the pizza on the ground, then get back *into* his car, *then* you can open the gate and get it."

Callie rolled her eyes, doubting the pizza would be worth the effort.

"Your total is $16.86. Thirty-five minutes."

Callie ended the call and stepped into her sneakers; she'd kill the half-hour pizza gap with a leisurely walk—anything to keep from diving back into that jewelry box filled with handwritten notes from the grandmother she'd never see or speak to again.

She'd managed to distract herself all afternoon, unpacking while Mr. Marston took Mom to get reacquainted with her animals. Callie spent hours organizing her clothes in the closet and antique dresser, knowing full well that Mr. Marston's pending remodel would likely negate the chore. She could picture the dresser (which she actually kind of liked) being unceremoniously tossed in favor of something new and expensive.

She headed down the stairs, let the door bang closed behind her, and set out on the crumbling path toward the gate.

Why had Gram written on those scraps? What did they mean?

Following what she hoped was the correct path to the entrance, Callie caught the salty bite of seawater in the air and wondered how far they were from the beach. It was one thing about Florida she thought she might actually enjoy.

For years, VanDrexel's Family Circus had made their "winter home" in Sarasota, where Quinn would spend their seasonal break bunking in an RV on-site to be close to the animals. Callie, however, rarely spent more than a day or two there. Instead, she would travel with her grandmother, the two of them teaching tightrope classes to children at summer camp or appearing as guest performers in circuses across the country and around the world.

Once she and Gram had taken advantage of a booking in Maine to spend a weekend at a drafty old cabin on a sparkling lake that Victoria had visited as a little girl, and once they'd gone to Italy, to enjoy *Un Piccolo Circo Familiare,* a small but highly respected show run by the dashing Marcello Ricci, a trapeze aerialist who'd been a visiting performer at VanDrexel's seventeen years before. He and Quinn—both in their late thirties at the time—had embarked on a whirlwind romance, and as Marcello had described it the time he'd happily recounted the story to Callie, *"Ecco fatto, aspettiamo una bambina!"*

The *bambina,* of course, was her.

Callie had only met her father in person a handful of times; he'd come to the States for her fifth and tenth birthdays, and when she was thirteen she and Gram had visited his circus in Italy. There she'd had the thrill of performing with him in the century-old *piccolo circo* he'd inherited from his family. Callie was quick to pick up the trapeze skills he so eagerly taught her, and their father-daughter act had delighted their European audiences. Marcello had been beside himself with pride, and for the first time Callie truly understood that the circus was indeed in her blood—on both sides of the DNA helix. She only hoped that when Marcello received her letter, begging him to let her come tour as a tightrope walker in his Circo Familiare, he would understand too.

Callie arrived at the front entrance at the exact same moment a battered Volvo convertible came screaming up to the gate, shrieking to a brutal stop. In the driver's seat was a girl with a blond haystack of a ponytail and retro sunglasses.

"Pepperoni and mushroom, right?"

Callie nodded and pressed the code Mr. Marston had given her into the keypad—Grover and Agnes's wedding anniversary. The ornate iron gates slowly began to part. At the same time, the driver's door flew open wide, and a girl hopped out, completely violating the agreed-upon safety precautions.

Callie blinked, confused. "I thought you were going to wait until—are you Shana?"

"Please! All that stuff about not having the balls to enter the grounds—that was Brody, the delivery guy. Total fucking bonehead, and major chicken shit. He acts like this place is Jurassic Park or something. Everybody around here does. So I volunteered, making me what you might call the 'substitute cuisine-transfer personnel.'"

Callie watched as the girl reached back into the car to snatch the pizza box.

"I'm Jenna, by the way. Officially, I'm a waitress, but since I'm the only Benigno's employee whose brain has fully evolved, I frequently step in to do the things my IQ-deficient coworkers can't handle. Basic math, for example . . . folding napkins. And delivering delicious pizza products to the poor shunned folks who live on dangerous wild animal reserves."

"Can I have my pizza please?" Callie asked, slightly dazed. "And it's exotic."

Jenna cocked her head. "I'd hardly categorize pepperoni as exotic."

"Not the pizza. The animals. You said wild. They're actually exotic."

"There's a difference?"

"Yes." Callie frowned. "No. Actually, I don't know. It's just how my mother always described them."

"Hmm. So maybe the animals *prefer* 'exotic' to 'wild.' But really, how would we know? Have they ever *objected* to being classified as wild?"

"Can I just have my pizza?" Callie repeated.

"Only if you let me come inside."

"What?" Callie was caught off guard. "Why?"

"Are you kidding? I've been dying to get a look at this place since it opened. I love that all these abused animals are being rescued from those skeezy circuses."

"They weren't *abused*!" Callie spat. *Well, not all of them.*

Jenna gave her a challenging look. "Were they kept in cages?"

Callie rolled her eyes. "No, they all lived in luxury condos."

Jenna snorted out a little laugh. "Good one, pepperoni and mushroom." She flipped the box open and helped herself to a slice. "I'm all about the sarcastic wit. So, you're telling me these animals weren't starved and beaten?"

"Ours weren't. Never. My mother wouldn't have allowed it. She always used to say, 'Cages are a necessity. Cruelty isn't.'"

Jenna considered this, taking a bite of the pizza. "So what happened to her?"

"Who?" Callie was having difficulty keeping up. Perhaps it was because she was close to dying of starvation. "What happened to who?"

"Your mother." Jenna popped a piece of pepperoni into her mouth. "She's gone, right?"

"Yes, she's gone."

"So what happened to her?"

"She went to dinner with her boss."

"Oh. So she's alive."

"Last I heard. Why would you think she wasn't?"

"I dunno, just the way you said, 'My mother *always used to say.'* Sounded very postmortem."

"I meant she used to say it when she was working with the animals in our circus," Callie clarified with an exasperated breath.

"Ah. Gotcha."

Callie reached for the pizza box, but Jenna jerked it out of reach. "First, clarify what you mean when you say 'your' circus?"

"I don't have to clarify anything to you."

"You do if you want your pizza."

Callie felt her cheeks beginning to burn. She hadn't planned on sharing her life story with this pizza person, but that's certainly where this seemed to be going. She might as well get it over with so she could eat. "My mother and I were both born into VanDrexel's Family Circus, which was founded by my grandfather's ancestors but got sold to a big entertainment company way back in the sixties. Then the animals retired, so she left, and now we're here." Callie held out her hand for the pizza box.

"You were *born* into the circus?" Jenna echoed, gnashing into her pizza and gulping it down. "That's really . . . well, to be honest, I'm not sure if that's extremely cool or hella freaky. But you do get big points for transparency."

"Gee thanks. Your turn. Why do you want to come inside so badly?"

Jenna took another bite of pizza, shrugged, and swallowed. "Because, the opening of this Sanctuary was a big fuckin' deal around here and I like to stay informed."

Snatching the pizza box, Callie dropped two ten-dollar bills into Jenna's hand and turned to head back through the gate.

And without being invited to, Jenna followed.

For some reason Callie didn't stop her.

∽

They had just reached the carriage house when Brad's Range Rover glided up behind them.

"I'm guessing these are the parents?" said Jenna, eyeing the terrific-looking couple climbing out of the vehicle.

"One of them is."

"Who's the other one?"

"Oh, y'know . . . just some billionaire."

"Well, hello there," said Quinn, her smile bobbing back and forth curiously between Callie and their unexpected guest. "Calliope—who's your friend?"

"Cuisine-transfer personnel," Callie muttered, throwing open the door to the stairway.

"Jenna Demming," said Jenna, stepping forward to shake Quinn's hand, then Brad's. "I delivered the pizza." Then she turned to Callie. "Your name is *Calliope*?"

"Her grandmother named her," said Quinn. "She always said a name should be a kind of enchantment. Didn't work out so well for me, though; *my* full name is Quinn Emily Sharon VanDrexel."

"Yikes," said Jenna. "Sorry to hear that."

"Callie fared far better. She got her name because the sound of the calliope was one of the first things my mother fell in love with at the circus."

"That is so cool!" Jenna said. "I'm named after some great-aunt in Tuscaloosa. Nothing particularly enchanting about that. Although family lore does suggest that she was a bit of a slut in her day, so I guess that's something."

Quinn looked momentarily taken aback, and Callie smirked. *You were the one who wanted me to make friends.*

"You live here in Lake St. Julian, Jenna?" asked Brad, unloading plastic grocery sacks from the back of the SUV.

"Yep. And let me just say right up front, I don't hate y'all anywhere near as much as the rest of the people in this town do."

Brad laughed. "Well, thanks, that's nice to hear. I think."

Taking two of the bags from him, Jenna followed Callie and Quinn up the stairs.

While Callie ate pizza on the couch, Quinn and Brad unloaded the groceries and fielded Jenna's questions about the Sanctuary, starting with why visitors weren't allowed on the grounds.

Halfway through Quinn's slightly preachy "these animals spent years performing in front of crowds" speech, Jenna interrupted. "Your reasoning is sound, but is there any chance you'd rethink that policy? I'm not suggesting you start selling souvenir rain ponchos or serving up corn dogs on sticks or anything like that, but what about inviting the neighbors in for an informational tour? I'm sure one day wouldn't compromise the natural habitat angle."

Abruptly, Brad straightened up from where he'd been bent over the refrigerator's crisper drawer (which, incredibly, still functioned). "Y'know, that's actually not a bad idea. I've been operating this place for a year now and I never thought of that. The pizza girl's been here half an hour and already she's got a better handle on PR than I do."

"Guess it's a good thing you *inherited* your money," Callie mumbled under her breath.

"An open house could go a long way toward generating good-will," said Quinn thoughtfully. "It's something to consider."

"Hell yeah it is," said Jenna. "People would be a lot less eager to run your collective human and nonhuman asses out of town if they understood what you were trying to accomplish here behind those fancy gates. After all, it's a truth universally acknowledged that people fear what they don't understand. You've gotta believe me on this. We Lake St. Julianites—or is it St. Julianians?—whatever . . . we don't *want* to hate you. That pretty much goes against everything we stand for."

Taking the empty pizza box to the kitchenette, Callie rolled her eyes.

"I know to the uninitiated, Lake St. Julian looks like some tropical mash-up of Stars Hollow and Twin Peaks," Jenna went on, "but don't let our quirkiness fool you. It's really just a sweet little town where people look out for one another. We may not have apple pies cooling on the windowsills, but you can knock on any door in town, ask for a bowl of gator gumbo, and you're guaranteed to get it."

"Who would *want* it?" Callie wondered aloud.

"Don't knock it till you've tried it, Calliope," Jenna advised, then turned to Quinn and Marston and gave them a glowing smile. "So what do you call that lion of yours?"

"We named him DiCaprio," said Brad. "Because—"

"Leo was just too obvious?" Jenna finished, grinning. "Excellent. Can we go say hello?"

Brad and Quinn walked Jenna up to the mansion in the hopes that some of the big cats would be making an evening appearance.

Callie opted out, which annoyed her mother. Good. She wasn't exactly crazy about the way Quinn and Jenna were acting as if they were long-lost soul sisters just because the girl liked animals.

The minute they were gone, she put on her tightrope shoes. Seconds later she was in the backyard, mounting the wire.

It almost hurt to feel the tightrope under her weight. The rightness was both soothing and agonizing as a rush of memory swelled— Gram's voice, her wisdom, the pressure of her hands as they'd adjust the position of a younger Callie's tiny feet. But the memories didn't just exist in her mind or her heart—her *toes* remembered, her arches, her heels, the bend in her knees, the thrust of her shoulders: that's where the recollections lived most vividly. For Callie, being a tightrope walker was both physical and spiritual, and she sensed her grandmother's spirit in every step she took, every careful breath that passed in and out of her body.

Alone in the yard with only the wire, she walked, she knelt, she spun. She scooted backward, then forward in the fading Florida sunshine that would never be a spotlight, with no one watching but a lizard clinging to the trunk of a royal palm. She was not ashamed to admit she'd always loved the applause. But there was no applause for her here, there was only—

"Holy shit!"

Startled, Callie lost her balance, causing the wire to rotate. Instinctively, she bent deeper into her plié and extended her arms. Her body commanded, the wire obeyed, and like the talented professional she was, she remained on her feet.

"Oops," said Jenna, stuffing her hands into her pockets. "I guess shouting out profanities when somebody's standing on a piece of string is a bad idea."

"Isn't shouting out profanities pretty much always a bad idea?" Callie retorted, lowering herself into a slow lunge that lengthened into a full split, then twisting to a side sit and rising up again with ease.

"Sorry. Couldn't help it. You're good. Like . . . *really* good. Like an Olympic gymnast or something."

Keeping her eyes focused straight ahead, Callie broke into a series of high kicks, jumped into a turn, then walked several quick steps to the end of the wire.

"Whoa." Jenna's eyes were wide. "That was *amazing*."

"That was nothing," said Callie. "In the eighties, my grandmother walked the wire in stiletto heels."

"Stilettos, huh? Sounds like your grandmother would have gotten along well with my great-aunt."

"Depends. Did she talk as much as you do?"

"Don't know. Never met her. So I guess you perform with a whole team of tightrope walkers? Like those Flying Influenzas?"

"*Wallendas*," Callie corrected with a roll of her eyes. "And no, I do a solo act."

"Solo . . . as in so-lonely?"

"It's not lonely. It's empowering."

"I guess it would be—for you. You don't seem like much of a team player."

Callie stopped walking to shoot Jenna an angry look. "Just because I happen to prefer working alone doesn't mean I *can't* perform with a partner. My grandmother taught me everything I know, and when I was really small she and I were billed as a team." *But it was never just the two of us; never just Gram and me. It was Gram and me and the VanDrexel family name. Whatever you do, Callie, don't let that name hit the ground.* "I even did a trapeze act with my father in Italy once."

"Sounds like a real swingin' time."

"You're hilarious."

"Yeah. I get that a lot."

"But on the wire, I'd just rather be alone. That way I'm only responsible for myself, for my own steps."

"Ah. So you're a control freak."

"Ugh, I'm not a control freak! Working alone is just less stressful. It's all about me."

"Ah. So you're an egomaniac."

Callie narrowed her eyes. "I didn't mean it like that. I mean, if I had partners, I'd have to constantly be worrying about them screwing up."

"True. But to be fair"—Jenna folded her arms—"wouldn't *they* have to worry about *you* screwing up too?"

Callie glared at her, rose up on her toes, and executed a perfect aerial backflip, landing on the bouncing rope without even the slightest wobble.

Jenna grinned. "Okay, so maybe they wouldn't."

Callie stayed on the wire until the moon showed itself in the cobalt sky. Pretty, but still not a spotlight. Jenna had parked herself on the ground, watching Callie go through her routine.

"I'm tired, I'm going in," Callie announced, jumping down from the rope and peeling off her shoes. "That was a hint, by the way."

"Yeah, I got that. But I'd like to say goodbye to your mom, if that's okay with you."

Since Jenna had already followed her into the garage, Callie figured it would have to be.

"It was cool of her and billionaire boy to show me around. Great head of hair on that guy by the way, huh? And Quinn really knows her shit when it comes to tigers. We spotted three from the terrace and even at like five hundred yards she knew which two used to belong to VanDrexel's."

"Antony and Cleopatra," said Callie, recalling them as newborns and feeling an unexpected tug at her heart. She'd found the cubs ridiculously cute for like five minutes. Then Quinn decided to make them the center of her existence and Callie lost interest soon after. "One of the elephants is ours too. Gulliver."

"Yeah, according to your mom he's ticklish."

"I wouldn't know. I try to avoid tickling elephants whenever possible since it seems like a good way to get crushed to death."

Upstairs, Callie went straight to her bedroom and tossed her tightrope shoes into the closet. She could hear Jenna chatting up Quinn, and decided she'd just hole up in her bedroom until Jenna left.

Turning toward the bed, Callie froze. On the floor beside it was the tattered cardboard carton with Victoria's name on it. Sitting on the quilt was the blue vinyl jewelry box.

"Mom? *Mom!*"

Quinn came rushing into the room with Jenna close behind.

"What's the matter?"

"How did this get here?" She pointed to the jewelry box as though it were a live grenade.

"I found it in the garage. I thought you might like to keep it on your nightstand, since it was Gram's."

"It's definitely more upbeat than your other knickknack," Jenna observed, eyeing the pewter urn.

Quinn ran her finger across the lid of the jewelry box. "I know the style's a little dated, but it's such an interesting blue, isn't it? I was thinking we could use it as our inspiration for the new paint."

Callie just stared at the jewelry box. *The color isn't even remotely the most interesting thing about that box,* she thought, remembering the notes inside.

"If you don't want it, I can bring it back down—"

"No! I want to keep it here."

Quinn eyed Callie curiously, nodded, and left the room.

Jenna, of course, stayed put. "I'm gonna go out on a limb here and speculate that your grandmother has shuffled off her mortal coil."

"If that means she's dead, then yes. As of three weeks ago."

"Oh. Sorry." Jenna's eyes dropped to her beat-up Jack Purcells, and for a moment—just a moment—she was quiet. Then: "So what's in the box?"

"None of your business," Callie snapped. But as if to confirm that she hadn't imagined them, she said, "Notes. Handwritten ones."

"Cool. Let's see."

Before Callie could refuse, Jenna had crossed the room, opened the box, and was staring at the black-and-white snapshot Callie had found earlier. "Wow. Is this your grandmother? Check out that bouffant flip."

"Other one," said Callie, her voice dull. "With the long hair."

"Oh. Yeah, I see the resemblance now. Where was this taken?"

"I have no idea. I've never seen it before."

"Really." Jenna settled onto the bed. "I thought you two were close."

"We were."

It suddenly occurred to Callie, like a punch to the gut, that this was the reason the box and its contents had bothered her so much.

LISA FIEDLER

Clearly it had been important, meaningful enough for Victoria to have saved it all these years. But she'd never bothered to share it with her granddaughter.

There was a narrow drawer at the bottom of the box, which Callie hadn't noticed before. Jenna gave the glass knob a tug. "Locked," she pronounced. "The plot thickens."

"There's no plot," Callie snapped. "It's just a jewelry box filled with little notes."

"Love notes?" Jenna waggled her brows and lifted the velvet shelf. "Maybe the glamorous tightrope walker was having a steamy love affair with the sword swallower."

"They're not love notes. They're more like inspirational quotes. Sayings, observations. Lessons, I guess."

"So . . . what?" Jenna pulled out what appeared to be an old Camel cigarette wrapper and examined it. "She never heard of a diary?"

When Callie slammed the lid closed, Jenna turned her attention to the cardboard box, withdrawing an old VanDrexel's program from 1971. It looked like the ones Callie herself had been featured in since the age of seven, except the graphics were less flashy and the color photos were faded.

Watching Jenna flip through, she spotted a full-page shot of Victoria on the wire executing a graceful arabesque. The caption read *Dainty and Death-Defying. Beautiful but Brave. Sassy yet Sweet.*

"Not exactly a feminist manifesto, is it?" Jenna joked. Putting the program aside, she examined another snapshot of the same black-and-white glossy variety as the one taken in the pickup truck. It was a picture of Victoria, at about Callie's age, standing in front of the lion's cage, holding hands with a handsome boy. The photographer had obviously caught the young couple unawares, and in so doing had captured a truly magical moment.

"Who's the hot guy?"

66

"That'd be my grandfather," Callie rasped, taking the photo and studying it. "James VanDrexel. He was the lion tamer."

"Of course he was," said Jenna, chuckling. "Which would make him, like, the coolest grandpa ever."

"I wouldn't know. I never met him." Callie traced the edge of the snapshot with her fingertip. "Neither did my mom. And actually other than a bunch of publicity photos of him and my great-uncle Gideon posing with their cats, this is the first picture I've ever seen of him."

Jenna reached into the box again, removing the threadbare T-shirt and a pair of denim cutoff shorts. "These are totally in again. You should wear 'em." Setting the clothes aside, she thumbed through sheet music for a song called "The Lion Sleeps Tonight," accidentally loosing a flurry of dried rose petals. She quickly collected them and scattered them back between the pages.

"You realize this stuff might be considered personal, right?"

Jenna ignored her and pulled out a brittle page from the *Boston Globe*. "Woah, TBT," she remarked, scanning the yellowed newsprint. "This is from April 1965. Look, there's a sale on girdles at Filene's Basement, and—ooh, bummer—an article about a local girl who went missing, and the details of a bombing on the Viet Cong." She folded the newspaper and placed it on the bed. Callie didn't spare it a glance; she was still staring at the picture of James and Victoria. She knew she was being silly and overly romantic, but from the way they were looking at each other in the photo, she couldn't shake the feeling that this may very well have been the exact moment her grandparents fell in love.

Jenna moved on to a photo album that was so old the pictures were held in by little paper triangles stuck at each corner. The first several pages were all photos of Victoria in her teens. Halfway through, Quinn appeared, a chubby dark-haired baby with two deep dimples.

"Weird," said Jenna.

Callie stiffened. "Weird that she's a teenage mother?"

"No." Jenna rolled her eyes. "Weird that there isn't a single photo of your grandmother as a little girl. No baby pictures, no first-day-of-school photos. It's like she was born at sixteen. Why is that?"

Callie had no idea. It *was* weird, but she had no desire to encourage further discussion. She just shrugged and continued to stare at the photograph of Victoria, James, and the lion.

"Ms. VanDrexel?" Jenna called. "Can you come in here?"

Callie snapped her eyes up from the photo. "What are you doing?"

"Can't help it if I'm naturally curious." Jenna smirked and flipped to the next page. "Look, here's a shot of your mother—I'm guessing it's her eighth or ninth birthday—surrounded by clowns and . . . Wait, is that a llama? Shit! It *is* a llama. This is awesome. She's *at* the circus and she's actually having a circus-themed birthday party."

"Well, technically she was having a circus-themed life."

"Exactly. Totally meta, right? Like, the essence of meta, even before meta was a thing. So cool."

Quinn returned to the doorway. "What's up?"

"I was just flipping through your photos and I thought perhaps a bit of color commentary was in order."

Callie glanced up in time to see her mother's face brighten, the crinkles around her eyes deepening as she smiled. "Really?"

"Yeah. Like, for example, this little kid with the baldy-sour haircut and the buckteeth. Who's he?"

"Oh! That's Toddy Harris." Quinn sighed, dropping onto the bed. "My first love. His parents were Francie and Dennis. Francie was the elephant trainer, and Dennis ran the lighting crew. Lovely people."

"Lovely people who let their nine-year-old son get a neck

tattoo?" Jenna queried, indicating the reddish-brown markings encircling little Toddy's throat.

"It's just henna. Genevieve used to draw those on us kids all the time. Completely temporary, but they wreaked havoc on the laundry." Quinn laughed; it was a faraway sound, filled with memory. "I got one once, without asking Gram. I thought she was going to flip her lid, but it turned out she was delighted. Kept congratulating me on my sense of adventure! Even after the henna paste stained my new white piqué culottes and all of our sheets."

Meta? Henna? Piqué culottes? Callie scowled. When did these two start speaking a foreign language?

"Who's this?" Jenna prodded, pointing to a lanky man in a starched cotton shirt and the 1960s version of cargo pants.

"That's my uncle Gideon."

Callie leaned over to peer at the pale colors of the snapshot. She had only the faintest recollection of her great-uncle, since he retired when she was three, but she knew that as a child her mother had been very close to him. In fact, he was the reason Quinn had decided to work with the animals.

So I guess I can blame him for all this, Callie thought.

Jenna waggled her eyebrows. "Uncle Gideon was quite the— what would be the historically appropriate term?—dreamboat."

"Well, he was no Toddy Harris, but yes, he was handsome." Quinn laughed. "So, Jenna, I bet there are some handsome boys here in Lake St. Julian."

Callie snorted. *Subtle, Mom, real subtle.*

"A few," said Jenna.

"And what sort of things do kids your age do for fun around here?"

"Well, along with your basic all-American teen rituals—house parties, football games, hooking up in parked cars on dark side streets—a lot of kids around here are into surfing. Crescent Beach is basically Mecca for my demographic." Jenna aimed her knowing grin at Callie. "There's also a fairly competitive teen croquet league, which is not, as one might expect, a dorks-only enterprise." When Quinn looked skeptical, Jenna laughed. "I'm not making this up. We've even got team jerseys and a league slogan, compliments of yours truly: 'Croquet is wicket cool.'"

Quinn was charmed. "So you play?"

"I used to." Jenna shrugged. Or was it more of a squirm? "Haven't lately. But I could sign Callie up if she's interested."

"Not a chance," said Callie, at the same time that Quinn said, "Great idea."

Quinn and Jenna continued to gush over the album, with Quinn giggling her way through stories of her circus childhood, including her many failed attempts to learn to walk the tightrope, and her first heartwarming encounter with a mischievous baby elephant named Schlubby.

In fifteen years, Callie had never heard a single word about Schlubby, or even about Toddy Harris for that matter, but she refused to let it sting. Instead, she focused on reading her grandmother's handwritten notes.

What's going to happen next?

Home is everything.

Mothers and daughters.

Quinn had progressed to recounting the adolescent escapades undertaken by herself and her two best friends, two fellow VanDrexel's "lifers," Harriet DuMonde, and a boy who was a few years older— Arthur, whose parents were clowns. A photo from Harriet and Arthur's wedding in the late 1980s showed Quinn as Harriet's maid of honor, both of them with hair so big it was amazing they even fit it under the Big Top. Harriet was now the head of advertising for VanDrexel's, and Arthur and their son, the infamous crush-harboring Dabney, had taken over Arthur's parents' clowning act and were regarded as some of the best jugglers in the business.

"So I guess VanDrexel's was a lot like Lake St. Julian," Jenna mused. "Essentially, a small town where people tend to stick around for generations."

"Present company excepted," Callie muttered. "My mom's more of the cut-and-run type."

Quinn frowned, rose from the bed, and headed for the door without another word. When she was gone, Jenna closed the album and cleared her throat.

"So, I assume you'll be matriculating at good ol' Lake St. Julian High? Go Conquistadors!"

"Go who?"

"Conquistadors. School mascot. 'Cause of Ponce de León? He was the Spanish explorer who landed in Florida and supposedly discovered the legendary Fountain of Youth and—"

"Yes, I am going to Lake St. Julian High," Callie huffed; after Quinn's walk down memory lane, she wasn't in the mood to hear any more rambling stories from the past.

"Great. 'Cause I was thinking we could meet in the library before homeroom Monday morning. Y'know, so I can give you a tour of the learning facility and generally start showing you the ropes."

Callie shook her head. "No thanks."

"Why not?"

"Because I'm from the circus, not the moon. I think I can handle finding my way to homeroom."

"Maybe. But a very wise woman once said, 'Learn from those who know.' "

Callie threw her a skeptical look. "Which wise woman was that?"

"Your dainty yet death-defying grandmother." Grinning, Jenna placed the Camel wrapper on the quilt and smoothed it out to reveal what Victoria had written there.

Find someone to show you the ropes. Learn from those who know.

"Looks like Victoria still has a few things left to teach you."

Looking smug, Jenna popped up from the bed. "Gimme your phone. I'll put my number in it."

"I don't have a phone."

"You're kidding."

Callie shrugged.

"So much for not being from the moon. I guess I'll be seeing you Monday morning—homeroom bell rings at seven thirty so let's say six forty-five in the library."

"She'll be there," came Quinn's voice, calling from the kitchen.

"Says who?" Callie shouted back.

"Says the person who'll be arranging your ride."

Biting back a chuckle, Jenna headed for the door. "See you at school, Calliope." Then she scooted out without waiting for a reply.

When she was gone, Callie went into the living room and scanned the remaining packing boxes.

"Way to eavesdrop, Mom."

"Small house, Cal. What can I tell ya?" Quinn looked less than contrite. "And I think it's great that Jenna offered to show you around."

"Show me the *ropes*," Callie, muttered, using Gram's words.

She opened the box marked OFFICE SUPPLIES and rummaged until she found a two-by-three-foot corkboard, dotted with colorful tacks.

"Can I have this?"

Quinn looked up from where she was putting an old kettle on to boil. "Sure."

Callie took the bulletin board back to her room. Since the walls were dotted with nails from long-forgotten artwork, she had no trouble finding a place to hang it.

First she tacked the photo of Victoria and James in the middle. The black-and-white image looked stark and artsy against the cinnamon-colored cork.

Then, one by one, she took each handwritten note out of the jewelry box and tacked them to the board around the photo.

Know when to call a John Robinson.

When in doubt, juggle.

Applause sounds better when you've earned it.

She pinned them up with no particular design in mind, no plan, no rhyme or reason.

A paper napkin advising: *When in the lion's cage, show no fear.*

And on the back of a business card, *Trust the net.*

Callie did this until there was not a single scrap left in the box. When she stepped back to admire her work, she noticed her mother was standing in the doorway holding a cup of tea. "There's still water in the kettle if you—"

"Did you know about these?" It sounded like an accusation.

Quinn shook her head. "Honestly, Cal, I really never knew much about my mother, except that she loved me. I did know that. And she *adored* you. But she was a very . . . *private* person."

"What do you mean?"

"When I was small I'd ask her about her childhood, and she'd always somehow manage to change the subject. I got to the point where I started to believe that she'd sprung fully grown from the head of Cornelius VanDrexel." Joining Callie in front of the corkboard, Quinn smiled over the rim of her teacup. "One time I asked her why she decided to become a tightrope walker. And do you know what she said?"

Callie shook her head.

"She said, 'Because I wanted to walk the sky. Because in the sky, I was lighter than I was on earth.'" Quinn put a hand on Callie's shoulder. "Poetic, isn't it? It also happens to be a scientific fact."

"I know how gravity works," Callie sneered, shrugging off Quinn's hand.

Quinn sighed and left the room.

Callie's eyes remained on the board as she remembered what Jenna had said.

Victoria still has a few things left to teach you.

With steady fingers, she removed one of the scraps. *Observation is the beginning of understanding.* A proverb? A lesson? A rule?

Callie wasn't certain, but whatever it was, tomorrow she would try her best to follow it.

SIX

New Jersey, 1965

BACK IN MY TRAIN car, I strip out of my filthy blouse and pants. Since I don't have a towel, I pull the top sheet off my cot, only to find the job application Mr. VanDrexel so pointlessly presented me with two nights earlier tangled up in it. I toss the form back onto the cot, and then head for the bathroom, wrapped in the sheet.

While I'm showering, Sharon manages to cobble together a wardrobe of cast-offs and hand-me-downs, cheerfully donated by some of the female performers. It consists of a few VanDrexel's T-shirts and sleeveless tops, a pair of blue jeans, one cotton sundress, and some shorts—a pair of collegiate-style madras Bermudas and some fraying denim cutoffs.

"We'll worry about winter when it comes," Sharon decides.

Come winter, I'll be gone.

I put on one of the T-shirts and the cutoffs. Then I remember the brooch and quickly retrieve it from my discarded pants, transferring it to my new pocket.

Cornelius VanDrexel gives me a cash advance on the salary we never got around to negotiating. It's the first money I've ever earned, though technically I haven't even earned it yet. Still, when Cornelius places the bills in my hand, they feel different from any money I've ever held before.

The red-haired dancer who is now officially my roommate gets us a ride into town. Her name is Valerie, and her father, Gus, is Van-Drexel's chief mechanic. Her mother is Hasty Pudding, the prettiest clown in the troupe. At nineteen, Valerie has never known any life but the circus.

"I was born in Minneapolis, between shows," she tells me, as we wait for her father to bring the truck around. "Mama went to the hospital in full makeup. The doctors thought it was a publicity stunt."

"Speaking of Minneapolis," I say, "where do we play next?" It's not a flawless segue, but at least I've broached the subject. I need to get a sense of when and where I'm going to land.

"Tonight we head to Delaware for three shows in two days, then Ohio—one night only. Then Fort Wayne. After that, we'll spend a few days in Chicago."

My father has a third cousin in Chicago. "Then where?"

"St. Louis. Then Podunks. July's just a bunch of Podunks."

"Podunks?"

"Little burgs nobody's ever heard of," Sharon explains. "Ass Kiss, Colorado; Pole Up the Butt, Connecticut; Bee Sting, Georgia; Snot Rag, Louisiana."

I'm only half certain she's making these up.

"Next big city after St. Louie'll be Houston," Valerie says, her eyes misting up slightly. "One night there, then two in Austin and after that we'll—well, *you'll*—start heading back up north."

Okay, then, Austin it is. It's not so much a decision as it is a slamming of my heart against my rib cage. I will slip away from Van-Drexel's and disappear for good in Texas.

"I'm not looking forward to giving you the ol' 'See you down the road,'" says Sharon, reaching over to squeeze Val's hand. Then for my benefit, she explains, "That's what we say when someone moves on. It's kind of a circus tradition, like 'The show must go on.' We don't like goodbyes, so we just say, 'See you down the road.' It's less . . . permanent." She turns back to Val. "But it still hurts."

A forties-era Ford pickup appears and Gus waves us in.

As we ride, Valerie explains to me that she'll be leaving Van-Drexel's before the end of the season. "Most circus performers are lifers," she explains, "but I guess you could say I have other aspirations." The statement contains no malice, it's simply a fact—and a hopeful one at that.

"What will you do?" I ask.

"I've got a cousin in San Bernardino. She and I are going to open a dancing school there, so I'll be parting ways with VanDrexel's from Austin."

"Much to Hasty's heartbreak," Sharon notes softly.

"Mothers and daughters," Val says with a sigh, as if that sums up everything in the universe. Then she reaches into her purse and produces a shiny little Instamatic camera. "Remind me, I need to buy flashcubes."

It's a short ride from the fairgrounds to town. Gus lets us out in front of Woolworth's and tells us we have an hour to shop. I follow Sharon through the glass door and breathe in the scent of new plastic mixed with the lunch counter's daily special.

Valerie heads straight for the record department, fearing the new Beatles 45, *Ticket to Ride*, might already be sold out. "Everybody thinks Paul's the cute one," she says, jangling her little change purse. "But if you ask me, George is the one with all the sex appeal." Then she glides away quickly, as if she can't bear the thought of Sharon or me disagreeing with her.

I buy shampoo, a toothbrush, toothpaste, and some other basic toiletries. Sharon guides me to the cosmetics section, where I am mystified by the array of brands and colors. In my father's house, makeup was on the list of forbidden things, so Sharon chooses a Revlon blush compact, some Maybelline eye shadow in the most perfect sky blue, a frosted coral lipstick, and waterproof mascara. In the apparel department I grab two three-packs of white cotton underwear, a Maidenform bra, some knee socks, and a pair of frilly baby doll pajamas (which are entirely Sharon's idea). As we wander on, I add to my collapsible shopping basket a hairbrush and a laundry marker (to write my name in the aforementioned underwear; Sharon says this is imperative and that I will thank her for it later).

"And this!" She zealously points to a very large jewelry box, sheathed in shiny pale-blue vinyl that makes it look as if it once belonged to the tooth fairy. It has a hinged lid and a shallow bottom drawer with a crystal knob and tiny keyhole.

"It's beautiful . . . but I don't have any jewelry." I'm lying on both counts; my mother's brooch, which is worth more than the aggregate cost of every item in this store, is still nestled deep in my shorts pocket.

"Then think of it as a treasure chest," Sharon suggests, tugging it off the shelf. "A keepsake box. The circus has a way of throwing memories at you, sister. You're going to need a place to keep them."

Since I can't tell her I'll be leaving before I've amassed enough memories to fill a pillbox, let alone this vinyl monstrosity, I agree to purchase it.

We rejoin Valerie, whose shopping basket is brimming with film cartridges and flashbulb packs. In addition to *Ticket to Ride*, she's also got 45s of Herman's Hermits' *Mrs. Brown, You've Got a Lovely Daughter* and *I Know a Place*, by Petula Clark.

Emily's favorites. The songs we would have danced to in the rumpus room if I'd made it to the sleepover. My heart cracks a bit.

"Val's single-handedly keeping Kodak *and* the British Invasion in business," Sharon quips.

Valerie helps me pick out sandals, a straw purse with leatherette handles, a faux-silk kerchief, and some sunglasses, while Sharon struggles to tote the unwieldy jewelry box.

When all is said and done, the objects of my new life come to just over thirty-four dollars.

Then we're back in the rusted bed of Gus's pickup, rumbling

toward the fairgrounds. I close my eyes, letting the marshy Jersey breezes caress my face, feeling for the brooch in my pocket.

Through the whisper of the wind I hear a plasticky *snap*, and open my eyes to see Valerie grinning; she's just photographed me with her trusty Instamatic. She advances the film and aims again.

"Smile!"

Sharon leans in and we both mug for the lens.

But even as I pose for the picture, I'm wondering what my father will tell our friends and neighbors in the aftermath of my escape. *Where is Catherine?* they'll want to know, and he'll come up with a good explanation for my inexplicable absence—a visit to some distant relative, perhaps, to distract me from the heartbreak of my mother's worsening illness.

But what will *he* think? That I've been kidnapped? Maybe he'll worry that I'm dead.

For all I know, he'll *hope* I'm dead.

And in a way, I am. The old me, at least.

But as the truck turns onto the dusty path that leads back to the Big Top, I realize that I've never felt more alive.

Back in our room Valerie opens the lid of her portable record player, snaps a yellow plastic adapter into *Ticket to Ride* and places the disc on the turntable. There's a brief crackling sound as the needle finds the grooves; then John Lennon's voice fills the air: *"I think I'm gonna be sad, I think it's todaaaaay . . . yeah."*

I empty the shopping bags, nestling my purchases among the hand-me-downs in the bureau drawers Valerie has sacrificed on my behalf. I neatly arrange my mysterious collection of dime-store makeup on top of the vanity, then turn my attention to the bulky "treasure chest" Sharon convinced me to buy. Sitting down on the cot, I haul it onto my knees and open it. Just like my antique jewelry box at home (passed down from a wealthy great-grandmother I never met) this one has a removable upper tray lined with velvet, divided into compartments for rings, bracelets, and necklaces. I lift the tray out and see that the cavernous interior is all ruched satin—pale blue to match the vinyl. A key sits on the bottom, small and silver. I pluck it out, jiggle it into the lock, and open the drawer.

I glance over at Valerie, who is lying on her cot with her back to me, singing along with the record at the top of her lungs.

Reaching into my pocket, I palm the brooch and place it in the drawer. It's not that Valerie has given me any reason to mistrust her, but she's a stranger from a strange world, and I want to keep this piece of my mother safe.

I close the drawer, silently, secretly, and twist the key in the opposite direction until it clicks. My father would call me stupid for bothering to lock the drawer, since even a half-witted thief would be smart enough to steal the whole box, then bash it open with a hammer and take whatever he wanted.

Still, I breathe a little easier now that the brooch is hidden, as close to safe as it can get. I wonder what old Louis-François Cartier would think about the great incongruity of his pricey bauble taking up residence in a four-dollar-and-fifty-cent jewelry box from Woolworth's, which, I realize, is a fairly apt metaphor for my life at the moment.

Before putting away the laundry marker, I grab the job application from my bed and write down the words Cornelius said to me: *Everything will eventually come full circle.*

Followed by: *Observation is the beginning of understanding.*

Seeing the words in black and white sets off a slight tingling in my chest; I feel as if I've stumbled onto something useful. Unlike my father's rules and demands, maybe my short time in this colorful world will offer me an unexpected education. So I place the application in the box. Sharon told me to fill it with "memories," but it seems "lessons" will have to do.

Lessons. I took so many of them back in Brooksvale—ballet, French, violin, deportment—all of my father's choosing, and all designed to result in getting a girl properly married. Maybe now it's time for me to learn something I'll actually enjoy.

Plucking my dirty pedal pushers from the floor, I wriggle my fingers into the pocket where the cotton candy cone and the Camel package are still crumpled. I fish them out and unroll the cone first, flattening it out on the lid of the jewelry box to scrawl across the sticky surface: *Everyone has a job to do.*

I un-ball the cigarette package and remove it from its outer wrapper just as the hi-fi's needle reaches the end of the record and the song fades out. The firecracker noise of the cellophane has Valerie glancing over her shoulder.

I smile sheepishly, and she turns away again, humming.

Pulling apart the corners, I smooth out the cigarette package and write on the blank side: *Find someone to show you the ropes. Learn from those who know.* I place these notes inside the jewelry box as well, then close the lid with a muffled *thunk.*

I've just slid the box under the cot when Sharon pokes her head in the door.

"Everything okay?" she asks.

"Great," I tell her. "So how's tomorrow, right after lunch?"

"For what?"

My reply is a smile and an expectant lift of my brows. When she finally gets what I'm asking for, she lets out a whistle and claps her hands. "You got it, sister," she says on a chuckle. "Tomorrow, you learn to walk the sky!"

SEVEN

~

BEAUTY ON THE OUTSIDE, danger on the inside.

"Well that's grim," Callie muttered, standing in front of the bulletin board on Monday morning, pondering the array of handwritten notes that represented either her grandmother's wealth of wisdom or a long-hidden desire to become a writer of fortune cookies.

When Quinn came into the room, Callie didn't even bother to turn around.

"Brad'll be here in ten minutes to drive you to school."

"Can't wait. We can bond all the way there."

Quinn stiffened but didn't take the bait. Instead, she dropped an apple into the nondescript blue backpack Callie had purchased yesterday under duress, during a ritual Brad identified as Back-to-School Shopping. But she was hardly going "back" to anything. School was just another step further away from things that used to be, and everything about it would be unfamiliar and miserable.

And with any luck, temporary, she reminded herself.

Next, Quinn held out a couple of dollar bills. "Lunch money."

Callie took the cash without looking, her eyes still leaping from scrap to scrap. She was hoping to find something that might work as an incantation to ward off even the most evil of high school demons—whatever they might turn out to be.

Observation is the beginning of understanding.

No thanks. Callie had already *observed* Quinn flirting incessantly with Brad Marston and had come to the somewhat disturbing *understanding* that her gracefully aging mother could not be accused of suffering from a diminishing estrogen supply.

When in doubt, juggle.

Much better. It was pithy, circus-specific, and unlike some of the other—what should she call them? Insights? Warnings? Mantras?—from the jewelry box, this was one that she'd heard her grandmother invoke a thousand times. So she removed the thumb-tack and slid the note—which was written on the back of an index card featuring, of all things, a recipe for cherry pie—into one of her new backpack's numerous outside pockets.

"Need anything else?" Quinn asked.

"Nope."

"You sure?"

"Positive."

"Well, what about . . . *this*?" Smiling, she produced a brand-new iPhone from behind her back.

Callie almost smiled. "When'd you get that?"

"I didn't. Brad did. When I mentioned I was planning to get you one, he just went out and took care of it. Pretty sweet, huh?"

Callie took the phone, remembering how Beatrice, Bianca, and . . . the other one . . . had basically been addicted to their touch-screens. Now she could see why. This one was certainly sleek, and knowing Brad it was probably the best model money could buy. She wondered how long it would take her to become proficient. Odd that she could do a backflip on a wire roughly the circumference of a nickel, but she didn't know the first damn thing about how to down-load an app.

Quinn gave her a quick tutorial, which included adding both herself and Brad to Callie's contacts.

"Maybe Brad can give you some more pointers on the ride to school."

There was that helium voice again. Dropping the phone into her backpack, Callie gave her mother a cool look. "So what's his deal, Mom? I mean, I thought you came here for a *job*."

Quinn's left eyebrow rose, the universal mom sign for *I don't think I like your tone, young lady.* "I *did* come here for a job. Or didn't you notice all those tigers prowling around the backyard?"

"So then what's with the dinners, and the grocery shopping, and the cell phones? I mean, he knows he's not my father, right? Because I have a father." Callie made an exaggerated rolling gesture with her hand, pretending to jog Quinn's memory. "You remember him, don't you? Guy about your age, speaks with an Italian accent, makes his living swinging from a trapeze."

"Oh yeah," Quinn snapped, perfectly matching Callie's sarcasm. "And by the way, be sure to let everyone in school know about *that*."

"What's that supposed to mean?"

"It means . . ." Quinn closed her eyes and let out a long rush of breath in an attempt to compose herself. "Just be aware that some of your new classmates might have preconceived notions when it comes to . . . circus people."

Circus people? The only thing that could have made that phrase more insulting was if Quinn had surrounded it with air quotes.

"So you're saying everyone's going to think I'm a freak because I walk the tightrope and my father is an aerialist and my mother knows what it means when some dumb monkey smiles at her?"

"Maybe," Quinn replied honestly.

"Great." Callie folded her arms and cocked her hip. "You force me to come here, you insist I make friends, and now you're like, 'Just don't forget you're a freak.' Helpful."

"I'm *not* saying you're a freak. I'm just saying . . ." Quinn paused and took a breath. "Look, I know you're proud of where we come from, and you *should* be. You, my darling girl, are a star.

I just . . . want you to be prepared. I want you to understand that not everyone will get it. So maybe just don't . . . I don't know . . . *lead* with the circus thing."

"So what *should* I lead with?" Callie shot back. "That I live on the estate where all the roaring is coming from and pizza delivery guys fear to tread?"

The Range Rover's horn sounded in the driveway. Callie scooped up her backpack and bolted down the stairs.

Per Jenna's directive, Callie arrived at Lake St. Julian High School a full forty-five minutes before the first bell. She still had no intention of taking Jenna up on her offer to show her around, but she'd spent the better part of the car ride trying to figure out how to connect to the Internet on her new phone and had come up empty. So she'd satisfy Gram's "learn from those who know" adage by letting Jenna help her with that.

After a few wrong turns she found the library, stepped into the silence, and positioned herself near the circulation desk to wait. At least she had the place to herself.

Five minutes later, no Jenna.

But lots of Ponce de León.

The explorer's name seemed to be plastered all over the building—on posters, flyers, even a banner strung across the main corridor announcing something called the Ponce de León Fountain of Youth festival.

Eight minutes. No Jenna.

Callie sighed and snatched a flyer off the circulation desk:

COME DRINK FROM THE FOUNTAIN OF YOUTH

AT LSJHS'S ANNUAL

FESTIVAL DE PONCE DE LEÓN

FRIDAY, APRIL 8 — 11:00 A.M.

THE ST. JULIAN INN

ALUMNI, DON'T FORGET:

COME DRESSED IN THE MOST POPULAR FASHIONS

OF YOUR HIGH SCHOOL YEARS!

Next to the flyers was a clipboard pinning down a sign-up sheet for something called the Surfing Conquistador Competition.

And they're going to think I'm *the freak?*

Twelve minutes. No Jenna. Callie was beginning to doubt the girl would show up.

At the far end of the long desk, Callie spotted a bin marked LOST AND FOUND. Riffling through the contents she found phone chargers, a dog-eared paperback copy of *The Catcher in the Rye*, an empty Vera Bradley makeup case, a lacrosse ball, several plastic travel mugs from Starbucks, a zip-up hoodie with LSJHS VARSITY SWIMMING AND DIVING emblazoned across the back, and a small plastic container of something called Mr. Zog's Sex Wax.

Moving to the center of the still empty library, she positioned a few of the items in her hands and began to juggle.

The items took flight, chasing each other, rising and falling, leaping from one of Callie's hands to the other, as if playing a game of aerial tag in which all of the objects were "it," but never came close enough to each other to tag or be tagged.

"'Scuse me . . . I think that's my sex wax."

The voice startled Callie, breaking both her concentration and her rhythm. The lacrosse ball hit the floor hard, followed by the plastic mug.

Luckily, or perhaps not, she managed to catch the third item.

"I'm sorry," she muttered, because, really, what else do you say to a boy who's just accused you of juggling his sex wax?

"It's okay." She noticed that his nose was sunburned—not too much, just enough.

"So, if you're done . . ."

"Done?" His hair was the kind of perfect mess usually reserved for magazine covers. For some reason, she found this very distracting. He held out his hand.

"Oh, right." Callie handed him the wax. It wasn't like she'd never seen a cute boy before. Cute boys came to the circus all the time, but then, she was always either looking down at them from a height of approximately sixty feet, or waving to them from a float in the Spec, or signing autographs for their little sisters. One-on-one conversations like this were more of a rarity.

"Thanks." He smiled. "I . . . don't know you, do I?"

Callie shook her head.

"Didn't think so. I'm Kip."

"Calliope," she said, instantly regretting it. "Callie."

"Calliope? After the Greek muse of poetry?"

Callie's cheeks burned. "After the steam organ actually."

"Oh, okay, well, still very cool. And hey, I totally feel ya."

"I'm sorry . . . you . . . *what*?"

"I get where you're coming from. About the name. Kip's short for Kipling, as in Rudyard, because my loving-but-slightly-pretentious parents happened to meet in a college literature class, and decided to commemorate it in a way that I will be paying for as long as I live. I figure I got off easy, though. I could be standing here introducing myself to you as Mowgli. Or Shere Khan."

"We had a Bengal named Shere Khan once." *Shut up, Callie.*

"Did you just say you had a Bengal? Like, a Bengal *tiger*?"

"Well, *I* didn't. The circus did."

"You had a *circus*?"

Jesus, what is wrong with me? "Yeah, kind of."

"Well, I guess that explains the juggling." Kip grinned. "Anyway, it was nice to meet you, Calliope."

"Nice to meet you, Kipling."

A name is a kind of enchantment.

Kip was about to put the sex wax in his backpack but stopped. "Hey, think you could teach me?"

"To juggle?"

"Yeah. I've always wanted to learn how." He held out the plastic container and grinned.

Panicked, Callie glanced around the library. "Um ..." *Seventeen minutes, and Jenna still MIA.* "I should probably get to homeroom."

"C'mon. I mean, it's not every day you come across a girl juggling coffee mugs and sports equipment in your school library. I feel like this is the kind of opportunity a guy shouldn't let slide."

Seeing no way out, Callie commenced with the instructing, talking him through the basics and giving him the standard slow-motion demo. Then she handed over the mug, directing him to practice tossing it from hand to hand a few times. Next came the wax, which she placed in his other hand and told him to toss upward, but under the mug before it came down. Lastly, the lacrosse ball entered the mix, and she proceeded to watch him go down in flames, dropping all three.

"It's easy once you find your rhythm," she assured him, picking up the objects and setting them in motion again herself. "There's an apple in my book bag. Would you toss it to me?"

"Four? You're kidding." But he was already rummaging past her new pens in search of the fruit.

"Okay, so just sort of lob it when I say ... *now.*"

Kip lobbed; Callie caught. Four items, rising and falling like popcorn—slightly more difficult than three, but nothing she couldn't handle. She often incorporated juggling into her wire routine.

When Callie heard the library door swish open, she glanced toward the entrance, expecting to see Jenna.

Not Jenna. *So* not Jenna.

She let the four objects drop out of the atmosphere, catching each one expertly—*plunk, plop, slumpfff, plip.*

"There you are, Kip Devereaux," purred the redhead who was now strolling into the library. "Who's your friend?"

"Kristi Baylor, this is Callie. She's new."

"Yes, she is." Kristi launched a smile at Callie. "So . . . you *juggle*? That's so . . . unusual."

Not where I come from, Callie thought, but caught herself before blurting it out.

"She was trying to teach me," Kip explained. "Turns out I'm not very good with my hands."

"Well, I happen to know *that* isn't true." Kristi flexed her hazel eyes at him, picked up the clipboard from the circulation desk, and handed it to Kip. A stubby pencil dangled from a ratty piece of string. "Also, the Surfing Conquistador contest is Friday and the best surfer in school still hasn't signed up. Unacceptable."

"Yeah, that's actually why I came in here."

"So *not* for a juggling lesson, then?" Kristi threw another bright smile in Callie's vicinity.

"Nope, that was just kind of a bonus."

"I bet it was," Kristi sang as Kip added his name to the list of Conquistador hopefuls. "So, Callie, where you from?"

"All over actually."

"Ooh, how mysterious." Kristi's smile broadened expectantly.

Gripping the lacrosse ball, Callie decided she might as well just get it over with. With any luck it would put an end to this unbelievably awkward conversation, and would also carry the added bonus of defying her mother's advice. "I was in the circus."

Kristi let out a snort of laughter that somehow managed to sound lovely, then abruptly pressed her perfectly polished fingertips to her perfectly glossed lips, as if that were the only way to keep her hilarity from escaping. "I'm sorry, I'm not laughing *at* you, I swear. I've just never met anyone from the circus before."

Callie had the distinct feeling the subtext of that statement was *nor have I ever wanted to.*

"So what was *that* like, being in the circus?"

"I'm gonna guess amazing," said Kip, sliding the pencil stub back into the clip.

"Well, *yeah*." Kristi bobbed her head enthusiastically. "You must have some great stories. So what did you *do* in the circus? You weren't, like, one of those really pretty clowns, were you?" She laughed again. "I didn't mean that the way it sounded. And *obviously* you were something way cooler than a clown. Clowns are so creepy. Even the pretty ones. I just thought, with the juggling and all . . ." Her greenish eyes shot quickly to Kip before recoiling back to Callie like a Ringmaster's whip. "Please tell me you weren't a clown, or I'm going to feel like a complete bitch."

"I wasn't a clown," Callie assured her.

"Oh, thank God. That would have been embarrassing."

For you, or for me?

Thirty-one minutes. No Jenna.

"Maybe you could sign up to juggle at the Ponce de León Festival," Kristi suggested. "I mean, unless you're worried about people finding out you were in the circus."

"Why would she be worried about that?" asked Kip, a bit archly.

Kristi dodged the question. "Jugglers were a thing in the Renaissance, weren't they? They called them fools, right? Anyway, Callie, the PDLF is a celebration of Ponce de León's discovery of Florida, which is why there's a Renaissance theme. It's also our spin on homecoming."

"It's a pretty big deal," Kip confirmed. "It's held on Ponce de León's birthday, so when it falls on a weekday, like this year, we get the day off from school. And since basically everybody in Lake St. Julian is an alum, the whole town shows up."

"And this year, *I'm* Isabella!"

"I thought you were Kristi."

"*Queen* Isabella," Kristi clarified. "It's like homecoming queen. Actually, it's kind of better than homecoming queen, because I get to wear this awesome Renaissance gown. It's an authentic reproduction." Turning to Kip, she slid the clipboard out of his grasp. "Now let's talk about how you're going to blow everyone else *away* at the Conquistador Competition on Friday, and how you should definitely wear those Billabongs I got you for Valentine's Day."

Kip smiled evasively. "Maybe."

After tossing Kip a final pouty look, Kristi left.

"So . . ." Kip slid his hands into his pockets and rocked back on his heels. "That was Kristi."

"Yeah."

"She's . . . a lot."

No argument there, thought Callie, walking back to the lost-and-found box to return the items she'd borrowed.

"What *did* you do in the circus?" Kip asked. "Besides juggle, I mean?"

"I walked the tightrope."

"No shit, really? That must have been terrifying."

Callie shrugged, because it wasn't, not for her. "Is surfing terrifying?"

"Nah. Well, sometimes. Actually I bet you'd pick it up pretty fast. You must have ridiculous balancing skills. Hey, we should—"

Just then, Jenna came bombing through the door—a whopping thirty-nine minutes late. One leg of her skinny jeans was stylishly rolled at the ankle, while the other was haphazardly tucked into her Chuck Taylor high-tops; her blond ponytail resembled not so much a hairstyle as a nuclear mushroom cloud.

"Sorry, sorry, I know I'm late. Crazy morning. Let's get go—" Noticing Kip, she stopped in her tracks, going from frenzied to awkward in a single beat. "Oh. Hey, Kippy."

"Hey, Jenz. Long time no chat."

"Yeah. Well, I've been . . . ya know . . ." She trailed off, adjusting her ponytail with a tug.

"Missed you at croquet practice the last few weeks. Everything okay?"

"Fine. I've, uh, just been picking up some extra shifts at work. Which, unfortunately, didn't stop them from firing me yesterday."

"You got fired?" said Callie. "From Benigno's?"

"No, from my CFO position at Google." Jenna forced a smile. "Yes, Benigno's. Which means you can forget about ever having another pizza delivered to the Sanctuary."

"The animal rescue place?" Kip grinned. "You live there? Wow, this just keeps getting cooler."

"Okay, VanDrexel," said Jenna. "First stop, homeroom. Your last name starts with *V*, so that'd be Mr. Kurtz, room 127. Let's roll." And she swooshed back out the door.

"Wait," said Kip. "I feel like I owe you one, ya know, for the juggling tips. Maybe I can buy you lunch?"

"Oh, um, thanks, but I think I'm good." Flustered, Callie gave him a clunky wave, grabbed her backpack, and dashed into the hall, where Jenna was already in tour-guide mode. She seemed determined to cram an hour's worth of orientation into the few remaining minutes before homeroom began.

"So you've seen the library. Stay out of the periodicals section—that's where all the drug deals go down. And that way"— she flung her arm noncommittally to the right—"is the gymnasium corridor. Self-explanatory, yes? Hey, have you got anything to eat by any chance? I didn't have breakfast."

Callie handed her the apple she was still holding, which Jenna crunched loudly as she hurried on.

"The science wing is off by itself, that way." She jerked her thumb to the left. "It's got orange lockers, no one knows why. The rest of the school has gray ones including the locker rooms, girls *and* boys, but don't ask me how I know that because it's a long story with a PG-13 rating and has nothing to do with our current undertaking. FYI, only science classes take place in the science wing, while all the other academic subjects pretty much peacefully coexist throughout the other three wings of the building, except AP History, which for some reason got exiled last semester to a lecture space behind the band room, maybe to underscore the historical significance of Napoléon Bonaparte? Just a theory. More likely it's because the super smart kids don't mind walking those extra six and a half minutes in exchange for weighted grades and college credits. Full disclosure, I'm one of the super smart kids, and it's not bragging if it's true.

"Cafeteria, down that ramp. The burgers are respectable, but the quality of the salad bar operates on a sliding scale, meaning that on Monday everything's fresh and crisp but by Friday it's all basically inedible so don't even attempt. The bathrooms are fair-to-partly-cloudy vis-à-vis cleanliness, but you might want to avoid the one just outside the in-school detention classroom for what I believe are obvious reasons." Tossing the apple core into a trash can she added, "Oh, and I think you'll find that most of the teachers here actually give a shit about their students and have a vested interest in helping us to become upstanding citizens and decent human beings. Or, at the very least quasi-literate."

They arrived at room 127, which Jenna indicated with a triumphant flourish. "Your homeroom, Ms. VanDrexel. Any questions?"

"Yes. What's sex wax?"

"Um . . . I think it's a brand name for this stuff surfers rub on their boards. *Not* a euphemism—it goes on their actual *surf* boards, for traction I think." She eyed Callie and grinned. "Shall I assume this is a Kipling Devereaux–related inquiry?"

Callie said nothing.

"*Well?*" Jenna prompted, bending down to roll her unrolled pant leg.

"He caught me holding his Mr. Zog's—also not a euphemism—

93

because you were late and I was bored so I took it out of the lost-and-found and used it to juggle with."

"Yeah, that would make sense—well, not the juggling part, the Mr. Zog's part. Kippy surfs before school whenever he can. He's been doing it since elementary school. The boy's obsessed."

"Was it my imagination or was it weird between you two back there?" Callie asked. Getting involved in the LSJHS social drama wasn't exactly high on her priorities list, but the awkwardness of the interaction seemed so bizarrely out of character for Jenna she couldn't help feeling curious.

"It wasn't weird," said Jenna, brushing it off. "And you should probably go inside and get your schedule and your locker combination from Mr. Kurtz before the—"

She was interrupted by a shrill clanging that had Callie jumping out of her skin.

"Warning bell," Jenna finished, grinning. "So how 'bout we meet in the lunchroom fifth period, unless you have a double-period science lab, which would take place in the . . . ?" She trailed off in an upward pitch prompting Callie to fill in the blank.

"Orange locker wing," Callie grumbled.

"Very nice." Jenna popped up from fussing with her jeans and started to walk away. "Remember, we rendezvous at lunch."

"That's not really necessary."

"Callie, it's *lunch*. So if you think having someone to sit with isn't necessary, your circus upbringing clearly did not include adequate access to the classic John Hughes comedies of the eighties, or *10 Things I Hate About You*, or—hell—*any* teen movie ever made starring anybody, in any decade, because if it had, you would know that eating lunch alone in a high school cafeteria is pretty much the worst possible thing that can happen to a carbon-based life-form."

"I'll risk it," Callie said coolly. "And if I change my mind, Kip offered to buy me lunch. Or maybe I'll sit with Kristi." She had no intention of doing either, of course, but if it would get Jenna off her back, she wasn't above pretending she was considering alternate dining partners.

Jenna stopped walking. "Are you talking about Kristi Baylor? You've only been in this building for ten minutes—"

"Forty-nine actually. *You've* been here ten."

"Fine, I was late. I get it. The question is how do you even know there *is* a Kristi Baylor?"

"She came into the library when Kip and I were juggling."

Jenna let out a hoot of laughter. "So how'd *that* go?"

Horrible. "Fine. She thinks I should juggle at the Ponce de León thing."

Another hoot. "Yeah, I bet she does. Callie, let me put this in terms you'll understand. Having lunch with Kristi Baylor is not something anyone should attempt without a safety net. I'm gonna have to strongly advise against."

"I don't remember asking for your advice."

"It's part of the 'showing you the ropes' job description. See, you're the new girl in our delicate public high school ecosystem, which makes you the algae to Kristi's red-bellied piranha."

"I know," said Callie, a defensive edge creeping into her voice. "She's a lot."

"A lot." Jenna snorted. "Where'd ya get that?"

"From Kip."

"Well, he should know since until about a month ago they were the proverbial 'it' couple. She actually wanted people to refer to them as 'Kripling,' which, I'm happy to say, never caught on for what I believe are obvious reasons. Ultimately, they broke up, because the boy does have a brain—and a soul—but my point is he's a nice guy and he can't help giving her the benefit of the doubt, even when she doesn't deserve it. Whatever. Bottom line, end of the day, when the smoke clears and any other idiom you may wish to apply . . . Kristi is about Kristi. This, b-t-dubs, is still me showing you the ropes."

"Or maybe this is just you being really aggressive and pushy and out of line, and maybe I'd rather let Kristi show me the ropes."

Jenna shrugged. "Go ahead. Knock yourself out. Put your trust in Queen Isabella, although I really hope it turns out better for you than it did for the Emirate of Granada."

"I have no idea what you're saying right now."

"I'm saying," said Jenna, walking away, "if you decide to let Kristi show you the ropes, don't be surprised when one of them has a noose at the end of it."

EIGHT

New Jersey, 1965

THE NEXT MORNING, VALERIE wakes me up with this:
"Payday."

I scramble out of bed and into another borrowed ensemble, taking the time to fasten my mother's brooch to my collar—not out of any sense of style, of course; it's just that I'm still a little uneasy about letting it out of my sight.

"Nice pin," Valerie notes. "Looks expensive."

"Kind of," I fib. "I wasn't going to wear it, but—"

When Valerie smiles, she looks like a cross between a prima ballerina and a dainty wood nymph. "If you're worried somebody's going to steal it, don't be. Despite what you may have heard about 'circus folk,' that's not how we operate. Everyone around here's pretty happy with what they've got, even if it isn't a whole hell of a lot."

It's such a simple statement, but it shoots a pang of longing through my heart. I come from a life where the price of diamonds was nothing compared to the cost of happiness.

"And I suppose that's a good thing," she muses, "since lately there's been a lot less to go around."

She doesn't elaborate, and since I'm only here temporarily, I don't see any reason to ask her to.

We exit the train to find everyone gathering outside the Big Top. Cornelius stands at the front of the crowd. There's a boy on his left—his older son, Gideon, according to Val—holding a thick pile of envelopes. James is on his right, with his hands in his pockets,

97

looking uninterested, impatient. For all I know, he's got the governor's niece waiting for him in his train car.

He catches me looking at him and he throws me a wink; I'm irritated by the way it makes my stomach flip.

When everyone has assembled, Cornelius chortles out a hearty "Good morning, my darlings, my coconspirators, my beloved children."

Nodding to Gideon to start handing out the pay envelopes, Cornelius goes on. "As you're all acutely aware, we have recently come up against some . . . *unexpected* . . . costs."

Here, Gideon pauses in his distribution duties to shoot James a ferocious look, to which James responds by casually giving his brother the finger. This doesn't seem to surprise anyone.

The air fills with the sound of envelopes crinkling open as the circus performers check their weekly pay. Given the Ringmaster's announcement, I expect to hear some rumblings of disappointment, but there isn't a single grumble nor sigh of complaint. As Cornelius continues, I can't shake the feeling I'm witnessing King Henry delivering his St. Crispin's Day speech to the troops.

"Take heart, my good comrades," Cornelius urges, his voice as booming and jovial as if he's announcing the fire-eater's entrance into the center ring. "I have every confidence our revenue stream will steadily increase as this incomparable season progresses. For the time being, we'll all just have to tighten our belts—or in my case, cummerbund—as we've done so many times before. Please do accept my heartfelt apologies for this week's financial inconvenience, and remember, the show must go on!"

The cast echoes his expression in a rousing chorus, like a wedding toast. Or a battle cry: "The show must go on."

As the crowd disperses with their meager earnings, undaunted—perhaps even inspired—to carry out their morning tasks, Gideon approaches me. Thanks to the advance Cornelius gave me yesterday, I will not be receiving a pay envelope.

"Cornelius would like to see you in his office," he says.

It feels like the circus equivalent of being sent to the principal. An icy tingle ripples across the back of my neck.

I follow Gideon toward the Ringmaster's train car, where both Cornelius and James are standing just outside the door. I wonder fleetingly if James is waiting for me. Then I wonder why I wondered; for God's sake, the boy taught me to shovel shit—we're not exactly courting. Besides, it's immediately clear from the way he's glaring at his father that he's barely even registered my arrival.

"You didn't have to say that," James snarls at Cornelius. "About the extra costs."

"Why wouldn't he say it?" snaps Gideon. "They have a right to know why their salaries are being cut. Veterinary specialists don't come cheap, little brother. And neither does hush money."

"First of all, Boo needed that medication and you know it. And second of all, it wasn't hush money."

"Really? What would you call being forced to pay off the Montpelier police commissioner because his daughter came home from your date with her dress inside out?"

I immediately drop my gaze to my sneakers. I shouldn't be hearing this.

"What were you thinking, James?" Gideon persists. "You're so damned impulsive. So reckless. Just like your mother."

I sense Cornelius stiffen, and keep my eyes low. I *really* shouldn't be hearing this.

"Couldn't you have behaved responsibly for *one* night?" Gideon thunders.

"*I* could have," James fires back, "but apparently, the commissioner's daughter couldn't. And neither could the motorcycle-riding juvenile delinquent she ditched me for five minutes into our date. So whatever was going on with that chick's dress had nothing to do with me."

This revelation brings Gideon up short, which has James looking smug.

"Maybe next time *you* should be the one to squire the local girls around," James baits. "I mean, what girl wouldn't be thrilled at the prospect of dating the guy the newspapers keep calling VanDrexel's *assistant* lion tamer—"

Gideon cuts him off with a right hook to the jaw. The next thing I know, the two are rolling around on the ground, throwing punches.

To my shock, Cornelius doesn't intervene. Then after a minute of letting them get it out of their system, he bellows, "Enough," and the brawl comes to an immediate and definitive halt. Both boys clamber to their feet, brushing the dirt from their clothes. Unfortunately, Gideon isn't quite finished.

"You know what it means if we're broke, James? It means we can't afford to send you on the ridiculous European tour you're always blathering about. Did you ever think about that? Christ, if I had the money, I'd send you myself. It would be nice not to have to clean up your messes for a while."

"You'd like it if I was gone, wouldn't you," James retorts, rubbing his jaw. "Then maybe Dad would start paying attention to you for once."

Gideon makes to lunge again, but Cornelius's hand goes to the whip at his waist and Gideon steps back. I suspect the gesture is purely symbolic, as I doubt that this man would ever resort to violence against anyone, let alone his own sons.

Now Cornelius turns to James. "Why didn't you just tell us the girl went off with someone else?"

James gives his father a wry smile. "What would have been the point? The money was gone, and Gideon had already convinced you I was to blame. Did he tell you again that I can't be trusted? That I should have no say in the business? Be honest: how long did it take him to remind you that I'm so damned much like my mother?"

A shadow of heartache darkens the Ringmaster's eyes. "My boy, the fact that you are like Helen is not a flaw, but a blessing. It is precisely what makes you—"

"The favorite," Gideon mutters under his breath.

"The charismatic, free-spirited, charming young man that you are," Cornelius finishes.

Strangely, James does not look particularly pleased with this assessment. Slicing one last look at Gideon, he turns and stomps off. A moment later, Gideon does the same.

With a toss of his head, Cornelius turns to me, as if only just remembering he's called me to his office. Then he flashes his Ringmaster's smile.

"Now then," he says, stepping aside for me to enter the train car. "Shall we have our little talk?"

The first thing I notice when I enter Cornelius's office is that there are two open newspapers on his desk.

One is the *Boston Globe*.

My heart turns to ice. He sees that I've noticed.

"I always make it a point to read the reviews of our previous shows," he says breezily. "In my line of work, it's important to know what sort of impression you've left behind."

I nod feebly, and he gives me a smile, all sparkle but no mirth. Then he fishes into his pocket, pulls out some change, and tosses a dime onto the open paper. "I thought perhaps you'd be interested in having a gander."

He makes to leave, but on his way to the door he pauses to give me the rest of the change. Then he places his hand gently on the crown of my head, like a blessing. And he's gone.

I all but dive for the newspaper, my eyes going directly to the shiny little coin, which has landed, not accidentally, beside a small headline.

BROOKSVALE GIRL GOES MISSING
FOUL PLAY SUSPECTED

*Sixteen-year-old Catherine Hastings, daughter of Davis
Hastings, vanished from the home of a friend . . .*

There's no picture. Shouldn't there be a picture? Isn't that what
they do when they want to find a missing person? They print a
photograph so law enforcement and good Samaritans will know who
to look for. My attention shifts to the other paper, today's Newark
Star-Ledger where I see the same article.

There's an *AP* in the dateline, which means the article has gone
out on the wire.

On the wire. The irony is not lost on me. Or is it some strange
poetic injustice?

Either way, I don't waste time reading further. I grab Cornelius's
dime and go.

Woolworth's again. I blow past the luncheonette counter and go
straight to a pay phone, where I drop my dime into the slot and tell
the operator I'd like to make a long-distance call to Brooksvale, Mass.
She tells me how much the first minute will cost, and I clank more of
the Ringmaster's change into the hungry telephone.

Then I dial the number of Emily's private line.

It rings once, twice . . . I picture the princess telephone on her
night table bleating like a pink plastic lamb.

"Hello?"

"Emily!"

She hesitates. "Petula!" she says loudly.

I could cry. Her parents are probably just down the hall and can
hear every word. "I'm all right," I tell her.

A grateful rush of breath comes through the phone's earpiece like a hurricane-force wind. Then she lowers her voice and rambles in a whisper: "When you didn't show up, I knew. I just . . . knew. And I wasn't worried because . . . I don't know, Cath, I just had this *feeling*. I thought, 'Wow, this is it, she's finally going to get away from that son of a bitch.' I was so sure of it I wasn't even surprised when your father showed up at our house."

My heart slams against my ribs. "Emily, what did you tell him?"

"I told him I didn't know where you were. I told him that we went to the circus last night, but this morning you were gone."

Oh, God. Oh no. I am reeling from how close her lie was to the truth.

"I told him the show was sold out when we got there, so we just played some games on the midway, and then we met some college boys and flirted with them and got them to buy us ice cream."

I bet my father just loved that.

"I also said you were acting kind of weird all night, like you had something on your mind, and you kept talking about this place in Maine . . . about some cabin you and your mother stayed at once when you were little."

My hopes lift slightly. "You said I went to Maine?" I'd only told her about that cabin once, and I'm oddly touched that she remembered. That trip was the one time my mother ever considered leaving my father, and those two days away were the most peaceful two days of my life. Even though, in the end, she got scared and went back.

"You're *not* in Maine, are you? Because right after I said it, I thought maybe I shouldn't have just in case—"

"I'm not in Maine," I tell her.

"Good." She takes a deep breath to go on with her story. "I told them we fell asleep in the rumpus room the minute we got back—you know my parents never check—and when I woke up the next morning, you were gone. And I swear, Cathy, they believed every word. Then your father used our phone to call the police. And he said right after he finished the call, he'd go straight to the newspaper."

"I know," I say, my chest tightening. "I saw the article. But it was so weird, Emily . . . There was no—"

"Photograph? Well, here's what happened with *that*." I can picture her flopping onto her flowered bedspread, tugging on the spiral phone cord like she always does when she talks to Cliff Parker. "While your father was talking to the fuzz, I snuck out and went to your house. I wanted to tell your mother . . . well, I wasn't sure what, maybe just that I was sure you were okay. And, Cathy, do you know what she was doing?"

I swallow hard. "What?"

"Somehow she'd managed to gather up every single picture of you that there was in that house! She'd gotten all the photo albums and the pictures in frames—oh, Cath, it must have been so exhausting for her." I imagine her shaking her head, just like I am, in disbelief. "She was *burning* them! Right there on the living room carpet! She was destroying all your pictures . . . even your cotillion portrait. At first I didn't understand. Then I realized it was so he couldn't print them in the paper, so you'd be harder to find."

My face is wet with tears. My chest is heaving. I'm nodding in agreement but of course Emily can't see. I have no voice, no words. *Mothers and daughters. Amazing.*

"We let the fire burn until there was nothing but ashes and then I helped her up to bed."

She pauses, and I reach for a napkin from the lunch counter to dry my eyes because somehow, I sense what's coming next.

"Cathy, I'm so sorry." Emily pauses again. She doesn't want to say it, but I need her to, and she knows it. "She died, Cathy. She died in her sleep."

"Probably so she wouldn't have to listen to my father scream at her for ruining the living room rug," I say, because I need to hear Emily laugh, and because my mother would want *me* to laugh.

"Probably," Emily agrees, and I can hear her smile through the phone. Then, again: "I'm sorry."

"Don't be. She's getting away from that son of a bitch too." I take a long, shuddery breath. "Please don't tell anyone I called, okay?"

"Never! I swear. And if they ask me more questions, I'll just keep right on lying. You've done it for me enough times." She's crying now too. "I'm going to miss you so much, Cath."

I want to say it back to her. I can't, but I don't have to. She knows.

Now the operator breaks in, asking for change. And it's almost funny. *Change*.

Rather than depositing Cornelius's remaining coins into the slot, I simply place the receiver back on the hook.

Goodbye, Emily. I say it in my heart and I'm sure she hears me.

As I walk slowly back to the circus, I can't help wondering if my mother actually willed herself to die in her sleep, if only as a means of distracting my father from searching for me long enough to give me a head start.

Mothers and daughters, indeed.

When I reach the fairgrounds, I send up a prayer for my mother's soul, and another one, thanking the Lord Almighty for making Emily Davenport the excellent liar she is.

NINE

~

CALLIE'S MORNING WAS ONE big game of catch-up.

Her English class was already three-quarters of the way through *To Kill a Mockingbird*, and the teacher, Ms. Connelly, seemed genuinely saddened by the fact that she didn't have a single copy left for Callie, who'd either have to check the book out of the library or buy her own on Amazon.

Too bad they weren't reading *The Catcher in the Rye*; Callie knew where she could get her hands on one of those.

"You can try Mr. Anderson," Ms. Connelly suggested. "He teaches AP English Lit. They read *Mockingbird* in the fall, so he might be willing to lend you his copy. He shares the AP History space with Dr. Wu, behind the band room."

Unfortunately, Callie didn't know where the band room was. She thought maybe Jenna had alluded to it in her turbo-tour spiel, but she wasn't sure, as she'd been suffering the lingering effects of sex wax at the time.

In chemistry class, a teacher whose name she couldn't remember (despite the fact that it was embroidered on his lab coat) handed her a textbook and a syllabus, informing her from behind his safety goggles that she was roughly nine chapters behind on said syllabus, and suggesting that it might not be a bad idea to brush up on her Bunsen burner protocol. She'd never heard the word *syllabus* in her life; she was also a little fuzzy on what a Bunsen burner was.

(At the circus, sticking to the curriculum was at the sole discretion of their teacher-slash-poodle-trainer, so science class often consisted of watching a baby llama be born or analyzing the cotton-candy-making process.)

Gym was a total nonstarter. Coach Fleisch explained that the only classes that would fit into Callie's academic schedule were full to capacity, so she'd have to earn her PE credit for the semester by joining an extracurricular sports team. Her enthusiastic recommendation: croquet.

In history, Callie was told by Mr. Carson that she had missed the entire Industrial Revolution. He advised her to pick up a study guide from the Peer Tutoring Center, the sooner the better as there was a quiz on Thursday.

Callie had no idea where the Peer Tutoring Center was. And the thought of asking one of the 890 strangers who were her new schoolmates had her feeling slightly nauseous.

Finally, lunch.

She remembered Jenna saying that the cafeteria was down a ramp. Or was it up a staircase? It wasn't in the hall with the orange lockers, she knew that much.

After wandering for a bit, Callie caught the unmistakable scent of tater tots and followed it to the lunchroom. Taking advantage of the fact that it was Monday, she helped herself to a salad, scanned the gigantic space for an empty table, and sat down.

She took out her new phone and, between bites of red pepper and raw broccoli, resumed her struggle to get online. She couldn't really imagine Marcello would say no to her request to join him in Italy, but it couldn't hurt to have a backup plan. There were circuses all over America, all over the world, and with her reputation as a gifted young tightrope walker preceding her, Callie doubted she'd have trouble finding a new position.

She knew she couldn't work without her mother's permission

of course, but she'd cross that bridge (or high wire, as it were) when she came to it . . . *if* she came to it.

She was so engrossed in navigating her touchscreen that it was a moment before she noticed someone had taken the seat across from her.

Callie snapped her gaze up to see a boy studying her from the opposite side of the table.

"Hot girl riding a horse?"

Callie frowned at him. "*Excuse* me?"

"Hot girl riding an *elephant*?" This came from a second boy, who'd sidled up on Callie's right. "Which I'm guessing is *definitely* better than the other way around."

Callie's heart slammed once, twice. She didn't feel threatened exactly—she was sitting in a crowded cafeteria with teachers posted like sentinels at every corner—but whatever this was, it was both very uncomfortable and extremely unwelcome.

The second boy had dropped his lunch bag onto the table and was sliding into the plastic chair next to Callie. "You're the circus freak, right?"

Her stomach flipped; a trickle of sweat began to snake its way between her shoulder blades.

"Dude, I'm pretty sure you can't say circus freak," the first boy admonished. "It's not politically correct."

"It's not any kind of correct, you idiot." A tall girl with long blond curls was taking the seat on Callie's left. She offered a genuinely friendly smile, and Callie felt a wave of relief—until she said, "Contortionist! No, wait . . . *acrobat*—but not the regular kind, the kind with those swirly, ribbony things."

"Rhythmic gymnast," the boy on her right clarified, with enough authority to earn himself a raised eyebrow from the boy across the table. "What? It's girls in leotards. I pay attention to that stuff." He turned a goofy grin to Callie. "Hot girl on a tiger? Clown-car driver? *Hot* clown-car driver?"

So they were trying to guess what she'd done in the circus. Callie couldn't tell if this constituted a clever and good-natured way to meet the new girl, or if they were simply trying to humiliate her. The fact that she'd begun to feel nauseous told her it was probably the latter.

And it was about to get worse.

Kristi came sauntering across the lunch room as if she really were Queen Isabella. "Hope you don't mind," she said, clearly hoping no such thing. "We just thought it'd be fun to make a little contest out of trying to figure out what you did in the circus."

"Right," came a familiar voice from behind Callie. "'Cause that's what every new kid in school wants . . . to have their actual life turned into a guessing game."

When Kip slid into the chair beside the first boy, diagonally across from Callie, she could have collapsed from gratitude. Reaching for her water bottle, she realized her hands were shaking.

"We're just goofin' around," said the second boy, helping himself to the pudding cup on Callie's tray. "Hey, I'm Zach. Sorry if things got weird."

Was he? Was he really sorry?

"Jacob," said the boy next to Kip. "And by the way, tiger or no tiger, you're still pretty hot."

The blond girl reached behind Callie to give Jacob a smack in the back of the head, then introduced herself as Emma-Kate. "Okay, so the suspense is killing us. What *did* you do in the circus?"

Callie sighed. "I was—am—a tightrope walker." Somehow, it felt less like a simple explanation than it did a confession, and a pretty dirty one at that.

"Hot girl on the high wire!" said Jacob, slapping his hand on the table as if he'd known it all along. "That was definitely gonna be my next guess. And also . . . pretty freakin' cool."

"Yeah," Zach agreed. "Puts a whole new spin on 'getting high.'"

"That must've taken a lot of guts," Emma-Kate allowed. "I'm

not crazy about heights. And Kristi has panic attacks in Nordstrom's mezzanine."

Kristi glared.

"Hey, Callie, I think I saw you getting dropped off this morning," said Zach. "Your dad drives a Range Rover, right?"

"Wait, so . . . *not* a clown car?"

"Jake!" Kip took a tater tot off his plate and lobbed it at Jacob. "Game's over, pal. Move on, okay?"

"He's, uh, he's not my dad," Callie said, her cheeks flushing. "He's . . . I guess you'd call him our landlord."

Kristi looked stricken. "You *rent*?"

"Yeah. Well, no. We just kind of live where my mother works."

"So she's a maid?" *Sounds like: So she's a topless-dancer-slash-serial-killer.*

Apparently, Brad and Jenna hadn't exaggerated the town's opposition to the rescue facility. But her classmates were going to find out where she lived sooner or later, so she might as well get it over with. "She's not a maid, she's an animal specialist," Callie said. "She works with exotic animals."

It took Kristi exactly three sips of Vitamin Water to make the connection. "You live at the *Sanctuary*?"

Apparently, this was even worse than having a homicidal stripper for a mom.

"So lemme get this straight," said Zach, intrigued. "You're a hot circus girl who lives at the zoo for fucked-up animals."

"Oh, that is so *definitely* not politically correct," said Jake.

Kristi gave Callie a chilling smile. "My father's the mayor of Lake St. Julian. He's been trying to close down that disgusting place for almost a year. According to him, the Sanctuary is a hazard. And if anything tragic ever happened there, it would bring down the property values of the entire town."

And there was the noose.

So Jenna was right. And so was Gram: *Beauty on the outside, danger on the inside.* Kristi Baylor, in a nutshell.

Jake shrugged. "I gotta say, K-Bay, I never quite got why your pops has such a grudge against that place. What's he got against endangered species? They're not bothering anybody. They're just trying to, like, remain on the planet."

"It's not a grudge, it's politics." Kristi's eyes flashed. "And public safety. What if one of those tigers gets loose and winds up in your backyard?"

"Chowing down on your stupid little English bulldog," Zach added with a snort.

"Fuck you, Zach. Pugsly isn't stupid."

Callie stared at her lunch, wishing she could disappear.

"Did you know the town council offered to buy the estate from Mr. Marston?" Kristi went on. "They had all these investors lined up, who were planning to turn it into a five-star resort. But Marston wouldn't sell."

"Seriously?" Zach huffed. "Well, that sucks. Can you imagine the awesome summer jobs we could've gotten at a place like that?"

"Sidenote," said Emma-Kate. "I saw Brad Marston buying a latte at Starbucks once, and he's pretty hot for an old guy."

"I don't think you're gonna care how hot he is when his elephants trample your house," said Zach.

"Oh my God, Zach."

Callie whirled at the sound of Jenna's voice.

"Did you take *another* croquet mallet to the skull? Nobody's house is going to be trampled by elephants. Marston has them in secure enclosures with like a zillion different fail-safes. And, Kristi, if you're really taking an interest in your father's political agenda, why don't you start with something you can actually get behind personally . . . like talking him into supporting the principal's plan to hand out condoms in school."

"Whoa." Jake scowled. "Your old man's against free condoms?"

"Like you'd ever have a reason to use one," drawled Emma-Kate.

During all of this, Kristi had been shooting Jenna looks that could melt glaciers, but Jenna didn't seem overly concerned. Completely ignoring Kristi's death glare, she leaned down to whisper sharply in Callie's ear.

"*Mean Girls.* Rent it."

Without another word to Callie or anyone else, Jenna turned and walked away.

TEN

New Jersey, 1965

WHEN I TOLD SHARON I wanted to learn to walk the high wire, I meant the "high" part literally. I'd pictured myself strapped into an elaborate safety harness, traversing the Big Top at sixty feet, with my arms outstretched, and my feet slipping tentatively across the wire.

But Sharon believes strongly in starting with the basics, and that makes the exercise a whole lot less exhilarating. We're working at ground level with an ordinary hemp rope laid out on the grass; my assignment is to walk back and forth on it, barefoot.

On the upside, the simplicity of the exercise will allow us to carry on a conversation, which I begin with this question: "What's with James and Gideon? They don't seem to get along very well."

"That's putting it mildly," says Sharon, lighting a cigarette.

"But they're brothers."

"Half brothers," Sharon corrects.

"Have they always been at each other's throats?"

"Nah. That nonsense didn't start until a few years ago." Sharon blows out a series of smoke rings. "I hate to say it, but I blame Cornelius. He's a great man, truly, but he *is* only human. I know he doesn't see it, but everyone else does."

"See what?"

"That he's got a favorite."

"James," I say, and Sharon nods. He'd told me as much, but I assumed he was just kidding. "So Gideon's jealous?"

"To the very marrow of his bones." Taking a long, fortifying puff, she launches into a tale that could only be true in the circus:

"Gideon was born the winter I joined VanDrexel's, but Cornelius divorced his mother about a year later. Trust me when I tell you, nobody was especially sorry to see her go. Bitch on wheels, that one was, and we all knew Gideon would be better off without her." Sharon pauses to wag her cigarette in the direction of my toes. "You need to get familiar with the sensation of the wire underfoot. Feel your soles molding to it. Grip without gripping. Ankles strong, knees bent . . . heel to toe, heel to toe . . . that's it."

I do as she says, but this is without a doubt the least challenging activity I have ever undertaken—and I spent a month learning how to curtsy for the coming-out ball. "What about James's mother?"

"Helen." Sharon's eyes mist up as she takes another drag. "Now, there was a gal who lived up to her name. As beautiful as Helen of Troy, and every bit as fickle. She showed up out of nowhere one morning with an Arabian stallion and no personal history to speak of—not one she was willing to share with any of us, at any rate. But the second Cornelius laid eyes on her he was over the moon."

"So they got married?"

"Oh no. Marriage was much too conventional for the likes of Helen. She called herself a free spirit."

"So you didn't like her?"

"Are you kidding? I adored her. We all did. She was like walking happiness, ya know? Gorgeous, charismatic, fun-loving, smart."

"Like James," I say, then wish I hadn't.

"Yeah." Sharon grins. "Just like James."

I turn abruptly and walk the rope back in the opposite direction. "What happened to her?" I ask over my shoulder.

"Well, when James was born the Ringmaster was beside himself with joy. The only one happier than Cornelius was Gideon. God, he was crazy about that baby. Proudest big brother you've ever seen. And James of course worshipped the ground Gideon walked on."

I try to picture it—the two young men who were just on the verge of killing each other, playing together as children.

"But then, one day, Helen just . . . ran off. Gone. Just like her mythological namesake."

"She *left*?" I stop walking and jerk back around to face her. "She abandoned her child? Just like that?"

"Just like that. Cornelius was devastated. Would have drunk himself to death if it hadn't been for Duncan. Dunc saved his life, saved him from himself. At first we were afraid that little James looking so much like Helen would make it harder for Cornelius to forget her. But instead of it breaking his heart, Cornelius actually took comfort in the resemblance. James was the one precious bit of magic she left behind. Which is why he'll never let that boy out of his sight. I think he's scared if he does, James'll do the same thing his mother did—vanish."

Sharon is about to say more but something in the distance catches her eye and she begins to bark out orders instead: "Balance and concentration, Victoria! Control your center of gravity! Open yourself up to the deeper philosophy of wire walking."

"And what would that be exactly?" comes an amused voice from behind me. "*Try not to fall to your death?*"

"Says the guy who pals around with full-grown tigers," Sharon teases back, flicking her cigarette butt into the dirt.

I swivel my head around to see who's addressing us and immediately lose my balance (Center of Gravity: 1, Victoria: 0) because Gideon VanDrexel has just sauntered up. He stands there with his arms folded and his feet apart, looking like an old-time matinee idol. Or a lion tamer. Which he is.

No wonder Sharon changed the subject so quickly.

"What can we do for you, Gid?" she asks.

"First of May is wanted in the wardrobe car. Something about a missing-button epidemic." He throws me a friendly smile. "You sew, right?"

"I, um . . ." Brooksvale Junior High School, seventh-grade home ec: I made a quilted tea cozy and embroidered half a handkerchief. "A little."

"Perfect." He jerks his head in an invitation to follow him. I brush the dry grass off my feet, slip them into my new sandals, and do exactly that.

"To be continued," Sharon calls after me, lighting another cigarette. "In the meantime, think *posture*."

I fall into step beside Gideon, who's taller than James and slimmer. He must have his mother's eyes because I'm not seeing the twinkle that James and Cornelius share.

"We haven't been properly introduced," he says, shaking my hand. "Victoria, is it?"

"Yes."

"Good to meet you. How's it going so far?"

"Going great!" I say with more gusto than I intended. "Well, except for that bit with the elephant trailer."

"Elephant trailer?' Gideon frowns. "James?"

I nod.

"Damn it. I've told him to quit hazing the new people. It's childish."

"Maybe he thinks it builds character," I offer, though why I feel the need to defend him I don't know. "And I did enjoy meeting Rabelais."

Gideon laughs. "Well, who wouldn't?"

We're delayed briefly by Vince, who has a few questions for Gideon. Tonight we close in Jersey, which means we're "on the jump," and he wants to be sure the animals will be ready for the "all out." Gideon assures him they will, but Vince stalls, stroking his chin. A shadow of concern darkens his weathered face.

"Listen, Gid . . . I'm not sure if James told ya, but Boo-boo didn't eat this morning."

Gideon's mouth twists. "I was afraid of that."

"James is actin' like it's no big deal," Vince goes on, taking off his slouchy fedora to mop his brow. "'Boo-boo's cool,' he says to me. But I can see it in his eyes. Somethin's off."

"And 'off' is just another word for 'unpredictable,'" Gideon murmurs glumly.

"And 'unpredictable' is just another word for 'deadly.' I hate to say it, Gid, but we might need to start thinkin' about positioning a sni—"

Gideon cuts him off with a meaningful look. "Not yet, Vince. And please, don't even *suggest* that to James."

"What am I, crazy?" Vince drops his hat back onto his head. "I'd sooner suggest it to Boo-boo."

He waddles off and we walk on. Gideon is quiet until we reach the wardrobe car. When he opens the door for me, I notice a long, jagged scar on his forearm, but I don't dare ask how he got it. The boy *is* a lion tamer after all.

"Hey, Myrtle," he calls inside, gesturing for me to enter. "First of May, reporting for button duty."

I suppose I'm not really qualified for much else, but that doesn't stop me from cringing. Gideon reads my expression and smiles for the first time since we left Vince. "Just see how it goes," he says softly. "If you don't like it, we'll try something else."

His tone is so genuine that I'm suddenly committed to becoming the best damned button-sewer this, or any other circus, has ever seen. Even if it *is* just for a couple of weeks.

"Thank you," I say.

"No problem. Good luck." And he's gone.

Inside, the wardrobe car is a jungle of tulle skirts, feather boas, and oversize silk jumpsuits in colorful, clownish stripes. A woman with a brassy beehive hairdo kneels beside a worse-for-wear dress-maker's dummy, repairing the fringe on a satin romper.

"Myrtle?" I venture.

Without looking up from the fringe, she explains that there are currently eight shirts, four pairs of overalls, and three tailcoats requiring new buttons. She talks me through the clutter until I have located scissors, a needle, and several spools of thread. Then she points me to an old coffee can filled with buttons.

I poke around until I find a few copper ones and start on the overalls. After several attempts and a great deal of squinting I manage to thread the needle.

By now, Myrtle has finished mending the romper's fringe and is struggling to outfit the dress dummy with a gorgeous little full-skirted dress—canary yellow, very short, with a fitted bodice and a deep sweetheart neckline trimmed in turquoise sequins. Judging by the number of pins, it is still very much a work in progress. But the dress is too small for the dummy and Myrtle is getting annoyed.

"You," she says. "Try this on."

"Me?"

"Yes, you. You're about her size."

"Whose size?"

"Evangeline, the flaming baton twirler." At my look of disbelief, she clarifies, "The *batons* are on fire, not the girl." Then she tosses the dress in my direction. "Put it on. Quickly, please."

"But—" I blush just thinking about that neckline. "I'm on button duty."

"Consider yourself promoted. Evangeline needs this tonight!"

I look around the wardrobe car. There does not appear to be a fitting room.

"Quickly," Myrtle repeats, turning her back.

I guess this is the closest thing to privacy I'm going to get, so I hurry out of my clothes and wriggle cautiously into the dress. The skirt barely skims the tops of my thighs.

When Myrtle zips me up, my breasts react by plumping into

the plunging V of the neckline and swelling up over the scalloped edge.

"You're bustier than Evangeline," she observes.

Thanks?

Myrtle spins me around a couple of times, as if we're embarking on an extremely serious game of pin the tail on the donkey. After she's checked me from all sides, she positions me in front of the mirror.

"D'ya think a drop waistline would've looked better?" she asks.

Since my expertise lies solely in the area of tea cozies, I shrug. This gives my breasts an excuse to peek even higher over the sequined edge of the bodice. Myrtle notices and her reflection smirks at mine. "Maybe *you* should think about learning to twirl batons."

Before I can respond to that peculiar compliment, the door opens and James VanDrexel comes breezing into the car. And judging from the way his eyes widen at the sight of me in Evangeline's dress, I'm thinking *he* wouldn't mind seeing me take up baton twirling either.

ELEVEN

~

CALLIE DIDN'T SEE JENNA again all day.

But Kip showed up at her locker after the final bell.

"Sorry about lunch," he said, leaning one shoulder against the lockers, a pose Callie suspected he didn't even realize qualified as a pose, but packed a whole lot of adorable nonetheless—a fact she really wished she hadn't noticed.

"Guess I should have given you more of a heads-up about Kristi, huh?"

"Gee, ya think?"

"You're mad."

"Actually, I really don't care enough to be mad, and I'm not going to be living here long enough for Queen Is-a-bully to even matter. But if I *were* planning to stick around, then yeah, I'd be furious. They were basically interrogating me, and you just sat there eating tater tots."

"Only because you seem like a girl who can take care of herself, and I didn't think you'd want me to come charging to your rescue, like some cocky, self-important knight in shining armor."

"Don't you mean conquistador in shining armor?" Callie snapped.

"Whatever. I didn't want to come off as some big strong macho dude who thought he had to stand up for you. I figured you had it under control."

"Not sure I'd classify you as a 'big strong macho dude.'"

Kip cocked an eyebrow.

"And when exactly did it appear to you that I 'had it under control'? Was it when Kristi was making fun of where I live? Or maybe when Jake was calling me the-hot-girl-on-a . . . insert exotic animal name here?"

"I threw a tater tot at him, didn't I?" Kip dragged a hand through his hair. "Look, they aren't usually that bad . . . well, except for Kristi, who's pretty much always that bad, and occasionally worse." He spun around so that his upper back was now pressing against the gray metal of the lockers, and the rest of his lean surfer's body sloped away at an angle; unfortunately, this stance managed to be even cuter than the first one. "But Emma-Kate's actually okay, and Jake and Zach are just suffering from a really bad case of teenage-boy humor, which, I know, is pretty much a public service announcement waiting to happen, but I swear, they honestly weren't trying to embarrass you. And if they did, I'm sorry."

He actually sounded like he meant it. Callie stuffed some books into her backpack, shut her locker, and started walking. Annoyingly, Kip fell into step beside her. She was about to politely ask him to go away, but her mother had decreed she make friends in the non-circus world, and so far he seemed like the only person here who might actually be tolerable.

Okay, slightly more than tolerable. And he did have a name her grandmother would have approved of. She was also fairly certain that K-Bay would absolutely hate it if Callie and Kip became friendly. So there was that.

"I didn't realize the Sanctuary issue was that much of a hornet's nest," Kip was saying. "Sounds like there's a good chance the place'll be shut down."

Callie was about to invoke the "not my monkeys" proverb, but didn't when she realized she'd probably have to explain it. So instead, she simply said, "I'll be gone long before that happens."

"Gone?"

"I'm going to be joining my father's circus in Italy pretty soon, so I'm really not all that invested in whether it closes or not."

"What about the animals? Don't you care about them?"

Callie sighed. "You know how in every family, there's always this one needy sibling who gets fussed over and hogs all the attention?"

Kip nodded.

"In my family, that sibling was the tiger. And the black bear. And the poodle-beagle mix who could never quite remember his routine on the balance beam. So yeah, I care about them, but I'm not going to be overly sad to move on. And Marston's animals will be fine. He'll just place them in other rescue facilities around the country. And my mother's good at what she does, so she shouldn't have any trouble finding a less controversial place to work." An image of Quinn grooming golden retrievers at some overpriced pet salon flashed in Callie's mind. She pushed it out.

"So when are you moving to Italy?" Kip looked genuinely disappointed. "Because you can't leave before I have a chance to perfect my juggling skills. Unless you'd be willing to coach me over Face-Time. Which reminds me . . ." He took his phone out of his pocket and handed it to her.

"What's this for?"

"So you can call your phone?"

"Why would I call my phone?"

"So I'll have your number and you'll have mine." Kip laughed; he seemed to find her obliviousness charming. "Looks like you know less about cellular devices than I do about juggling. No worries, I'll show you what to do."

Mortified, Callie handed over her phone and let Kip walk her through the process. When he noticed she didn't have Jenna's number, he tapped the screen a few times and said, "There ya go. You have just experienced your first 'Share Contact.' Wasn't so bad, was it?"

"Painless," said Callie, feeling overwhelmed. It had already been a ridiculously long day, and what she'd hoped would be a stress-free walk to the parking lot was turning out to be the most exhausting part of it. All she wanted to do was go home and get on the tightrope.

Through the exit's glass doors, she could see Brad's Range Rover pulling up to the curb with Quinn in the passenger seat and Brad behind the wheel. Callie reached for the door handle, but Kip stopped her.

"Before you go . . . I was sort of hoping you might be willing to help me out with an experiment. I've been formulating this theory," he explained, grinning, "since, oh, just about seven o'clock this morning—and you happen to be uniquely qualified to help me prove my hypothesis."

"Why me?"

His grin broadened. "Because you're not like everyone else around here."

Callie stiffened. Everything her mother had said to her that morning came back in a cold rush. She didn't want Quinn to be right. And she didn't want Kip to be . . . well, she didn't know what she wanted Kip to be. She was in unfamiliar territory—at the circus they'd have said she couldn't read the crowd. Her feet arched in her shoes, wishing for the safety of a wire beneath them. "What does that mean?" she asked, bristling. " ' I'm not like everybody else.' "

"Well, for starters, you're the only girl I know who can walk a tightrope, which kind of makes you—"

"A circus freak?" Her voice broke on the phrase, which somehow made it sound even more shameful. Tears burned behind her eyes, but she refused to let them fall in front of Kip. She'd already experienced enough embarrassment for one day.

Shoving the door open, she bolted for the Range Rover and climbed into the back seat.

"Well," said Quinn, smiling anxiously. "How was your first day?"

"I definitely didn't have to suffer the humiliation of eating lunch alone, if that's what you're wondering."

Quinn beamed.

"How about your classes?" asked Brad. "Learn anything exciting?"

"Oh yeah. Tons of great stuff. I learned all about Queen Isabella, and property values." Tossing her backpack onto the floor, Callie sunk into the Rover's lush upholstery and sighed. "Oh . . . and nooses."

TWELVE

New Jersey, 1965

MY ARMS CROSS OVER my chest in an attempt to hide what Evangeline's sequin-trimmed neckline doesn't. "Well, if it isn't Billy Bongo, the monkeyless boy."

"That's *Baby* Bongo," he corrects, grinning. "Nice dress."

Myrtle's face breaks into a smile of pure delight. "Hello, handsome," she coos, giving his cheek a motherly squeeze. "Problem with your costume?"

"Nothing fatal." *Seems like a risky word choice for a guy who performs with lions*, I think. "I just suddenly find myself in need of a button."

"Oh, I bet you do." Myrtle chuckles.

Her knowing eyes flick from James to me, standing there half-swathed in satin.

It takes a moment for realization to dawn. She's implying that the button emergency is just an excuse. *He's here to see me.* And given my sudden foray into the world of fit modeling, he's seeing a whole lot more of me than he expected.

But James is sticking to his story. "It's a pretty important one, as buttons go," he says pointing to the empty place on his waistband where the button should be—they're the safari-style pants he wears in the show. *Nice touch.*

Myrtle, who was not born yesterday, heads for the door. "I think I'll just run over to the pie car for a cuppa tea," she singsongs. "Victoria, you know what to do."

If she means "stab him with the scissors," then, yes, I do. But murdering one of Cornelius's star attractions—not to mention a blood relative—might be construed as ungrateful, so I grab a black velvet cape from a hanger and slip it on over the dress I'm almost wearing. Then I dig around in the coffee can again until I'm holding a flat taupe-colored button that looks to be the right size. I clear my throat and say in as professional a voice as I can muster, "Take off your pants."

His smile is pure gloating as his fingertips go obediently to his fly. "Would you mind turning around?"

I spin away from him; unfortunately, I now have a perfect view of his reflection in the full-length mirror.

The next thing I know, James VanDrexel is standing there in his—

"Boxer shorts," I blurt, stupidly.

"What were you expecting? A loincloth?"

"Shut up and give me the pants," I hiss. I'm not about to tell him I've never seen a boy in his underwear before.

Oozing smugness, he steps out of the khaki puddle that is his trousers and hands them to me. I thread the needle—first try, thank *God*!—and set to work, dipping the point in and out, in and out, again and again through the four tiny holes, pulling tightly each time, until the button is secure. Then I thrust the pants back at him over my shoulder, keeping my eyes averted until I hear the zipper go up.

"Are we done?" I snap. "Or is there some camel spit somewhere you need me to mop up?"

"Oh, c'mon," he says, tucking in his shirt. "It wasn't that bad. You got to hang around with Rabelais, didn't you?" Without warning, he breaks into a dead-on impression of Rabelais's trumpeting noise and I smile in spite of myself. The next thing I know, he's whinnying like a horse, then roaring like a lion, then hopping around like one of the poodles until I'm laughing so hard I can barely catch my breath.

"You have a great laugh," he says.

"And you have a great whinny." I tilt my head at him. "You, James VanDrexel, are a one-man menagerie."

"I've been called worse." When he winks at me, I quickly glance away, but without any permission from me, my eyes go immediately back to his and hold there. I've seen Emily do this a million times with boys, but I didn't know why until just this moment.

"Thanks for the button," he says, his voice dropping one sultry octave.

"You're welcome," I murmur.

His eyes slip to half-mast and he gives me the full voltage of his showman's smile. The next thing I know, he's leaning in to kiss me.

Slaaaappp! My palm connects with his cheek smartly enough to send him staggering into a rack of jugglers' costumes; the impact knocks a mountain of crisp white tutus from a shelf, and they tumble down on him like a crinkly avalanche.

I am immediately sick to my stomach. While it's true that in my world, girls are *supposed to* slap boys who get fresh, I know that my reaction is more about me than about James. My hand trembles. I've spent my whole life ducking cheap shots like that one—hitting, I realize, feels almost as shameful as being hit.

James squirms his way out of the pile of crinoline and gold lamé. "I guess I had that coming," he concedes, dragging a hand through his hair. "I'm sorry."

I get the feeling he doesn't use that phrase very often, but since *I* was about to apologize to *him* for resorting so readily to physical violence, his mea culpa brings me up short. How can a person be so smarmy *and* so charming at the same time?

So . . . *smarming.*

To my surprise, James actually starts tidying up the mess we've collectively created, righting the tutus and replacing the juggling suits neatly on their hangers. I'm basically paralyzed, so I just stand there and watch him do it. And then I hear myself saying the silliest thing:

"Well, at least your pants stayed up. Maybe I've got a future in wardrobe after all."

He smiles, turns to leave, then turns back. "Hey. Come with me, okay? There's someone I want you to meet."

"What? No."

"C'mon."

"I'm . . . I'm on button duty." I wince at how ridiculous that sounds.

"And I'm the heir apparent to this little dog-and-pony show, and I say the buttons can wait. So can the snaps. And the eye-hooks." His broadening smile brings out a pair of rugged dimples in his cheeks. "I know the belt buckles have a reputation for being impatient, but screw them, they can wait too! Let 'em complain to the zippers. Just come with me, Victoria. I swear, I won't be a jerk." Pointedly, he rubs his jaw.

"Are you sure Myrtle won't be mad?"

"I'm positive," he promises. "She kind of adores me."

Of that I have absolutely no doubt.

Moments later, I've changed back into my own clothes and we're on our way to the menagerie, the section of the grounds where the animals are displayed before showtime.

On the horizon, the final shimmer of daylight is melting like candle wax out of the sky; a jewel-toned twilight swells above, coaxing out the stars. The show won't begin for another hour, but already a crowd is on hand to experience VanDrexel's oversize petting zoo. The more docile animals are enclosed in portable gates, ready and willing to be cuddled.

"Popcorn?" James offers, plucking a bag from a vendor's cart.

As we walk, he tells me little anecdotes about each animal. He talks about them like most people talk about their families—openly, honestly, critically at times, but always with the deepest affection: the horses are spoiled but lovable. There's a camel called Toast who loves ice cream, and Chubs, the black bear, who "talks" in her sleep. We pause to watch a troupe of dancing dogs billed as the Barkettes, all of whom are former strays rescued from dog pounds around the country. A terrier named Miss Kelly politely shakes my hand, and Shakespeare, a collie, sits up on his hind legs to wave hello. A quintet of poodles delights the spectators with what can only be described as a canine kick line.

"To be honest, most of them don't have any rhythm at all," James confesses in a stage whisper. "But we let 'em dance anyway. They dig the applause."

"Do all circuses do that?" I ask. "Adopt abandoned dogs, I mean?"

"Some do. Not all. But Gid and I insist on it. Another thing we insist on is no beatings."

For a second I think he's exaggerating, but there's something somber in his tone that makes me understand he's not.

"There's a right way to interact with an animal, and there's a wrong way," James goes on. "The right way isn't about control, it's about mutual respect."

I think of all those times my father raised his fists to me in an effort to exert control, and I realize James is right. The fact that I am here proves that control doesn't come with any guarantees.

"At least you and Gideon agree on that," I venture.

"Yeah," he says. "I just wish he had a little more respect for *me*."

Emboldened by his candor, I ask, "What did Gideon mean about you going to Europe?"

James hesitates. "Just this plan I've got," he says vaguely. "Well, kind of a plan, kind of . . . I don't know, a dream. But I guess everybody has one, right?"

I shrug, thinking of the things that passed for my own dreams before I joined VanDrexel's, and feel strangely empty inside. I want to ask him the details of his, but something tells me he wouldn't be willing to share it with me.

Yet.

We're quiet for a moment, and I watch Toast steal a Creamsicle from a giggling child. I marvel at three white horses bowing to an elderly woman who curtsies back to them as if they were knights in shining armor. Chubs, the black bear, happily shakes her enormous bottom to the music of the calliope. It horrifies me to imagine that anyone could ever hurt any of these creatures in the name of entertainment, or for any other reason. I'm already in love with them.

Rabelais is holding court beside his trailer. A gaggle of children fawn over him and he seems to be enjoying himself—every time a child shouts hello, he waves his trunk and the magical noise of their giggles gives the calliope a run for its money. A woman in a spangled dress stands beside the elephant, watching proudly.

"That's Francie," James tells me, munching the popcorn. "I guess you could say she owes you a favor." When I give him a curious look, he explains that Francie is Rabelais's official trainer and handler, and confesses that he purposely sent her on an errand yesterday morning so that *he* could be the one to introduce me to the elephant and instruct me in the finer nuances of shoveling shit.

I remember how James and the elephant had behaved as if they were best buddies. "That elephant's as smitten with you as everyone else around here."

James laughs. "Can I help it if I'm charismatic?"

"You probably could if you tried."

We arrive at two colorful wagons containing four fabulous cats—three tigers share one of the ornate cages, while in the other, a regal-looking lion enjoys the privacy befitting his King of Beasts status. The tigers peer out through the bars as though they believe it's we humans who are on display for *their* enjoyment. The lion knows better.

"They're gorgeous," I say, cautiously taking in their silken coats and bright green-gold eyes from a gap of no less than three feet. "What are their names?"

James points to the smallest of the three tigers, small being a relative term in this case since, if I had to guess, I would put the cat at about three hundred pounds. "This is Clementine."

The tiger makes a sound like a powdery drumroll, which she repeats several times. James responds in kind.

"She's chuffing," he explains. "It's their happy sound."

It's certainly making me feel happy.

"Clemmy's our only female," James goes on. "Very mischievous, very smart. She's kind of like the little sister I never had."

"I'm not sure whether that's the cutest thing I've ever heard or the weirdest," I tell him. Then I let out a little shriek, because James is reaching into the cage to stroke Clementine's orange fur as casually as if she were a pampered housecat, and not one of the most dangerous creatures on the planet.

"How's it weird?" he challenges. "I've known Clemmy since she was a cub, I watched her grow up. I protect her and I teach her stuff, just like any big brother."

"Quizzed her on her multiplication tables, did you?"

"Taught her to jump through a fiery hoop." His forehead wrinkles with a frown. "Didn't want to, but the crowds were seeing it elsewhere, and this is a competitive business so we gave it a shot. Once. She totally cleared the flames, but I nearly had a heart attack watching her do it. The next day Gid and I decided it wasn't worth the risk and took it out of the act for good." He shrugs, then presses his lips together and lets out a whistle. A second tiger reclining near the back of the cage leaps up and lumbers over to us. He's much larger than Clemmy; instinctively, I step farther back from the bars.

"Scruff, say hello to Victoria."

Scruff lets out a growl that makes my knees buckle. I would have much preferred a chuff.

"He's Clemmy's brother. So's that big lug over there, but he's a little shy. Gideon named him Prince Edward."

"After Queen Elizabeth's baby?"

James nods. "These three were born last year in March, same day as the prince. They came to us when they were just four months old. Right after their mother died."

Again, my knees threaten to give out on me, and I feel an instant, heartrending kinship with these three enormous orphans.

"When we first got 'em, they'd take turns sleeping at the foot of my bed," James boasts, rubbing the tiger's massive neck.

"Interesting alternative to a teddy bear," I observe. "Or did you cuddle up in bed with Chubs when she was little too?"

"How else would I know she talks in her sleep? And for the record, she's a major pillow hog."

I laugh, then we both go quiet for a moment, letting Scruff enjoy his neck massage.

"So, I guess if this is going to work, I'm going to have to learn to be a whole lot more gallant," James says.

"If what's going to work?"

"Us." He looks at me sidelong. "Wait a minute . . . You didn't think I was done flirting with you, did you?"

I blink at him.

"Oh . . . you *did*. Well then, let's be clear . . ." He stops petting the tiger and places his thumb gently under my chin, lifting it until my face is nearly even with his. "It's gonna take a hell of a lot more than a few tutus to the head to discourage me, Victoria."

I hold my breath, certain he's going to kiss me.

But he doesn't. He lets go of my chin and nudges me on to the next wagon, where the lion is posing regally.

"I know I shouldn't say this," James whispers, "but this guy's my favorite." I can certainly see why. The lion's mane, his coat, even the tuft of his tail rival my mother's most expensive fur stoles, and his eyes are the palest shade of topaz. I know it sounds crazy but I'm sure I see wisdom in them.

"He's been with VanDrexel's as long as I have," James explains. "He's pretty old for a lion. Just turned eighteen."

The cat stirs, lifting his head from his paws as if he knows we're talking about him. I'm captivated by those glittering eyes, which somehow manage to soothe and terrify me at the same time. This animal is fully aware of his own might, of the threat he poses, and yet, despite his fangs and claws and staggering weight, he has made the choice to be gentle. Even so, I can't bring myself to step any closer to the bars.

"What's his name?"

"Baraboo. My father named him after the town in Wisconsin where a couple of brothers by the name of Ringling grew up. Maybe you've heard of them?"

I laugh. "Uh, yeah. I think it rings a bell."

"Technically they're the competition, but without them there'd be no us, so . . ."

"Baraboo," I echo, liking the tribute.

"Wanna pet him?"

He's kidding, right? I shake my head emphatically. "No thanks."

James rolls his eyes and reaches between the bars to rattle the metal food dish, but the lion doesn't budge. "When I was little, I couldn't say Baraboo. Best I could do was Boo-boo, and it stuck."

"Wait, *this* is Boo-boo? The one who didn't eat breakfast?"

"Didn't eat dinner either. I'm sure it's no big—" James snaps his gaze from the lion to give me a curious look. "How'd you know that?"

"Vince mentioned it." I muster the courage to knock on one of the bars of the cage. "Hey, big fella. Hello there, sweet boy."

Boo-boo's tail flicks.

"Not hungry today?" I prompt.

He tilts his head; one massive paw flexes as he curls his lip to make a sound that is the friendlier, less-threatening cousin of a snarl.

Again, James nudges the metal dish in the cat's direction, but he does not interrupt what is swiftly becoming a conversation.

"That meat looks reeeeally delicious," I croon. "C'mon, sweetie. Have a taste, just a little one. Please."

My chest fills with . . . I'm not sure what—Fear? Excitement?—when Boo-boo rises to his feet, stalking toward us with his nose twitching, his whiskers quivering.

"He understood me!"

"Not exactly, but he knows you mean well. Keep talking. He likes the sound of your voice."

But it's not *my* voice I'm using, I realize; it's my mother's. I've called it up from deep within me, from that nameless place where, unknowingly, I'd tucked away every reassuring word she ever said, every hopeful lullaby she ever sang—the only things she had to offer to make me feel safe in my unsafe world.

"Keep talking," James urges again.

So I lean closer to the bars and say, "Come on, Boo-boo. It's almost showtime. Big star like you can't perform on an empty stomach, can he? There you go, baby, that's a good boy. That's a good king of the jungle."

As the lion slinks closer, I notice with a jolt that his legs are shaking. There's also a slight heaving in his chest.

Baraboo reaches the bowl, glances at James, and emits a sound like tremendous gears grinding, a scrape from his larynx that isn't quite a roar. It's not an unhappy sound but there is some pain in it, I know.

Vince knows too, and Gideon.

And James knows. He doesn't accept it, but he knows.

And Baraboo knows, even as he lowers his majestic head over his bowl and partakes of his supper. The lion knows.

And it all but breaks my heart.

"Eat up, buddy," James murmurs. I'm not sure when he took my hand in his. Or maybe it was the other way around.

Snap.

I let my fingers slip from his and turn to see Valerie lowering the Instamatic from her face. "That'll be a good one!" she says, beaming. "Candids are the grooviest."

It's almost time for the Spec to begin, so James and I leave Boo-boo to finish his supper and make our way back toward the train.

We pass children squealing with glee, and their parents don't even try to shush them. The sense of anticipation, of joy, hangs in the air like the smell of roasting peanuts. *What's in store for us tonight? What's going to happen next?*

To be honest, I'm wondering the same thing myself.

"Do you ever get scared?" I venture softly.

"I wouldn't be much of a lion tamer if I said yes, would I?" James replies, with an evasive grin.

"But they're wild animals," I say, remembering the look in Baraboo's eyes, the look of peace and power, mingled. "What about their instincts? What about what's in their nature?"

"That's what makes it so exciting. A thing that's wild can be taught, but never tamed." He says this with so much conviction that his voice cracks over the words. "But a thing that's tame, on the other hand, can definitely become wild."

Strains of the most circus-y of all circus music—the plucky "Entrance of the Gladiators"—follow me as I head back to my room. I tear off a piece of the empty popcorn bag and use my laundry marker to record James's words there among the butter smears:

A thing that's wild can be taught, but never tamed. A thing that's tame can become wild.

I take a moment to consider the sentiment, then sweep away the stray kernels that are stuck to it and place it in the jewelry box, wondering if perhaps it is only half-true.

That night, I am invited to assist in Clown Alley during the show. It's a rare honor, as the area is generally off-limits to non-clowns, but this morning after my call to Emily and before my tightrope lesson with Sharon, I offered to look after a toddler named Arthur so his parents, Sir Bailiwick and Hopscotch—two of VanDrexel's most beloved clowns—could rehearse a new gag involving a bowling pin, a cherry pie, and a rubber chicken.

"Always remember, Arthur," Bailiwick had called to his son. "When in doubt, juggle! It keeps your mind from wandering and never fails to entertain the rubes!"

My reward for babysitting is being allowed to spend the night backstage among the clowns, filling their squirting lapel flowers, locating their giant bowties, and polishing their oversize shoes.

During a lull in the dressing room commotion, Bailiwick teaches me to apply some basic clown makeup. "Sad or happy?" he asks, referring to whether he should paint me with a smile or a frown.

The answer is happy. So, so happy.

Then Hopscotch loans me a pair of polka dot bloomers and some tennis shoes with pom-poms on the toes. Just before the grand finale, I run back to my room and pin my mother's brooch to the suspenders holding up my dotted pants. When Hopscotch and Bailiwick sneak me into the tent with the others, I wave and blow kisses to the crowd and even take a bow. The applause rains down around us and sounds like a beautiful storm.

I can only imagine how it feels when you've actually earned it.

THIRTEEN

~

THEY HADN'T EVEN GOTTEN out of the school parking lot before Callie heard a small, electronic warble. It took her a moment to realize it was her phone.

On the screen, Jenna's name had popped up, along with Callie's first-ever text message:

WHAT THE HELL IS WRONG WITH U?

Callie blinked at the phone.

Another warble, followed by a little red face giving her what could only be described as a very exasperated look.

Frowning back at the unfriendly emoji, Callie arranged her thumbs on the keyboard, and with a little help from autocorrect, managed to type a legible reply: WHAT DID I DO?

KIP SAID HE ASKED U ON A SURFING DATE AND U WERE A TOTAL B%*!H ABOUT IT.

Callie's eyes flew open, and her thumbs jerked over the keys. HE NEVER SAID ANYTHING ABOUT A DATE. HE ASKED ME TO HELP HIM WITH A SCIENCE EXPERIMENT.

There was a long delay, during which Callie's eyes remained fixed on her phone. At last—*warble*—Jenna's response materialized, consisting of no less than a dozen tiny yellow faces, each of which appeared to be laughing so hard there were tears streaming out of their eyes. Then: DO U LIVE ON THIS PLANET? HE LIKES YOU.

Again, Callie stared at the phone. She was so amazed by what she'd just read that she didn't even realize the car had come to a stop until her door flew open.

There was Jenna, holding her phone and smirking.

A new text: MOVE OVER.

"What's going on?" Callie asked as Jenna climbed in, forcing Callie to slide to the opposite side of the seat.

"We're picking up Jenna," Quinn said.

Callie rolled her eyes. "I see that. Why?"

"Because she called me at the Sanctuary and told me you were nice enough to invite her over for dinner, but she needed a ride, so could we possibly swing by and pick her up."

As Brad pulled out of what Callie could only assume was Jenna's driveway, Callie just gaped at her. The girl had audacity, Callie had to give her that.

"I would have liked to pop in and meet your mother," said Quinn, turning around in her seat to smile at Jenna.

"She was kind of busy. But next time, definitely."

"You're sure she's okay with you having dinner at our place?" Brad asked.

Callie scowled at the back of Brad's head. *Our place. Gross.*

"Yep, she's totally okay with it," said Jenna, glancing out the window.

When Quinn turned back around to segue into a conversation with Brad about adjusting Gulliver's diet, Jenna took the opportunity to give Callie an utterly disgusted look. "He feels really bad, you know."

"Who, Gulliver?" Callie hedged, swiping through her phone's emoji keyboard. "Well, he's always had digestive issues, so . . . Hey, in what context would anyone ever possibly use the fried shrimp emoji?"

"I'm not talking about your big old gassy elephant, and you know it, so stop trying to change the subject. Having said that, I feel compelled to add that fried shrimp happens to be an all-purpose emoji and one of my personal favorites. But I digress. The issue at hand, Calliope VanDrexel, is that Kipling Devereaux really wanted to surf with you—not a euphemism—and you completely dissed him."

"Then why was he talking about some stupid science experiment?"

"Because he was trying to be *cute*, you nitwit. Boyishly charming, irresistibly clever. Hashtag *flirting*; hashtag *read between the lines*."

Callie's mouth went suddenly dry. "Seriously?"

Jenna nodded.

Christ, it was Dabney the juggler all over again! *"Seriously?"*

"Well, I can get him to sign an affidavit if you want, but for now you'll just have to take my word for it. The boy. Was asking you. *Out*."

Maybe she *was* a nitwit. Or maybe she was just exhausted and overwhelmed. Either way, Callie honestly had no idea Kip's proposed experiment was actually a date. "I thought maybe he was making fun of me for being in the circus."

"Wow." Jenna leaned into the backrest and sighed. "You really are out of your element, aren't you? It's actually kind of amusing."

"I'm glad my lack of experience entertains you," Callie said tartly. "But it doesn't matter because I'm not going to be here long enough to get romantically involved with anyone."

"See? Perfect example. Nobody who's ever been romantically involved with someone would actually use the phrase 'romantically involved.'"

Callie made a face. "Noted."

"But the good news is that you, my friend, have caught the eye of one of Lake St. Julian's most eligible surfer dudes, who, in addition to maintaining an extremely impressive grade point average also happens to have a heart of gold and an incredibly cute ass."

"So why don't *you* surf with him? Better yet, why don't you go surf with yourself?" She shot Jenna a look. "And that *is* a euphemism."

"Yeah, I got that." Smiling, Jenna tapped on the back of Quinn's seat. "So, Ms. VanDrexel. What's for dinner?"

While Brad and Quinn were at the mansion preparing their meal, Callie treated herself to a quick workout on the tightrope. She couldn't afford to let her skills get too rusty, in case Marcello's reply came sooner than she expected. She knew it was rude to practice while she had a guest, but then again, the guest had invited herself, so Callie figured they were even. And Jenna seemed happy enough to watch Callie perform.

"No wonder Kipalicious wants to get you on a surfboard," she said. "You'll probably pick it up in five seconds flat."

"Well, I guess we'll never know, will we?"

Callie was in the middle of executing a perfect Russian split on the wire when Jenna's phone dinged.

"Dinner's ready," she announced.

"How do you know that?"

"Because your mom just texted me the words 'Dinner's ready,' so unless she's using some super-secret spy code language, I'm pretty sure she's telling us that dinner's ready."

"You," said Callie, pointedly. "She's telling *you* that dinner's ready."

"Well, *yeah*, probably because she figured since *I* wouldn't be the one doing backflips on a shoelace, I'd be more likely to answer my phone."

Callie slipped off her tightrope shoes and stepped into her sneakers. "Right. Probably."

Brad and Quinn had whipped up an amazing meal of grilled swordfish and sautéed vegetables, which they enjoyed on the mansion's back terrace. DiCaprio looked on from a distance, catching the last rays of evening sunshine, and farther away Gulliver trumpeted boldly, setting off a chorus of birdcalls from the trees.

Since the conversation revolved mostly around the Sanctuary's new website, Callie found herself without much to say. Jenna, however, offered several suggestions, all of which Brad pronounced revolutionary.

Halfway through the main course, Quinn reached over and patted Callie's hand. "I'm so glad you've found a friend," she whispered. "Jenna's a terrific kid."

"Yeah," Callie huffed. "She's just great." *And so was my Russian split, but I guess you're not going to ask about that.*

After dessert, Quinn headed out with Brad to walk the grounds, and Callie and Jenna went back to the carriage house, where Jenna spent some time studying the bulletin board plastered with Victoria's notes.

"It's cool that you have these," she said. "It's like you and your grandmother are still communicating. It's kind of sad that people don't write things down anymore, doncha think?"

Callie thought of the letter she'd mailed to Marcello, which was probably in the cargo hold of some jetliner that very minute, bound for Perugia. "Well, at least we've got emojis" was Callie's sarcastic reply.

"A distant second to old-school forms of expression." Running her fingers across a piece of a peanut bag, then a cardboard scrap torn from a red-and-yellow box, Jenna shook her head. "The Rosetta Stone, the Gutenberg Bible, Shakespeare's folios—and circus scraps. I told you my professional association with Benigno's Pizza has been permanently terminated, right?"

"Yeah. You got fired."

"So would you mind if I co-opted a little of your gram's

motivational mojo to aid me in my employment search?" Sliding her thumbnail under the head of a tack, she removed a white triangle-shaped scrap. *Everyone has a job to do*, it said.

"Go ahead," said Callie, walking into the living room and trying to imagine any or all of the Bertière triplets ever using the words *co-opt*, *motivational*, and *mojo* in one sentence . . . or lifetime. "Jenna, exactly how smart *are* you?"

"Well . . ." Jenna grinned, following Callie to the kitchenette. "Profoundly Gifted is the official designation, but the words 'borderline genius' have been bandied about on more than a few occasions."

Callie opened the fridge, took out two grapefruit seltzers, and handed one to Jenna. "About your job search . . . I have a proposition for you."

"I'm listening."

"I need you to teach me how to navigate the circus websites. I want to start reaching out to some of them to inquire about openings, but I'm not exactly tech-savvy, so I was hoping you'd help me fill out some applications, maybe download—or is it upload?—some videos of my performances, set up an email account."

"You're offering me an IT position. Nice. What's it pay?"

"Nothing."

"Hmm. Well, that's a little less than I'm used to, but what the hell? Count me in."

"I also need you to keep coming over here and acting like we're friends."

Jenna raised an eyebrow. "You're offering me a job as your friend? Isn't that a little desperate?"

"It would be if I were going to pay you. But I'm not, so it isn't."

"Sounds like another fabulous career opportunity."

"Look, my mother's worried about me making friends and fitting in, but I really don't see that happening here. First of all, why bother? And second, I'm just not the Ponce de León Festival type.

But if she thinks you and I are bonding and becoming great friends, she'll relax and stop driving me crazy about having a social life."

Jenna considered it. "Just out of curiosity, what would be so wrong with at least trying to foster a social life? I mean, you don't have to go out for head cheerleader or anything, but would it kill you to go to a slumber party sometime?"

"Are you *inviting* me to a slumber party?"

Jenna looked away. "Absolutely not. But you could join a club. Or a study group."

Callie felt a rush of anger. "Why are you taking my mother's side?"

"I'm not."

"And other than the Recently Fired from Benigno's Pizza Society, what clubs do you belong to?"

"I'm croquet captain, although I'm taking what you might call an extended leave of absence from my leadership responsibilities. But I used to do peer tutoring, and before Kristi became unbearable, she and Emma-Kate and I were on the tennis team."

"I'm hearing a lot of past tense."

Jenna shrugged. "So what happens if during the course of this so-called job of friend impersonator, we actually do become friends? Do I get a bonus?"

"Yeah. If we become actual friends, I'll double your salary."

"Nothing times two." Flopping onto the sofa, Jenna popped open her seltzer. "How can I possibly turn that down?"

"Excellent," said Callie. "And in return for you doing those things for me, I'm going to secure you a real *paying* job working for Brad and my mom."

"No shit?" Jenna's face lit up. "Done. But before we make it official, you're gonna have to do something for me."

Callie was immediately wary. "If you're going to make me agree to go on a surfing date with Kip Devereaux you can just forget—"

"I want to hear you say I was right about Kristi."

"You were right about Kristi."

"Damn straight I was!" said Jenna. "But to be honest, I wish I wasn't."

Callie took a long drink of soda. "So she and Kip used to date, huh?"

"Kip? Kip Devereaux? You mean the boy that you, for some unfathomable reason, don't want to go out with? Yeah, they did. Didn't last long, though."

"Why not?"

"Well, it was your classic teen-angst-ridden romance, based mostly on good hair and kick-ass pheromones. I mean, he's gorgeous, she's gorgeous, and they're both so freakin' charismatic they're practically made of neon, so I suppose they kind of had to take a run at it. But when she started channeling her inner Regina George, Kip was smart enough to walk away. Hey, will ya look at us, doing the whole girl-talk thing, pretending to be friends! I guess that means I'm on the clock, huh? So, lemme see . . . five minutes, at zero dollars an hour . . . yep, still broke."

"Do you think Kristi ambushed me in the lunchroom because she saw me juggling with Kip?"

"Word on the street is Kristi's still got it bad for old Kippy, so yeah, that's probably what put the target on your back. Then, when she found out about your connection to the Sanctuary . . . Well, let's just say that fed right into little Miss K-Bay's ever-evolving Daddy Issues."

"Daddy issues?"

"Not the creepy, deviant, unscrupulous kind, it's just that Mayor Baylor's a textbook example of the high-achieving distant father whose career comes before his kids. So there's poor little Kristi jumping up and down, waving her arms in the air determined to get him to notice her while we all just stand back and try not to get whipped in the face with that luxurious Pantene commercial hair of hers. I swear, if the Honorable Keith Baylor would just ask his daughter about her grades, or her field hockey stats, or her Miss America aspirations once in a while, we'd all be living better lives."

"One more question."

"Shoot."

"Did Zach really get hit in the head with a croquet mallet?"

"Twice," Jenna reported. "And both times, he was the one holding the mallet."

"Come on."

"Hand to God," said Jenna, and burst out laughing.

"What's so funny?" asked Quinn, appearing at the top of the stairs with her hair in its customary messy bun, and smelling a bit like, if Callie weren't mistaken, camel (also customary).

"Nothing," said Callie, her tone frosty. "But Jenna was just telling me how she lost her job at the pizza place, and I was thinking she'd make a perfect Sanctuary ambassador."

"What a wonderful idea," said Quinn, beaming at Jenna. "You know Mr. Marston and I were so impressed with your open house idea that we've decided to do it. But since we're currently dealing with acclimating two new tiger cubs we just rescued from a ghastly roadside zoo, it would be great if you'd jump in and handle the event planning."

"Absolutely," said Jenna, brimming with gratitude. "You know, the Ponce de León Festival is this Friday and it's a pretty huge deal. The whole town shows up. You've got to picture it. A decade-by-decade cosplay-a-palooza."

Quinn looked to her daughter, wide-eyed, for a translation, and since Callie was slightly further along in *Conversational Jenna for Beginners* she attempted to provide one. "I think she means everybody comes in costume."

"Right!" Jenna confirmed. "The theme is Fountain of Youth, so they actually fill coolers with like a zillion bottles of artificially flavored chocolate drink and call it . . . ready? . . . the Fountain of *Yoo-hooth*."

Quinn laughed. "Very creative."

"And in the spirit of recapturing said youth, all the alumni and their guests come dressed in the fads and fashions that were popular the year they graduated from Lake St. Julian High. So visually, you've got this Renaissance Festival meets Woodstock meets *Saturday Night Fever* meets MTV meets Kurt Cobain's Seattle Grunge Scene meets Britney's Breakdown meets the Obama Administration." She shrugged. "The PDLF is a valiant effort all around, although it seems the pre-Internet founders of the festival were a little fuzzy on the difference between the Renaissance and the Middle Ages, resulting in some pretty glaring historical discrepancies. Technically Ponce de León was more of a Middle Ages kinda guy rather than a true Renaissance man. But since I'm pretty sure Mr. Wu the AP History teacher and I are the only ones who've ever noticed, I say why spoil the fun?"

"What's any of that got to do with the open house?" Callie asked.

"Nothing, except that somewhere in all of that craziness there's a whole ton of small-town camaraderie. Which is why I think we should use PDLF as an opportunity to promote the open house. We can pass out flyers, sell tickets, maybe do a Q and A about the Sanctuary to get people interested. We could even take advantage of the festival momentum and hold the open house this Sunday."

Quinn was taken aback. "That soon?"

"Mayor Baylor's pretty determined to shut this place down."

Pursing her lips in thought, Quinn considered it. "Well, the animals certainly don't need any time to prepare. I'm sure Brad has catering connections, and the weather's going to be gorgeous. Okay, let's do it!"

Half an hour of rapid-fire brainstorming ensued, halfway through which Jenna and Quinn started finishing each other's sentences. The profoundly gifted borderline genius was smarter than the average bear when it came to . . . well, bears, and every other species represented at the Sanctuary. She asked all the right questions: What time were the tigers most likely to show themselves? Could they count on DiCaprio to make an appearance? What were the chances of the camels doing something cute? Because if they wanted the Sanctuary to remain operational, the animals were going to have to endear themselves to the townsfolk.

Jenna actually used that word . . . *townsfolk*. Callie wasn't sure why it annoyed her. After all, getting Jenna this job had been her idea—a means to the end of getting her mother to quit harping on her social life. But while she might not have been a borderline genius, she might have had something to contribute if one of them had bothered to ask.

"We should probably get started on the flyer," Jenna suggested. "Have you guys got a computer?"

"Not down here," said Quinn. "But Brad's offices are crawling with them, so we'll have to head back up to the main house. Maybe you should give your mother a call and let her know you're going to be here a little longer."

Callie thought she noticed the briefest dip in Jenna's enthusiasm, but she recovered quickly, assuring Quinn that her mother wouldn't mind.

Jenna and Quinn continued to brainstorm while Quinn quickly tidied up her hair and applied some lipstick. They were halfway down the stairs when she remembered to call out, "Callie, honey, you wanna join?"

Callie's answer was to march into her room and slam the door.

FOURTEEN

Delaware, 1965

I AWAKE TO THE rhythm of sledgehammers clanging against iron rods—percussion and promise—as gangs of men transform the empty acreage of this Delaware meadow into a kind of dreamscape. Vince is a magician and a mathematician, laying out the angles and corners of the tremendous Big Top with a precision that would impress Pythagoras himself. The sun is just coming up and the tent rises along with it, as if some great tectonic shift has occurred and a striped canvas mountain is being born.

Sharon has raised my practice rope to three feet above the ground. She teaches me a sit-mount, which requires me to first settle the right half of my bottom on the wire; as it bobs gently under my weight, Sharon, with her cigarette poised in the crook of a peace sign, talks me through bringing my right foot up, then my left, tucking it close to my body. We practice until I can lift myself to a standing position—which is to say *hours*. I feel clumsy and inept, but Sharon assures me that I'm making great progress. We work through breakfast and before I know it, it's time for lunch and I rush off to the pie car where the cook, Hank, enlists me in handing out dukeys—boxed lunches—to the crew. I spend the rest of the day learning the finer points of scouring a griddle and cleaning out the deep fryer.

Later, unseen in the far corner of the kitchen, I overhear a very glum conversation between the strongman, Alberto, and one of the dog trainers, Hale. Alberto is so enormous he barely fits in the booth. Hank brings them two cups of tea and a small mountain of shortbread cookies. Hale immediately slips one of the cookies into his pocket for Miss Kelly.

Soon enough, the topic turns to money. Or, more accurately, the lack thereof. It seems they're both dangerously close to being forced to look for jobs with other shows. Neither wants to, of course. But funds are low.

"I've talked to Cornelius," Alberto says, the quaver in his voice belying his monumental muscular bulk. "He says he understands if I decide to go, says he'll even help me find a position if he can. But this is home."

Hale sips his tea. "What do you think about that girl who came on board in Boston? The one who's always wearing that pricey hunk of gemstones?"

"Seems like a sweet kid. Why? Wha' d'you think?"

"I think if she can afford a brooch like that, she's got no business being here, taking pay out the mouths of poor workin' stiffs like us."

"Aahhh, you don't mean that, Hale," Alberto says. "Besides, far as I can tell, she's workin' just as hard as the rest of us."

"Yeah, I s'pose you're right." Hale frowns and takes one last long sip from his cup. "Don't mind me. This whole money thing's just got me cranky."

Alberto rises out of the booth like an iceberg swelling out of the sea. "So maybe you should give yourself one of them distemper shots like you give your mongrels," he jokes.

"Hey! Don't you be callin' my babies mongrels."

That night, I put my brooch in the bottom drawer of the jewelry box, turn the key in the lock, and vow not to take it out again until Austin.

Then I fall into bed exhausted and miss the show entirely.

I dream deep, of a girl tiptoeing across the sky, of horses with braided manes, and a ballet performed by clowns on tiny bicycles. In the dream I think I hear the far-off roar of a lion and the collective gasp of a crowd, but the dream tells me to ignore it, so I snuggle close into the gentle forgetfulness that encircles all our dreams, protecting us from waking, shielding us from the world.

In the dream an aging lion suns himself on the whitewashed steps of an elegant Brooksvale porch.

My father is bleeding. My mother is free.

And someone is humming—not Petula, not Herman, not John. But me.

She's got a ticket to ride but she don't care.

~

Ohio, 1965

Sharon presents me with a pair of pliable leather slippers. I execute my sit-mount, and when I'm vertical I attempt the slow heel-to-toe walk she taught me back on the ground in Jersey.

I only manage one step before I start to wobble.

"Redistribute your weight!" Sharon commands as the rope bounces, pitching me into the pile of crash mats she had Duncan arrange on either side of my makeshift tightrope. Thanks to my father's temper, I'm used to much harder landings than this; I immediately spring to my feet and return to the wire.

"*That*, sister," says Sharon, nodding through a halo of smoke, "that right there is half the battle."

She leaves briefly and returns with a long flexible pole for me to carry; it immediately improves my balance.

Sharon continues to shout out tips and corrections until the day burns off to evening. That night, I'm back in Myrtle's trailer, finishing up the buttons I never got around to in New Jersey.

This time, unfortunately, James does not make an appearance.

~

Indiana, 1965

I don't hear from him in Fort Wayne, either, where over hot coffee on a rainy morning Sharon regales me with stories of Charles Blondin and Maria Spelterini, two funambulists who were among the best ever. They each made their mark tightrope walking across Niagara Falls.

"Niagara Falls," she squeals. "Can you imagine? So many variables! Wind, moisture, not to mention all that ferocious water, roiling beneath them."

"Sounds like fun," I say absently, watching through the pie car window as James rushes past. He's flanked by Gideon and Cornelius. Cornelius looks glum; he's holding his ledger, which he's rarely without these days. Gideon, as though he's part of the storm, is gesturing wildly, trying to make his brother comprehend something.

But James does not appear to be in a comprehending sort of mood.

I glance away from the window when I sense Sharon popping up from the booth. Vadim, one of the Russian stilt walkers, has just entered and they're smiling at each other.

"Gotta go, sister," Sharon says, slugging back the rest of her coffee. "Got me a hot date with Mr. *Very* Tall, Dark, and Handsome."

"Does this mean I can take the day off?"

"You betcha," she calls over her shoulder. Then she molds herself cozily against Vadim and together they slink out of the car.

When I turn back to the window, the VanDrexel boys are gone.

I decide to head into the city, to the public library, where I can begin to do some research on Austin, Texas. Every day that passes brings me a little closer to the life I left Brooksvale to find, and I want to be prepared. They may even have copies of the Texas newspapers, so I can start calling ahead to inquire about jobs and lodging.

I've narrowed my job options down—in those moments when I remember to pause in petting camels or popping popcorn to think about my real future—to salesgirl, waitress, or (if I can find a family trusting enough to hire me without references) live-in nanny, which would carry the added bonus of room and board. I have no delusions about the kind of apartment I'll be able to afford on my own, but such is the cost of independence.

Exiting the pie car, I step into the downpour and head for the main road that will take me into town.

I feel the sound before I hear it, a direct hit to the heart. At first I think it's just the howl of the wind, but there is no wind, only rain.

And it's not a howl. It's a roar. A roar filled with agony.

Changing direction, I make my way through the deepening puddles and thickening mud to the menagerie, where I splatter past the tiger triplets. They're curled together against the storm, a warm knot of black-and-orange fur, bright against the damp gray world.

I find Boo huddled at the end of his cage, silent now, taking short, anxious breaths. The rain slices in through the bars but he doesn't seem to notice. I, too, am beyond feeling it now, though my clothes are drenched and my hair drips rivulets into my eyes and down the back of my neck.

"Hello there, handsome," I say, minding my three-foot comfort gap from the cage, speaking loudly above the relentless drumming of raindrops on his roof. "Nice day for a nap, huh?"

He lifts his head, only slightly. Another roar, weaker, more desperate.

Without intending to, I step closer. "I'm sorry you aren't feeling well."

His coat, where the rain has reached it, clings to his ribs, and I can see now how truly thin he is. With his chin resting on his paws he looks melancholy and resigned, all alone there in his cage. When I'd first seen his accommodations, I deemed them "private," seeing his solitude as an honor, a reward for his great and singular strength. Now it just looks like what it is—loneliness.

I take two more steps, needing to be closer, and when I press my cold wet face to the cold wet bars, a chill wracks me. "What can I do for you?" I whisper into the cage, feeling helpless. "Tell me what I can do."

He blinks his lion's eyes, which today hold no brightness.

Again, I hear myself speaking in my mother's voice, softly through the rain: "Poor baby. Poor, beautiful baby." I see my hand moving before I even realize I've lifted it, see it reaching through the space between the sturdy steel bars that separate us, and I watch my fingers settle near Boo's shoulder. My touch—unexpected by both of us—elicits a gasp from me and a rumbling sound from deep within his weakening body.

I hold perfectly still, feeling the slight rhythm of his breath. Then, slowly, I begin to stroke his damp fur, gently, carefully. To my relief, he does not object. He accepts the meager comfort I am suddenly so willing to give.

"You're not alone, Baraboo," I tell him. "Not here."

"Neither are you." The Ringmaster's son; the favorite one.

I don't turn away from the lion as James puddles his way closer to Boo and me. His footsteps throw muddy water onto the backs of my legs. He, too, is soaked from the storm. He's holding a metal dish, and in it I see, of all things, meatballs. Four of them. Raw.

"I hope that's not what Hank's calling the lunch special," I try to joke, but the words come out thick and dull.

James is able to muster a chuckle. "Didn't you ever wonder how medication is administered to an apex predator?"

"Sure. Doesn't everyone?"

We try so hard to laugh, and so hard not to cry as Boo gives another pathetic roar. I step back as James steps forward, angling the bowl into the cage. "Eat up, buddy. C'mon, pal. Eat up."

And miraculously, the lion does.

We stand there for a moment, watching him feed, but the effort is great and it's difficult to witness. So we step away for our own sakes, landing in front of the tiger cage, where the striped siblings untangle themselves, probably anticipating some James-devised fun. Scruff snarls; Clemmy chuffs hello.

But I don't think James even hears them. I want desperately to ask him where he's been, why we haven't talked, or laughed, in weeks. But I'm afraid of what the answer might be, so I just stand there, letting the rain have its say. And then:

"Victoria."

He speaks it like it's the only word he knows.

I shiver closer, lifting my face, feeling my lashes clinging to each other. I hold my breath; I hold *his* breath . . .

And then the lion tamer brushes a kiss against my lips, a whisper of a kiss; it's there and gone in the very same heartbeat, almost not a kiss at all.

The one that follows it comes from me—surprising us both. I hear myself sigh into it, and feel his arms going around me. I am aware of Clementine and Scruff ambling away from the bars toward the far side of the cage, and of Prince Edward nestling his face into his paws. In my altered state of awareness I imagine they find our public display of affection to be in very poor taste.

They're probably right.

But I have no idea how kisses end. Luckily (or not) James does.

When he pulls away I actually wobble. Sharon would be distressed to know that I'm having a great deal of trouble controlling my center of gravity . . . and a few other places, as well. The rain is coming harder and a streak of lighting rips through the sky, snapping like Cornelius's whip, making us both jump.

When I realize he's considering a third kiss, I press my hand to his chest. "I think we're making the tigers uncomfortable," I say, and immediately feel like a complete idiot.

James laughs, a soft, silky rumble from deep inside his chest. "Wouldn't wanna do that," he drawls. "C'mon."

Suddenly we're running, side by side, toward the train, pounding up the three metal steps and into the dry silence of the narrow corridor. We make our way to the door of my car. My hair is dripping, my heart is racing, my knees are trembling. By the time we reach my room, I'm dizzy with wondering.

What's going to happen next?

With my eyes locked on his, I open the door and back into the room. He smiles and swipes a wet lock of hair off his forehead.

And then I see it—the flicker of hesitation, the sudden change of heart.

I have to bite my lip to keep from urging him to follow me inside, to make this moment *our* moment. *Let what happens next be exactly what I want.*

But what happens next is this:

"Thanks," he says, "for going to Boo."

"Of course," I say, nodding hard but only as an excuse to pull my gaze from his. "I just hope he—"

But James is already halfway down the hall.

He's gone.

FIFTEEN

~

ON THE MORNING OF Ponce de León's birthday, Callie stood at her bulletin board and once again considered her collection of Victoria-isms.

Per Jenna's advice, she was wearing her bathing suit. "In case you feel like taking a dip in the Atlantic before the Conquistador competition," Jenna had said cagily.

When she'd pulled Gram's vintage denim cutoffs on over her swimsuit, she wasn't surprised to find that they fit perfectly.

In the living room, Quinn, Brad, and Jenna were frantically collating the literature they'd printed out for the open house marketing blitz. Considering they'd had only three days to prepare for it, the amount of material they'd been able to generate was mind-boggling. Callie probably should have been helping them pack up, but instead, she lingered at the bulletin board, her fingers tracing the outline of a cocktail napkin with the fading logo of a place called Husky Pete's printed in the bottom corner. Above the logo was a phrase written in a hand that was not her grandmother's: *James loves Victoria.* Her heart twisted, then flip-flopped, thinking of the surf date that wasn't going to happen simply because she was too naive to even know she'd been asked out.

It's better this way, she told herself. She'd never admit it to Jenna, but she had the feeling she could actually like Kip Devereaux, as a friend or maybe more, and that was definitely out of the question. She'd be leaving Lake St. Julian as soon as humanly possible—either for Un Piccolo Circo Familiare in Perugia, or some other circus—and she didn't want anything tugging at her heart when she left. She might not have had a lot of experience with missing people in the past, but losing Gram had been a crash course in misery. *Just keep moving forward—that's the only way to stay balanced.* On and off the wire she preferred the freedom of being a solo act; why suffer from someone else's missteps? And just because her mother kept calling this place "home" didn't mean it was. The thing about a traveling circus was that you got to bring home—however you chose to define it—with you wherever you went. For Callie, home was a moving train, a taut wire, and a cavernous Big Top ringing with applause.

The applause of strangers whose absence she wouldn't feel the need to mourn when the tent came down and the jump was made.

"Cal?" Brad peeked in through the open door. "Your mom wants me to tell you we're leaving in five."

To her surprise, he came over to stand beside her at the bulletin board, taking a moment to examine the scraps. "Quinn was telling me about these. Pretty fascinating."

"Four minutes and counting," Jenna announced, striding into the room.

Callie immediately took Jenna's arm and tugged her a few feet away from the bulletin board. "Hey," she said in a low voice. "I sent you a video."

"Was it the one of the squirrel making pancakes? Because I've already seen it."

"Quit playing dumb. It's of me performing last year in Ann Arbor. It's for my website. For my job search."

"Duh."

"So? Have you started working on my profile?"

"Not yet. I've been a little preoccupied with trying to help your mother not lose her job. But I'll get to it. I promise. Right after the open house."

They shuffled back to the bulletin board, where Brad was reaching for the Husky Pete's napkin. "This one's interesting."

Callie had to resist the urge to slap his hand away. But then she saw that he was removing the tack in a way that was almost reverent, and cradling the napkin as carefully as if it were a priceless artifact (which, in a way, it was).

Fine, he can hold it. But only for a minute.

"Husky Pete's," Jenna read. "I assume that's the name of some long-defunct drinking establishment. Question: before something becomes *de*funct, is it just considered *funct*?"

"I wouldn't know," said Callie. "You're the one who's profoundly shifted."

"Gifted, wiseass."

"Okay, Team Sanctuary," came Quinn's voice from the living room. "Time to go."

Jenna practically bounded out the door.

"Mind if I hang on to this for a bit?" Brad asked, indicating James and Victoria's napkin. "I'll bring it back," he added quickly. "And I swear, I won't let anything happen to it."

Something about the way his blue eyes were almost twinkling made Callie decide to trust him.

The parking lot of the St. Julian Inn across the street from Crescent Beach was already full when Callie slid out of the Range Rover. A replica of Ponce de León's fabled ship had been erected on the side lawn of the hotel. And while it didn't look seaworthy, exactly, it was still pretty imposing, especially considering it had been built by students from sophomore woodshop class.

The many teachers and students on the planning committee were rushing around, in and out of the inn, draping the veranda with floral garlands, setting up refreshment booths, and organizing game tables, everyone resplendent in their sixteenth-century attire. It was corsets and doublets as far as the eye could see; ruffs on ruffs on ruffs.

Glancing toward the beach, she could see several surfers taking practice rides before the official start of the Conquistador contest.

"Go, Callie."

She turned, surprised to find her mother standing beside her, smiling.

"You know you want to."

Want was a strong word. Maybe she wouldn't have *minded* watching Kip surf . . . Then again, maybe it would be too weird. Or maybe it might not be weird at all. She honestly didn't know. "I'm supposed to be helping you set up the marketing booth" was her somewhat lame excuse.

"We can handle it. Jenna told me what happened with the surfer boy."

"She *told* you?"

"You should go wish him luck in the comp—"

Callie was stamping across the lawn of the inn before Quinn had even finished her sentence. Not because she'd suddenly mustered up the courage to approach Kip, but because if she happened to find herself within five feet of Jenna Demming, she wouldn't be able to stop herself from strangling her.

"Hey."

Kip looked up from methodically applying Mr. Zog's to the surface of his board. One corner of his mouth kicked up—just one, as though he were only half convinced this particular encounter warranted a smile. "Hi."

"So . . . I just wanted to come over and, ya know, wish you luck."

"Thanks."

"And to say . . . well, to say I'm sorry about the other day at school. I didn't realize you were—"

"It's fine." Full smile: both corners, and as an added bonus, some very dazzling teeth. "Hey, as long as you're here, how about you let me repay you for the juggling how-to with a quick surf lesson?"

Callie hesitated.

"A friendly lesson," Kip said meaningfully.

So Jenna had gotten to him, too. Didn't that girl ever shut up? "Okay, sure."

Moments later, he'd borrowed a surfboard for Callie to use and was giving her a quick preliminary lesson on the sand, which basically amounted to three words: "Paddle, push, pop."

"Full disclosure," said Kip, as they waded into the Atlantic. "The east coast of central Florida is not exactly the surfing capital of the world, but if you're patient and not too picky, you can actually get some decent rides."

He left his own surfboard on the sand in order to help Callie with her first few attempts, treading water beside her board while she sat on it with her legs dangling over each side. While they waited for a decent curl to roll in, they discussed the overlap between surfing techniques and tightrope skills, agreed that Scout Finch was a total badass, and debated the merits of soft tacos versus crispy. Kip told her the reasons why he believed Childish Gambino was the greatest artist of all time, and Callie confessed that she wasn't familiar with his music.

"Well, then I guess we'll have to do something about that, won't we?"

They had to cover their ears a couple of times when the local rock band that would be providing the entertainment at PDLF was setting up their equipment on the hotel lawn; the squeal of their microphones was deafening.

"Are they any good?" Callie asked, skeptical. Peering across the sand, she thought the lead singer might be wearing a suit of armor.

"The Renaissance Renegades? They're okay for a band that mostly sings about famine and religious persecution. Most of their fans are partial to their haunting stadium ballad, 'My World Is Flat Without You,' but I prefer their heavy-metal Inquisition-inspired number, 'Love Is Torture, Baby, but You've Got a Great Rack.'"

Then Kip's eyes were lighting up at the sight of the Atlantic shrugging its crystalline shoulders to bestow the gift of a wave. "Here we go," he said, shifting effortlessly from music critic to surf coach. "Okay, now down on your stomach . . . good, get ready . . . perfect peak comin' atcha . . . okay, paddle . . . paddle . . . push . . . *pop!*"

And with Kip's voice cheering her on, Callie VanDrexel, the girl who walked the wire, became the girl who rode the waves.

Nobody was surprised when Kip won the title of Surfing Conquistador.

With her denim shorts pulled on over her suit, Callie had watched from the shore as Kip competed against some of the best surfers Lake St. Julian had to offer. Kristi, in her capacity as Queen Isabella, got to award Kip his trophy, which, in keeping with the contest motif, was a shiny metal morion helmet.

As Callie headed for the Sanctuary booth, which had been set up in the inn's gingerbread gazebo, she saw that the costumed crowd had certainly taken the Fountain of Youth theme to heart. There were poodle skirts and disco suits, and the tie-dye was running amok. She found Jenna and Quinn handing out postcards that had been printed up just yesterday, featuring the Sanctuary's newest arrivals, the rescued tiger cubs. Jenna had named them Tessio and Clemenza, and her idea was for Lake St. Julian to adopt the tiger babies as community mascots; each cub would have his own Facebook page, so the "townsfolk" (a word Jenna seemed to really like) could keep track of their escapades and enjoy watching them grow up.

As Callie sidled up to the booth, Jenna gave her an expectant smile. "So?"

"Kip won." The words were devoid of inflection.

"Of course he won. I wanna know what you said, and what he said, and if—"

"You know what's the best thing about being a solo act, Ambassador? It's not having to worry that somebody's going to blab every single thing that happens in your life to your mother."

Jenna looked a little sheepish. "It just sort of came out when we were working on the marketing stuff. She kept asking me about how you were interacting with the other kids, and I figured if I could get her to believe you were being, um—what's the word?— *normal* she'd chill out and leave you alone. Which, by the way, is exactly what you asked me to do when you offered me my unpaid faux-friend internship." Jenna fidgeted with the tiger postcard in her hand. "Look, Callie, you should be glad she worries about you like she does. There are worse things than having a mother who just wants you to be happy."

"If she wanted that, she should have left me at VanDrexel's."

"Great, you're here," said Brad, approaching Callie with a stack of flyers. "Would you mind taking a lap or two around the lawn to hand these out? Chat people up, tell them they can swing by the booth for more information."

"Isn't that what the ambassador's for?" Callie huffed.

"Excellent point. So how 'bout you both go? You can grab something to drink and pass out the flyers along the way."

The music of the Renaissance Renegades lent a true party atmosphere, and Callie and Jenna made their way to the refreshment area. Callie noticed how everyone just seemed to feel at home. Graduates divided by decades shared stories of big games and bad teachers; the older alumni spoke of the slow sweep of time and the changes it had brought, but more importantly of the changes it hadn't. Parents, children, neighbors, all on a first-name basis, all proud denizens of this quirky little town, were mingling and reminiscing, recounting disastrous storms and beautiful spring-times, restaurants that opened and restaurants that closed, noisy summer parades and solemn holiday pageants. And they all spoke, if not in an accent, with a cadence that seemed to belong to Lake St. Julian and Lake St. Julian alone.

The sense of community was powerful, and Callie was surprised to feel a stab of loneliness, remembering how, at the circus, she'd kept her distance from everyone but Gram.

Jenna led her to the beverage concession, the Taberna, where several large coolers filled with ice and cans and bottles were lined up under long folding tables. The festival-goers who had reached the age of majority (or who could produce a passable fake ID) could order up *cerveza*, sangria, and other cocktails. For everyone else there was the under-twenty-one drink station, staffed by Emma-Kate, who was fetchingly attired in a brocade gown with a starched ruff collar. Jacob's costume included a sheathed rapier, which Callie sincerely hoped was fake. Zach, who had been given the honor of playing King Ferdinand to Kristi's Isabella, was experiencing a major sugar high from the seven chocolate beverages he'd already downed. Callie half imagined his crown was vibrating.

"Care to drink from the Fountain of Yoo-hooth?" said Emma-Kate, holding out chilled bottles to Jenna and Callie.

Callie took a sip and found the taste to be both cloyingly sweet and strangely refreshing, though it was clear that any relationship the drink bore to actual chocolate was purely symbolic.

"Hey, Em," said Jenna, motioning to her fussy neckpiece. "Ruff morning?"

Emma-Kate laughed and threw her arms around Jenna. "Jenz! You're the best. I miss you, girl. I hate that you're never around anymore."

"Yeah," Zach agreed. "Why don't we hang?"

Jenna deftly avoided the question, slapping one of her flyers down on the table. "Look, I know things got weird at lunch Monday, but you have to come to the Sanctuary open house on Sunday so you can see for yourself what a cool place it is. And," she added, looking directly at Zach, "I have it on very good authority that the buffet is going to be awesome."

"In!" said Zach, cracking open yet another Yoo-hoo. "*Es bueno ser el rey!*"

But then things got weird.

Well, weird*er*.

"Jen, I think I see your mom," said Emma-Kate, sounding concerned.

Callie followed Emma-Kate's gaze to where a woman—who'd graduated LSJHS sometime in the late eighties judging by the fact that she was dressed for a Jazzercize class in a spandex leotard and leg warmers—was making her way to the Taberna. She was holding a martini glass.

An empty one.

Jenna looked at Jacob. "How many times has she been to the bar?"

Jacob hesitated. "A few. More than a few."

With a determined expression and a heavy sigh, Jenna stepped into her mother's path. If Callie wasn't mistaken, it took a second for Mrs. Demming to recognize that it was her daughter placing herself between her and the bar.

"Jenna, sweetie!" She pressed a loud kiss on Jenna's cheek. "How's the job going? How's my little ambasssssador?"

"Good. How are you, Mom?"

"I'm *fab*uloussss, honey! You know me! I adore the Renaisssss-sance! Tell me, how's the job?"

"You just asked me that. Hey, I think they're serving coffee inside."

"Jenna, it's a party. Don't you think we should be toasting old

Señor de León on his five-hundred-and-fifty-somethingth birthday with something a little stronger than coffee? Like a martini." Raising her empty glass, she cried out, "Many happy returns of the day, you crazy old explorer you!"

"Just curious, Mom—how many martini toasts have you made already?"

Mrs. Demming's eyes went chilly. "Only a couple. And that is the God's honest *troohooth*!" Skirting around her daughter, she slid her glass across the table to the bartender. "Martini please, with a twist, no olive. And this time, can you go a little heavier on the gin and a little lighter on the *vermoohooth*?"

Jenna grimaced.

"Oh, c'mon, honey. I'm just getting into the spirit of the day. You really need to lighten up, Jenna. Have a Yoo-hoo. In fact, have Two-hoo!"

Jenna turned away from Mrs. Demming just long enough to thrust the stack of flyers into Callie's hand. Then she grabbed hold of her mother's arm and firmly but gently led her away from the bar.

Nobody said a word until King Ferdinand piped up. "I gotta say, I thought that vermouth line was kinda funny."

"It's not funny," said Emma-Kate. "It's why we never see Jenna anymore."

"Kristi's mom told my mom that Mrs. Demming got a DUI last week," said Jake.

"Shut up," Emma-Kate admonished. "Don't spread rumors."

"It's not a rumor if it's true," Zach muttered.

"Oh, okay, King Ferdin-*ass*! Maybe you can pardon her then."

"I'm not trying to be a dick, Emma-Kate. I'm worried about Jenna too."

"Look, Callie," said Emma-Kate, her tone serious. "I know we didn't exactly make a great impression the other day, and I'm sorry about that. But we all care about Jenna a lot. I don't want you to think we're just gossiping. This is for real. Okay?"

Callie nodded, her eyes shooting to Mrs. Demming's empty martini glass, still waiting to be filled. Then she tossed the flyers onto the Taberna table and dashed off into the laughing crowd of hippies, bobby soxers, and popped-collar preppies to find Kip.

SIXTEEN

Illinois, 1965

IN CHICAGO, THE NOT-SO-DISTANT smell of the stock-yards, with all that blood and fresh meat, has the three tigers on high alert. Or maybe it's something else that has Scruff and Clemmy pacing in their cage while Prince Edward stays low on his haunches and keeps his ears pressed back. Among them, there is no chuffing to be heard.

I work with Sharon (on a wire that is now at four and a half feet) until Vince summons me to one of the concession stands outside the Big Top, where I start off the night selling Pepsi-Cola and hot dogs, felt pennants and full-color programs. But just before the Spec, there's a rush on snacks and souvenirs, and as I frantically dole out paper straws and mustard packets, I accidentally give change for a twenty to a man who paid with a five, and vice versa.

"I'm sorry," I tell Jolly Joe, the concessions manger. "But all of these people start to look alike after a while."

Joe cracks a smile at that remark, but it does not stop him from promptly releasing me from my sales duties. So I slip into the tent and take my usual place in the front row, just in time to watch the big cats perform, half wondering if, subconsciously, I messed up the money on purpose, just so I could see James.

Cornelius's voice booms through the tent when he announces his sons, who saunter in like a pair of Roman gods. Around me, girls point and giggle at the sight of the two handsome young men who are about to face down certain death with nothing but a leather whip

167

and a boatload of ego. Clemmy, Scruff, and Prince Edward appear behind them, trotting into the large fenced enclosure where they perform their act. Baraboo enters last, and although the effect is breathtaking, my eyes are locked on James.

Other than in passing, I haven't seen him since our rainy kiss in Indiana. I've been telling myself he's been busy, but I haven't asked myself *with whom?* Another mayor's daughter, perhaps? A councilman's pretty sister? Maybe he's been entertaining Evangeline in (or out of) her skimpy satin dress.

The band plays a fanfare and the performance begins. The tiger triplets are a huge hit, standing on their hind legs, bestowing kisses on James, and hurdling over each other like children playing leapfrog. Clemmy playfully swats Gideon's backside with her tail and he pretends to be insulted. All over the Big Top, females swoon. Baraboo, however, seems off. He's lethargic, inattentive, and missing his cues. Once, he even growls at Gideon, lifting one mighty paw as though he might swipe. The crowd gasps, but a sharp whistle and a clap from James have the animal retreating to his place. Gideon throws his brother a look, but James won't meet his eyes. Over the anxious whispers of the crowd, Cornelius's voice calmly fills the tent. "Will John Robinson please report to the main entrance? John Robinson . . ."

And as if a spell has been cast upon them, the VanDrexel brothers immediately take their bows. I've seen their act enough to know that they are, at best, three-quarters of the way through. But there they are, making their exit.

Fortunately the audience doesn't realize they are being given short shrift, and the VanDrexel brothers receive their usual standing ovation.

As I rise to my feet with the crowd, I sense a flicker of motion near the top of the tent and assume it's Sharon preparing for her act. But it isn't Sharon; the movement isn't even coming from the wire, rather from a small perch used by the lighting team. It takes me a moment to recognize Forget It, the roustabout with the indigo eyes. He is lowering an object from his shoulder to his side. Something long and narrow made of metal and wood.

A rifle.

My heart spins in my chest as he begins his long climb down. I am momentarily mystified, and then Vince's advice to Gideon in Jersey comes back to me in a nightmarish rush.

"*Another word for 'deadly.' I hate to say it, Gid, but we might need to start thinkin' about positioning a sni—*"

Gideon had interrupted before he could finish pronouncing the most important word in the entire conversation—the word, I realize now, used to define a gunman perched high above a crowd: *sniper.*

Forget It was up there in the event of something unpredictable. Something deadly.

I don't wait for the applause to die down; I run.

I sit there for almost an hour waiting for him to arrive. I've turned on one small lamp, which makes the atmosphere moody and strange.

He startles when he sees me. For a moment, only surprise registers on his face, but then a smile teases up the corners of his mouth. I'm not naive enough to imagine that this is the first time he's returned to his train car to find a girl sitting on his bed. But when he notices my hands folded tightly in my lap, my spine as rigid as the king pole holding up the Big Top, his smile wavers. Nothing in my bearing suggests that I am just another lovesick girl who's snuck into this room to surrender her virtue to a lion tamer.

"Hi, Victoria."

"Hello, Gideon."

A lock of his hair has shaken loose from the shiny hold of his Brylcreem; it flops over his eyes, making him look boyish and slightly nervous.

"This looks serious."

"It is. I saw him."

"Who?"

"John Robinson."

"*What?*"

"The roustabout up in the grid, Gideon! The one with the rifle. You know . . . the *sniper.*"

Gideon's hands slide into his pockets, and he stares at the toes of his boots for a long time. Through the train car's open windows I hear Cornelius introducing Bailiwick's bowling pin gag, which means the show will be ending soon; everyone else will be scurrying now, preparing for the finale.

But Gideon doesn't budge. Swearing under his breath, he sits down beside me on the narrow bed. "First of all, his name isn't John Robinson. It's Shaw."

"Then why did he climb down when Cornelius called for him?"

"He wasn't calling *for* John Robinson, he was calling *a* John Robinson. It's a signal to shorten the act, to go right into the final trick and get the hell out of the ring before something goes terribly wrong. My father saw how Boo was behaving and called a John Robinson before anyone could get hurt. Including Boo."

"In Jersey, you told Vince it was too soon."

"That was Jersey. This is Illinois."

"Thanks for the geography lesson."

Gideon lets out a chuckle that becomes a ragged exhale; he tries to smooth his hair back into place, but his oily pomade seems to have given up for the night. The hair falls back onto his forehead. "Baraboo is sicker now. I don't think you were watching that night in Delaware when he took a poke at me, and then he roared like he might . . ." He trails off, shaking his head. "I never heard a crowd gasp like that."

I do remember that night, although Gideon is right, I wasn't watching. I was dreaming. And even in my sleep I heard the roar.

"Every day he's weaker and in more pain," he tells me, "which means we can't anticipate what he might do in the ring. If something were to go wrong—"

"If something were to go wrong, a tent full of children will have to watch a beautiful lion get shot in the heart."

He snaps his head up. "You'd prefer they watch my brother and me get mauled to death instead?"

I open my mouth. I close it. Then I shake my head. "Of course not."

"And for the record, you don't euthanize a lion by putting a bullet in his heart. You aim for his brain, so death is instantaneous and painless. Shaw knows that. And Shaw doesn't miss. I chose him because he's a trained sharpshooter. He's supposed to be in Nam, but . . . that's another story. The point is, if he ever did have to shoot, Boo's death would be fast and humane." Gideon's face tightens on a sigh. "Miserable and heart-wrenching, but fast and humane."

We're quiet again, letting the magnitude of the dilemma set in. "What about a tranquilizer dart?" I venture. It's a term I heard once on *Mutual of Omaha's Wild Kingdom*, but really, I have no idea what I'm talking about.

"Not fast enough," says Gideon. "Ideally we'd just retire him, keep him comfortable, and let him die in peace."

Retire him. The absurd image of a lion receiving a handshake and a gold wristwatch flashes in my mind. "Why don't you, then?"

"Because James refuses to admit there's anything wrong with him." He attempts a wry grin. "You may have noticed my little brother can be a real pain in the ass. And besides, retirement only solves part of the problem."

"You mean because Boo's suffering?"

"The pain is bad but it isn't constant. Not yet. But he's weak, and he gets confused, and that's what makes him dangerous. Thank God he's still comfortable most of the time, but who knows how long he'll stay that way."

"What does Cornelius think?"

"He loves Boo just like the rest of us, but I'm willing to bet he'd rather lose a lion than a son." He rakes his hands through his hair.

"Willing to bet? You mean he doesn't know about Shaw? Gideon, he's the Ringmaster."

"I'm aware of that, Victoria." Dropping his face into his hands, he groans. "But my father has other things to worry about at the moment. We had to cancel three shows in Alabama. After that violence in Selma a while back, nobody down there is in much of a circus mood. Can't say I blame them. But that's a helluva lotta tickets that won't get sold, and a whole lot of cash that won't be coming in. Or going out in the form of paychecks. My father worries about that, and so do I."

I don't see any point in mentioning that after Texas, at least they'll have one less employee to worry about compensating.

The music rippling through the windows tells us it's almost time for final bows. Gideon quickly composes himself and rises from the bed. "The show must go on," he says, and it sounds almost like a prayer. "Promise me you won't say anything to James. It would only rattle him."

Since a rattled lion tamer sounds like a bad idea, I reply with a nod, though I don't see it as being an issue since, apparently, James and I don't speak anymore.

Outside, I watch Gideon head back to the big tent, but I don't follow. Suddenly I have no interest in watching the cast bid their raucous farewells to another adoring crowd.

Instead, I climb back up the train steps and head to my room.

When I open the door, I'm met by an explosion of light. Valerie and her Instamatic again—another candid, this time with a flash. She's in full costume for the finale. Blinking away the spots before my eyes, I notice she's got a goofy smile on her face.

"You've got company," she says, sweeping past me into the tight space of the train's corridor.

My first panicked thought is that my father has finally tracked me down.

Then I see James sitting on the vanity bench.

"Hey." That slow, seductive smile appears. "How've you been?"

"Fine."

"Haven't seen you since . . . Fort Wayne, was it?"

"I don't remember." *Yes I do.* And before that, Jersey. Thanks to Valerie, I even have a snapshot of the two of us holding hands by Boo's cage tucked into my jewelry box.

James stands and takes two tentative steps toward me. "I've missed you."

I feel the words like silk across my skin. "You have?"

When he smiles, it's like Delaware and Ohio never even happened. "Of course I have. It's been hell, you know . . . leaving you alone. It nearly killed me but I wanted to respect your wishes."

Now I'm confused—beyond confused. "What wishes?"

"Gideon said you told him to tell me to leave you alone."

"He said . . . I said . . . *what*? *Why?*"

"Because you needed to focus. He said you wanted me to keep my distance for a few weeks, because you were really committed to learning to walk the wire, and seeing me would be a distraction."

Of all of that, only the final six words contain an ounce of truth. James VanDrexel is the very definition of a distraction. But I never said anything even remotely like that to Gideon, and I certainly never asked for James to leave me alone.

I don't pretend to understand Gideon's motives—jealousy, perhaps, at the thought of his brother having one more person adoring him? Or maybe he feared that our extended flirtation might distract James from his more important responsibilities, such as staying alive in the lion's cage. Possibly, Gideon is interested in me himself. In any event, his trickery has been to my benefit. Without James to divide my attention I've thrown myself into learning the skills Sharon's been so eager to teach me. Not that I think I'll have much use for them once I'm gone, but the sense of freedom and power it gives me makes it a little easier every day to forget how it felt to be a prisoner in my father's house.

Something deeply cynical in me can't help but wonder if posting the sniper is not the altruistic act Gideon's insisting it is. Maybe he just wants to take Boo away from James. I don't want to believe that, but I can't shake the feeling that it's possible. Maybe Gideon himself doesn't even realize it.

"So . . . can you do it yet?" James asks softly, interrupting my thoughts. "Can you walk the wire?"

"I'm . . . getting there."

He steps closer and touches my cheek; flashcubes ignite in my belly.

"I had a feeling you'd be good at it."

"You did?"

"Yeah. I mean, you're kind of . . . well, you're basically amazing."

I realize society girls are supposed to play hard to get with *ordinary* boys, and I suspect that maxim is even more critical when it comes to lion tamers. But right now, James VanDrexel is settling onto my neatly made cot and he looks like Christmas lights and birthday cake and summer rain and all I want to do is put myself in his arms.

Which is exactly what I do.

His kisses are warm along my collarbone, and my hands are in his hair. His are on the snap of my jeans.

"Not yet," I whisper.

"Okay," he whispers back. "We've got all the time in the world."

We don't. But I won't think about that now.

Outside, the music of the finale swells, triumphant and thunderous. I am suddenly, deliciously without my shirt and he is without his. There is a bruise on my shoulder blade from falling off the wire, which he frets over in soothing little whispers; for several moments his lips linger there, just there. But I feel it everywhere.

"No more mayor's daughters," I tell him—it is both a wish and a command.

"No more mayor's daughters," he repeats; his voice is raspy but his hair is as soft as dandelion fluff as he moves from my shoulder to the small of my back. "No more anyone, Victoria. No one but you."

I nearly correct him. In the heat of my dizziness I nearly whisper *Catherine*. But it is suddenly clear to me that I was never as much the Catherine I was as I am the Victoria I've become. The girl who ran off with the circus.

The girl in James's arms.

The girl on a wire.

SEVENTEEN

~

KIP PARKED HIS WRANGLER in the Demmings' driveway, and he and Callie hurried up the crushed-seashell walkway to knock on the front door.

Jenna answered almost immediately, as if maybe she'd heard the Jeep crunching up the drive. Rather than inviting them in, she angled herself out through the half-opened door and joined them on the front porch.

"Hey," she said, her brows knit quizzically. "What are you guys doing here?"

"I was in the mood for some gator gumbo," said Callie. "You said knock on any door, so here I am."

Jenna managed a smile. "Ha. I see what you did there. Nice. But unfortunately we're fresh out."

"Personally I'm not a fan of the gumbo," Kip said. "I try not to eat anything that, if given the opportunity, would try to eat me first."

Everyone laughed; everyone fell silent.

"So what'd I miss?" Jenna asked at last.

"Well, Emma-Kate ended up making out with Jacob, but who didn't see that coming?" Kip reported. "Zach drank about fifty Yoohoos, as per Yoo-hoo-sual."

"The flyers seem to have had a huge impact," Callie added. "I heard lots of people talking about coming on Sunday."

"Great."

There was another brief silence, during which Jenna fidgeted and kept glancing behind her at the door.

"Is your mom feeling any better?" Callie asked.

"My mom's feeling nothing," Jenna said, and it was the first time Callie ever heard her sound bitter. Or was it scared?

"Listen," said Callie, "I need a favor. The only way I can earn a gym credit this semester is if I join a recognized sports league, and Coach Fleisch suggested the croquet team. Problem is, I've never played. So I was wondering if you'd give me a few pointers. Show me the ropes, I guess you could say. Kip says you haven't played in a while, but you're still the best."

"Well, that goes without saying," said Jenna, quirking a grin. "But just so I'm clear about the whole PE thing—you can swing by your ankles on a trapeze ten billion feet above the ground, and do backflips on a tightrope the approximate width of a hot dog, but the Holms County Board of Education is refusing to award you phys ed credit until you prove you can hit a pastel-colored ball through an oversize paperclip?"

"Pretty much sums it up," said Callie with a shrug.

"Go figure," said Kip.

Moments later, they were barreling through the paling sunlight toward the croquet courts. Callie noticed that Jenna's mood had improved the minute the Wrangler's wheels left the driveway.

"Hey, Kippy, put on your helmet!" Jenna shouted from the back, shoving the shiny morion between the two front seats. "I'm being chauffeured by the Surfing Conquistador, and I want the world to know it."

Obediently Kip put the stupid thing on his head.

With the Wrangler's roof and doors absent, the wind made it impossible to carry on a conversation, so Kip took the opportunity to introduce Callie to more of his favorite music.

Callie felt an unfamiliar tingle in her pocket and realized it was her phone. She fumbled it out and saw a text message from the girl in the back seat.

But it wasn't just a message. It was an image. A vintage photo of a female tightrope walker appeared on the screen. Callie had to guess it had been taken in the 1950s. The girl wore a tutu-skirted costume that looked like the sort of thing a toddler might wear in her first tap-dancing recital.

Before Callie could turn to give Jenna a questioning look, the phone warbled again and another picture appeared. Another tightrope, but this time two performers stood upon it, balanced in perfect symmetry.

Another alert, another image. Three men on a wire; one of them riding a bicycle.

Warble. Two men, two women; the women were standing on the men's shoulders.

Warble. A distant, fuzzy shot capturing one of the most dazzling tightrope performances of all time—the Wallenda family, seven of them, brandishing poles (and talent . . . and courage) to execute their signature stunt: a high-wire human pyramid.

Callie stared at the photo, then swiped back, and back again, experiencing a kind of pictorial countdown, until she was back to the solo performer in the tutu.

Another alert. Words this time. JUST WANTED TO SHOW YOU THAT SOLO ISN'T THE ONLY OPTION.

NOT AS EASY AS IT LOOKS.

NOTHING EVER IS.

EIGHTEEN

Missouri, 1965

IN ST. LOUIS, SHARON raises the wire to a height of six and a half feet. It has less give, and feels more dangerous.

"Just keep moving forward," Sharon instructs from where she's stretched out on a quilt in the sun, her skin coated in a gleaming mixture of baby oil and iodine. "We call that 'directional inertia.' It'll help you stay balanced, as long as you just keep moving straight ahead."

I remember thinking the very same thing the day I arrived at the Brooksvale fairgrounds, making my desperate beeline through the crowd, knowing that if I stopped pressing forward for even one second I would lose my nerve.

I take a tentative step, then another, and suddenly, it seems as if the wire is welcoming me . . . as if I've earned my place upon it simply by not giving up. Only now do I realize that this is not a solo act; the wire has life in it, motion and chance, and we must yield to each other because only by agreeing do we succeed in this ill-advised and astounding collaboration. A girl on a wire; a wire supporting a girl— for no other reason except that it can be done. It is all so remarkable and strange, and therefore miraculous. *Grace*, I realize, has two meanings, and right now, I am living both of them—the elegance of motion and the favor of the gods.

Sharon leaps up from the blanket. "Center of gravity!" she sings, and although she's said it a thousand times before, this time it has the effect of some mystical incantation . . .

The words hit their mark. All of me that matters is suddenly compressed into that tiny, all-important place right below my ribs and just above my belly button: that place where I engage in battle with one of the greatest forces the universe has to offer. Focusing all of my awareness into that spot, I let grace work its magic. Tipping is not an option; shaking is the beginning of the end, and falling . . . *I am just so goddamn tired of falling.*

So I don't. I decide to excel instead, choosing to remain upright, steady, in charge. By embracing the improbability of this task, I've made it conquerable. I am walking on a wire . . . a *wire*, less than an inch wide.

"Confidence, sister," Sharon shouts through her laughter. "That is what keeps us from landing on our asses!"

Standing taller, I toe-heel my way to the center of the wire, then summon my courage, and go up on my toes to perform one perfectly elegant turn. An about-face, in every possible sense.

I am not surprised to see James, standing a few yards off, watching. I think maybe I knew he was there all along. I think maybe I felt him, urging me to succeed.

Cornelius is with him. He looks pleased. Proud.

With the Ringmaster and the lion tamer watching, I widen my arms into a dainty half circle, as if I would gather the whole world into my embrace. Then I dip my chin, and bend one knee, letting my opposite foot drop well below the tautness of the wire—this is not the stiff curtsy of a debutante, but the grateful bow of a tightrope artist discovering what she can do.

Sharon lets out a little hoot of celebration, stamping out her cigarette into the dirt. "I didn't even show her how to *do* that!" she cries out, delighted. "Some things you just can't teach! Some things you just know."

Yes . . . some things you just know. Like when you're falling in love with a boy who's slept with tigers at the foot of his bed.

Sharon goes right on cheering. James is smiling—because, like he said that night in my room, he knew I could do it. And Cornelius is applauding.

"What d'ya think, Mr. VanDrexel?" Sharon calls out, planting her hands on her hips and shaking her head in awe. "Not bad for a beginner, huh?"

"Not bad at all," Cornelius agrees, rewarding me with a tip of his hat. "Looks as though we've got ourselves a natural."

It is the very best and very worst thing I have ever heard.

Because every day, we get just a little bit closer to Texas.

~

Oklahoma, 1965

We're somewhere in Haskell County. I'm sure the town we're playing has a name, but Sharon's just been calling it East Dung Beetle, and it seems like a good fit.

That night I watch her on the wire, feeling her steps in the soles of my own feet. There is no John Robinson during the big cat performance; somehow Gideon has talked James into giving Boo-boo the night off to rest.

After the show, a bunch of us go into town; Duncan has an old friend, Husky Pete, who owns a bar. The place is a real dive, a wonderful dive, with sawdust on the floors and dirty words scrawled on the walls. There's a jukebox and a dartboard, and the knife thrower, Tobias, places his partner, Angelique, in front of the bullseye and dramatically throws darts at her, delighting the bar patrons. Round after round of drinks and shots are purchased for us by the regulars. Recalling my hangover, I decide to go easy on the alcohol, so James orders me one drink called a Harvey Wallbanger, which is, in a word, yummy.

Duncan pops a few coins into the jukebox, chooses a song, and suddenly everyone is crowded onto the dance floor, dancing the Watusi, just like Luci Baines Johnson and Steve McQueen.

"Let's dance," I say.

James looks skeptical. "I'm not much of a dancer."

"Oh, come on!"

He grins, shrugs, slides off his barstool. "Okay. You asked for it."

I grab his arm and pull him into the crush, only to find that he wasn't kidding—he's got even less natural rhythm than the rescued dogs! But he refuses to be intimidated, and gamely wiggles his hips and even throws in a few of the requisite jerky arm movements, none of which are even remotely close to being in time with the music. Honestly, if I didn't know he was dancing, I'd be calling for a doctor—he looks like he's having some kind of convulsion. Duncan's laughing and Husky Pete is laughing and I'm laughing; I'm laughing so hard I nearly pee my pants. I've never seen anyone look so utterly ridiculous and so completely self-assured at the same time.

The song fades and another begins—The Tokens' "The Lion Sleeps Tonight." Without missing a beat James pulls me close.

"They're playing our song," he teases.

"We have a song? And *this* is it?"

"That's what you get when you fall for a lion tamer, sweetheart."

It's not your typical slow dance but neither of us cares. We sway against each other and he doesn't seem to mind that I'm leading.

"Told you I couldn't dance."

"And yet, you totally pulled it off. How did you manage it?"

"First thing I learned on the job," he whispers, kissing me just below my earlobe. "When you step into the lion's cage, show no fear."

"So to you, *this*"—I glance around to indicate the dance floor—"is a lion's cage?"

"No," he says, indicating me in his arms. "To me, this . . . is heaven."

Settling my cheek onto his shoulder, I sink into the song. Across the bar, Sharon is snuggling in a booth with Vadim. They look cozy, blissful, smitten. Our eyes meet and we share a smile. She's trying to tell me something. But at the moment I'm too lost in James to know what it is.

When the song ends, we go back to the bar where my watered-down Wallbanger waits on a cocktail napkin with the Husky Pete's logo printed on it. I borrow a pen from the bartender, turn the napkin over, and proceed to print carefully on the damp paper: *When in the lion's cage, show no fear.*

James watches me, taking a long swig from his beer bottle. "What's that about?"

"I've just been writing things down lately," I tell him, trying to sound offhanded, in case he finds it silly. "Life lessons." I grin. "Circus-life lessons, actually. Things I should know. Things I want to remember."

"Here's something I want you to know and remember," he says. Taking the pen from my hand, he turns the napkin back over, inscribes something on the front side and slides it back to me.

James loves Victoria.

I read it twice. Three times. My heart races. I'm afraid he doesn't really mean it.

I'm afraid he really does.

When I look up from the napkin to meet his gaze, his face is calm, almost unreadable, but there's something in those green eyes of his—something anxious and hopeful—and I realize he's just put himself back in the lion's cage. He's trying not to look frightened when, in fact, he's petrified.

Baby Bongo of the Congo is not in the habit of falling in love.

So I lock my arms around his neck and pull his mouth to mine, kissing him as thoroughly as I know how. More than anything, I want to tell him I love him back. I want him to know that I'd be happy to Watusi with him, however horribly, for the rest of my life.

But I can't. Because the rest of my life *can't* happen here in this loud, crowded, unpredictable traveling circus. Not that it isn't wonderful. But there are just too many connections, too many things to lose, too many people to miss when they're gone—*See you down the road.* I think of the brooch when it was pinned to my mother's bathrobe, this precious thing that ultimately served only to weigh her down. I think of those cherished photos she had to burn in a desperate effort to protect me from the law. The more you love a thing, the more it can, intentionally or not, bring you pain, so to love and be loved by a family as vast as VanDrexel's would be the most reckless kind of gamble I could take. I've been hurt enough already.

The rest of my life, by my own design, will be something different. Quietly manageable, normal in the extreme, unencumbered by wonderfulness, by connection. I can do without those, if it means I can finally know what to expect from tomorrow, and the tomorrow after that. And in place of excitement, and mystery, and love, I will give myself all the things my father took away from me long before I even had the chance to sample them.

Agency, self-reliance, freedom. That's my dream.

And it starts in Austin, Texas.

NINETEEN

~

THE LETTER WAS WAITING on Callie's dresser beside Victoria's urn when she got home from dinner on Saturday night.

Brad had taken Quinn, Callie, and Jenna to the priciest restaurant in Holms County for dinner, to discuss the final details of the open house and to celebrate their anticipated success. He'd even invited Mrs. Demming—Ellen—to join them, which had turned out far better than Callie had thought it would after the scene at the PDLF. At dinner Ellen had been polite and engaging, and it was clear that Jenna had inherited all that wit and intelligence from her. She was younger than Quinn by quite a few years, but the two moms really hit it off.

When Brad ordered champagne for the table, Jenna had gone pale. But Ellen politely declined, opting for sparkling water instead. And when Quinn made a toast to Jenna, lauding her creativity and hard work, Ellen had looked pleased and proud. By the time the salads were served Jenna had completely relaxed and they all had a terrific time.

Now, with trembling fingers, Callie tore open the envelope and read the response from her father, only to discover that the only thing worse than Marcello's attempts to write in English was his response to her request.

Cara Mia,

I am so sorry to hear that you and your mother have

leaving VanDrexel's. You know that wonderful circus holds a most especial place in my heart, as do you, my Calliope. Your question to be joining me here in Italia has truly to make me feel the joy and pride. And as much as I would enjoy to have my talented and beautiful bambina here with me, I cannot be able to say sì to your warming the heart request. We are traveling very much and I am busy always with the business of running Un Piccolo Circo. I fear it that I would have not the time to be the kind of devoted papa a girl the age of you is needing and hoping for. I invite you to please to come to Italia soon for the vacation when the time is for your school to be finished for the summer. Until then, per favore dai il mio amore a tua madre.

Con tutto il mio cuore,

Marcello

At eight o'clock Sunday morning, Callie stormed up to the mansion, strode across the marble foyer, and burst through the doors of Marston's office.

"What happened to my wire?"

Quinn and Brad looked up from the last-minute adjustments they were making to the open house schedule.

"I *said*, where the *hell* is my wire?"

"I had the landscaping crew take it down last night," said Brad, looking waylaid. "It was visible from the back terrace, and your mother and I were concerned it might be a distraction for the guests. I assumed she told you we'd be dismantling it for the day."

"She didn't."

"I'm sorry. It slipped my mind," said Quinn, rubbing her eyes. "I've been a little busy."

"Yeah, what else is new? And what's so distracting about a wire?"

"It interrupted the view."

"It's a wire."

"Still . . ." Brad gave an apologetic shrug. "It just looked out of place. And honestly, a little sloppy."

"It's a *wire*."

"Callie, stop it," Quinn warned. "You know it's not just the wire, it's the cross bar and the platforms and the legs—the whole apparatus looks like something out of a medieval torture chamber."

"Or out of—oh, I don't know—*a circus*."

"We're just trying to make a good impression today," said Brad. "A professional impression."

"And my tightrope was interfering with your posh, upscale aesthetic? You do realize this whole place reeks of elephant shit, don't you?"

"Callie!"

"She's not wrong," Brad allowed with a chuckle. "And, Callie, I promise you, we'll put the wire back up as soon as the open house is over."

"Lotta good that does me now." Callie stomped out the door and into the foyer. Seconds later she heard her mother's sandals clicking behind her on the marble tiles.

"Calliope, don't you dare take another step."

Callie stopped stomping.

"That was completely out of line. You know how important today is."

"How come only the things that are important to *you* are important?"

"I don't understand why you're making such a fuss about this. Brad told you he'd put the wire back up as soon the guests were gone."

"But I needed it *this morning.*"

"Oh, don't be so dramatic. You didn't *need* it."

"How can you say that? You have no idea what I need. Because I'm not a tiger, or a camel. Or Jenna."

Quinn looked taken aback.

"I'm upset about . . . something, and when I'm upset I feel off-balance. And when I feel off-balance I deal with it by walking the wire. Because I'm a VanDrexel and that's where I recognize myself. It's where I know who I am. How can you not know that about me, Mom, and yet you know the feeding schedule of every animal on this reserve? You know when Gulliver needs his toenails cut, and when Cleopatra has a goddamn ingrown whisker. But you can look your only daughter in the eyes and not even understand that her heart is breaking!"

With that, Callie turned and ran, pausing briefly to peek through the conservatory gate, in the hopes of catching a glimpse of d'Artagnan.

And there he was, pressing his lovably funny face against the bars, blinking at her with those golden-brown eyes. A moment later, he had dashed off into his man-made jungle.

It wasn't until Callie was back in the carriage house, sprawled on her bed, weeping into her pillow, that she realized why she'd wanted to see the chimp. Because like Callie, d'Artagnan understood how it felt to be completely and totally alone.

The curious Lake St. Julianians started arriving just after four in the afternoon.

Some were less curious and more concerned. Others were open-minded and a few were downright hostile. And one, Zach, was only there for the food.

But most of them seemed excited to be taking part in this one-time-only visit during which they hoped, according to the snatches of conversation Callie picked up while trying to be invisible, to glimpse DiCaprio the lion. Or perhaps a tiger. Maybe a bear.

"I just wish people would stop with the 'lions and tigers and bears' refrain," Quinn lamented, smoothing her hair—which was a far cry from messy-bun status today. "It's just not funny anymore. Why can't someone for once just say, 'tigers and bears and lions'? Or 'bears, lions, and tigers.'"

"Doesn't exactly roll off the tongue," said Brad, gazing at her adoringly. "Maybe we could try getting everyone to join in a rousing chorus of 'lynxes and wildebeests and ocelots.'"

"We could, but then we'd actually have to *get* some lynxes and wildebeests and ocelots."

Brad gave her a wink. "I'm sure it's just a matter of time."

"Speaking of time . . ." Quinn turned to Callie. "What time did Jenna say she was coming? I really expected her and Ellen to be here by now."

Frankly, so had Callie. And Jenna's tardiness was only making her mother more nervous than she already was. Quinn had never particularly enjoyed the spotlight, which was one of the reasons why it was Callie and not Quinn who had followed Victoria's example and become a tightrope star.

She knew it was mean-spirited, but Callie couldn't help feeling like her mother's current distress was exactly what she deserved for taking Callie away from VanDrexel's and dragging her to this ridiculous place, then promptly forgetting all about her.

Callie noticed Brad pressing something into Quinn's hand. A folded cocktail napkin—but not one of the safari-themed ones Jenna had ordered for today's event. This one was old, and stained, and very familiar. Callie's heart thudded.

"I know you don't like crowds," said Brad, as Quinn unfolded the napkin. "So I thought a little pep talk from your mother might help."

Quinn's eyes got misty as she examined the napkin. "Husky Pete's?" she read aloud, then gave a soft gasp, and turned to Callie.

"James loves Victoria? Callie, is this one of the scraps from the jewelry box?"

Callie gave a curt nod. *And if I'd known he was going to use it to profess his love to you, I wouldn't have let him borrow it.*

"Well, this is awkward," said Brad, with a chuckle. "That's not actually the part I wanted you to see." He took the napkin from Quinn's fingertips and turned it over. "This is."

Quinn read the handwritten words and laughed. "'When in the lion's cage, show no fear.' Okay, well, I suppose in this context that makes a lot more sense."

"It's excellent advice," said Brad. "And in that courageous spirit, I say we all split up and mingle. Remember, the idea is to educate these folks. Let them know the place is safe and secure, nothing to worry about here. Got it, Cal?"

"Yeah, got it." Snatching the napkin out of Quinn's grasp, Callie tucked it into her pocket and strode away.

All around the grand foyer, other Sanctuary employees had been posted to field questions on everything from the history of the grand mansion to the mating habits of the tigers. Jacob, not surprisingly, had a lot of questions about mating habits. Callie positioned herself at the buffet table, hoping people would be less likely to ask her questions with food in their mouths.

Emma-Kate had caught a ride with Kip, and they were now both making their way toward Callie across the foyer. "This place is incredible," said Emma-Kate, motioning to the high ceilings and marble floors. "No wonder Jenna's so into it."

"Where is she, by the way?" asked Kip. "I thought she was giving a speech or something."

"I guess she's running late," Callie muttered. The words on the Husky Pete's napkin—*James loves Victoria*—had reminded her of how her father had closed his rejection letter, that bold, masculine script looping out the phrase *dai il mio amore a tua madre.*

Give my love to your mother.

Fuck that.

"So what's over there behind those gates?" asked Emma-Kate.

Realizing that in Jenna's absence she had inherited the unwelcome role of ambassador, Callie led Emma-Kate and Kip over to the conservatory gate, where three furry little attention whores, Athos, Porthos, and Aramis, were peeking out through the iron scrollwork. A moment later, Zach and Jake had joined them.

"They look like Marcel from *Friends*," Jake noted.

"They're capuchins," said Callie, searching the flora for a glimpse of d'Artagnan, even though she knew he was far too skittish to make an appearance.

Suddenly, a ripple of interested whispers rolled through the crowd. Mayor Baylor and his family were making their grand entrance, and the next thing Callie knew, Kristi had floated over and was standing directly between her and Kip.

Closer to Kip. Big surprise.

"I totally have to Instagram these monkeys!" she said, aiming her iPhone, and snapping capuchin candids like some downgraded Jane Goodall with a social media addiction.

When a little girl came skipping over and asked to hold one of the monkeys, Sam, the Sanctuary employee posted at the conservatory gate, dutifully informed the child that although visitors were not allowed to hold or touch the monkeys, he had permission to take one out briefly to give the guests a closer look.

The little girl seemed okay with that, so Sam unlocked the gate—then unlocked it again; then once more.

"Jeez, it's like a maximum security prison," said Zach.

Emma-Kate gave a little snort. "You oughta know."

At last, Sam was reaching his arm inside the opened gate. Maybe the monkeys had drawn straws earlier in the day to decide who would get to make the personal appearances—if they had, then

Porthos had been the winner. He scuttled up Sam's arm and onto his shoulder, then (having obviously been coached) the monkey used his tail to pull the gate closed behind him.

The little girl squealed and giggled and blew kisses. More guests approached the conservatory, cooing and laughing at the conspicuous display of cuteness. Porthos lapped it up like a pro, waving and hopping and covering his face with his leathery little hands as if he were simply overcome by their adoration.

Callie almost wished he'd start behaving like a real monkey and start flinging his capuchin poop around the room. But no, Porthos was a public relations savant. Every flick of his tail and wave of his paw was another sympathy vote in favor of keeping the Sanctuary open.

The walkie-talkie on Sam's hip gave a staticky hiccup, followed by a voice crackling through the speaker. "Speeches are scheduled to begin in ten minutes. Please guide guests toward the presentation area."

Sam returned Porthos to the conservatory, locked and locked *and locked* the gate, then set about ushering the crowd to the part of the foyer where several folding chairs and a podium had been set up. The space overlooked the prettiest and most populated expanse of the reserve.

Cue the endangered animals, Callie thought, contemptuously. *Gulliver, are you ready for your close-up? Feel free to belch.*

Jake, Zach, and Emma-Kate went to grab a seat. Kip made to follow but Kristi reached out and pulled him back.

"Let's take a selfie with the monkeys in the background," she suggested. Or was it a command? "The Queen, the Conquistador, and the Capuchins."

"Sounds like the title of a horror movie," Kip joked.

Kristi didn't seem to find it amusing, but that didn't stop her from snuggling herself up against Kip and aiming the camera.

Callie turned away. She would have rather watched Porthos

flinging poop. She'd taken only two steps toward the presentation area when her phone warbled.

"Is it Jenna?" asked Kip

Callie nodded, opening the message to find that this was not one of Jenna's typical succinct, abbreviation-heavy, emoji-ridden messages; what Callie saw on her screen was an elongated gray column written entirely in proper, grammatically correct English.

"It's her speech. I don't think she's coming."

Kip squirmed out of Kristi's grip to read over Callie's shoulder, concerned. "Did she say why?"

"No. She just says somebody's going to have to give her speech." Callie gripped the phone, willing it to warble again. She'd sell her soul to the devil for a single tears-of-joy emoji, a JK, or even just a simple LOL.

Nothing.

Callie looked at Kip. He looked at her. They both knew Jenna wouldn't miss this event for anything. Unless . . .

"Go," said Callie, but Kip was already sprinting for the door.

"Callie?" Quinn was rushing across the foyer. "What's going on? Where's Jenna?"

Callie held up her phone. "She's not coming. But she sent her speech for you to read."

"Oh, dear Lord," said Quinn, wringing her hands as Callie held out the phone in her direction.

When she didn't take it, Callie's brows shot upward. "I hope you're not thinking what I think you're thinking."

"I think I am." Quinn offered a hopeful smile. "You're so much better in front of crowds than I am, Cal—you're a natural. I'll just get tongue-tied and make a complete mess of things."

Callie actually laughed. "Thanks for the compliment, Mom. It's kind of hilarious, though, how my natural ability with crowds is such a great thing when it's in your best interests, but when I want to stay with the circus, it doesn't seem to count for shit."

Quinn sighed. "That's not true and you know it."

Callie shot her mother a challenging look. "I'm not giving this speech."

"Callie, please." Quinn's face was ashen. "Please understand. I need you to do this for me."

"Well, I needed my wire this morning, but you didn't understand that, so I guess we can't always have what we need, can we?"

Kristi let out a little snort. Callie had forgotten she was there.

"Calliope," said Quinn, her jaw flexing as she tried to control the panic that was rapidly returning the color to her cheeks. "You have five minutes to get comfortable with that speech. Then I expect to see you at that podium. Or tomorrow morning you just might find your tightrope contraption has been donated to the capuchins as a playscape."

Quinn turned and marched away. If Kristi hadn't been in earshot, Callie might have shouted one last obnoxious barb in her mother's wake. But what would have been the point? Defeated, she began to scan the speech. With any luck her phone battery would die halfway through it.

Across the foyer, Brad was stepping up to the podium. He tapped the microphone, kicking things off with the requisite "Is this thing on?" gag. Then his movie-star voice was booming through the PA system, welcoming everyone to the Sanctuary.

Jenna's speech continued to unfurl on Callie's screen, elongated text-bubble by elongated text-bubble, replete with phrases like "worthy endeavor" and "collective obligation to all God's creatures, large and small." It was a good speech, a great speech.

A speech that might just succeed in keeping this place open indefinitely.

And in keeping Quinn—and by extension Callie—at the Sanctuary for years.

Callie was so engrossed in Jenna's words that she almost jumped out of her skin when someone tapped her on the shoulder.

Kristi. Still standing there. "Can you do me a favor?"

She's kidding, right?

"Can you get me into that monkey room?"

Callie blinked at her. "Didn't you just hear Sam tell the little girl it's not allowed?"

"Yeah, but you . . . live here. I'm sure the rules are different for you."

"Not how rules work," Callie muttered, glancing beyond Kristi to the doors of the terrace, flung wide to afford the eager spectators the best possible view. The tigers, including the cubs, perhaps sensing that it was in their best interest to do so, had come out to roam. Tessio and Clemenza romped and rolled, and as though he could not stand to be upstaged, the mighty DiCaprio, handsome and blond and regal, strutted through as if he'd been invited to do a cameo. All the while, Brad's perfectly modulated voice and crisply enunciated words continued to fill the marble space: "—so glad you all came out to explore our facility in an effort to clear up any confusion—"

"You know," said Kristi, toying with her phone, "if you were to help me get a close-up with those monkeys, it could be a really good thing for this place."

"You want to do a good thing," Callie echoed, scrolling deeper into Jenna's remarks: *community spirit . . . ecological advancement . . .* "for the place you and your father can't wait to shut down?"

"Maybe I've had a change of heart about that," said Kristi.

Callie, who was pretty sure Kristi didn't have a heart to change, refused to rise to the bait, prompting Kristi to go back to the gate and wrap her manicured hands around two of the iron bars, attempting to yank it open.

"What the hell are you doing? It's locked."

"So open it. I'm telling you, you won't regret it. Do you have any idea how many people will see these pics when I post them on Instagram?"

"Over one hundred animals representing thirteen different species—" Brad boasted to the standing-room-only crowd.

"And I'm telling *you* that you *will* regret it," Callie insisted, still trying to focus on the speech. "Those three little Marcel look-alikes aren't the only ones behind that gate. There's a chimp in there too."

"Currently residing on the grounds of the estate which, as some of you might not know, once belonged to my very own great-grandfather—"

"Can't you just let me in there for like two seconds?"

Was she really that stubborn, or just that stupid? "No."

"God, Callie. They're just monkeys."

"No, Kristi, they're not 'just monkeys.' They're my monkeys. And there is no way on God's green earth that I or anyone else is going to let you walk through that gate."

"Why not?"

"*Because*," Callie seethed, her volume rising as steadily as her fury, "if you were to set one foot inside that cage, the chimp you want so desperately to photograph will feel threatened. And if he feels threatened, then he will attack. And if that happens," she continued, her voice now risen to a shout, "it's very possible that the chimpanzee could actually . . . *KILL YOU!*"

The last two words came out in what could only be described as a full-on shriek, amplified by the echo-chamber-like acoustics of the foyer.

In the wake of it, Brad's voice fell silent.

And suddenly every eye in the room was trained on Callie.

TWENTY

Oklahoma, 1965

JAMES DOESN'T ASK ME back to his car. It is simply understood by both of us that I will be joining him there.

With the beer from Husky Pete's still bitter on his breath, and the sawdust still clinging to the bottom of my Keds, we burst into his room. Before the door even closes behind us we are tangled in each other, stumbling around the narrow space as though we are dying for each other.

We are.

Between ravenous kisses he asks me questions, which I answer with convincing half-truths.

"Where did you grow up?"

"Near Boston." *Nonspecific, but true.*

"Big family?"

Big mess. "Only child."

"Where are your parents?"

"Dead." *Well, one is. And if there were any justice in the world, the other would have been a long time ago.*

Enough. I kiss him more zealously, to the point of distraction; I kiss him right off the subject of who I am, and seduce him into telling me *his* dreams instead. He is more than happy to comply.

"Someday, I'm gonna visit the great European circuses," he tells me, pausing in unbuttoning my blouse just long enough to motion to the maps he's tacked to the walls. "Rome, Marseilles, Lisbon . . ."

"Is that what Gideon meant when he talked about your European tour?"

197

"Yeah. He thinks it's pointless. Or maybe he just thinks *I* am. But that doesn't mean he wouldn't want to be rid of me for a while. It's ironic, actually. He doesn't want me to have what I want, but he's constantly whispering in the Ringmaster's ear that I should go."

We fall into bed. I nip the bottom edge of his T-shirt between my teeth and tug—a request, which he fulfills by yanking the thing over his head and flinging it across the car.

"Why?"

"Because he hates that I'm Cornelius's favorite."

"I meant why *Europe*?"

"Oh." He laughs and kisses my eyelashes. "Because it's just *different* there—they respect the circus, they consider it a true art form. And I want to learn everything I can, and bring it all back here, to make VanDrexel's the best American circus there ever was."

And to prove to Gideon you can do it, I think.

"Can you imagine it, Victoria? Me, going from show to show, an itinerant performer, studying with every *Löwenzähmer* I can meet."

"Every *what*?"

"Lion tamer. German."

I laugh and repeat the word against his lips—*Löwenzähmer*—then giggle it into his chest, loving the way it makes him flinch. I move lower, whispering it over and over and over again as I nuzzle each carved ripple of his abdomen. "What else?"

"*Pitre*. Clown." He slides my open blouse from my shoulders, then his fingers find the buckle of my belt. "French."

I wriggle my slacks down my legs; the cot squeaks beneath me as I kick them off. "And . . . ?"

"*Direttore del circo*." He takes my hand and gently brings it to the front of his jeans, his thumb caressing my palm. "Ringmaster. Italian."

"More . . ."

"Acrobata, pagliaccio, Sprechstallmeister."

There is something so mysterious and romantic about those words, those circus words, spoken in his voice. My spine tingles with them as they tremble off his lips and onto mine. I sigh a slow smile, thinking, *Who else but a lion tamer, who else but James, could entice a girl with circus words?*

Now my fingers find the tab of his zipper and I ease it down— his turn to wriggle. His progress is impeded by the fact that I refuse to unwrap myself from his body. But his jeans come off, and when there is nothing but night between us, we revel in the feeling of being this close, me marveling in him, him marveling in me. His thumb traces the line of my jaw; my instep curves against his ankle.

"Why haven't you gone already?" I ask.

He rolls up on his elbows and settles above me. "Part of it is that Cornelius is afraid to let me go," he whispers, kissing my lips, my nose, my chin. "He thinks I'm too much like my mother, that I'll get swept up in the adventure and never come back."

The thought of James leaving VanDrexel's for good sends a stab of panic through me. I don't know why, since I'm leaving soon myself.

"Is he right?"

"No. I don't think so, anyway."

"But you can't be certain. Salzburg, Barcelona, Paris . . . you might be tempted."

He considers this, then shakes his head. "No. VanDrexel's is home. Home is everything."

Home is everything. I have to stop myself from looking around for something to write on.

"But it doesn't matter anyway," James laments, "since we don't have the money to fund a trip like that."

Good, I think. Not for me, of course. For Cornelius. And the circus. James will stay and the show will go on.

"But if I could go . . . damn, I know it would be one hell of an adventure."

I skim my fingertips across his chest to make him shiver. He smiles and dips his head; his bangs brush the base of my throat. I cradle his face in my hands to draw his mouth to mine. My eyes fall slowly closed; he is kissing me like I'm made of candy. A quiet rumble fills his chest—a tiger sound. I meet it with a sigh, then something softer: a promise.

"I love you."

"I love you too."

And all thoughts of European adventures are abandoned for the one we suddenly can't stop ourselves from embarking on.

Right here, right now.

James is already gone when I wake up.

He and Gideon left before dawn and will be away all day. Cornelius has heard rumors of a carnival that recently went belly-up, and he's sent the boys to see what the bankrupt owner might be willing to sell off, cheap.

It is just past sunrise when I creep out of his car to meet Sharon in the center ring.

Today I will graduate to the actual high wire—*sixty-six feet* high, to be precise—and I'm more than a little bit nervous. Although she never uses a safety net herself, Sharon's insisted that I have one and I'm not inclined to argue.

The crew has just finished setting up the net, and they're bouncing on it to make sure it's properly arranged. A giant's fishnet stocking. The only thing between me and the hard-packed dirt floor of the Big Top.

I have been doing fabulously well on the low tightrope Sharon's had me training on. And I love the feeling of holding motion at bay by creating motion of my own. I am, as Mr. VanDrexel pointed out, a natural. I am graceful, nimble, mighty.

I am also, as it turns out, slightly afraid of heights.

But when the crew guys are gone, I tamp down my nerves, make the climb, and position myself on the wire.

The band is having one of their casual practice sessions; they good-naturedly announce my moment with a long, exaggerated drumroll.

"Very funny," I shout down, but somehow their teasing makes me feel better, braver. "I'd like to see you fellas try this."

A rim shot: *ba-dum-tsh* . . . how drummers laugh.

I begin my walk and Sharon calls out corrections, encouragements . . . It's all as it always is except from here she looks much smaller. I think about how, for me, in Brooksvale, ground level was so much more precarious than this, and my fear begins to wane.

I do as I'm told and succeed in skipping, turning, bowing, even walking backward. I am an athlete, an artist, a magician. An angel, a daredevil, a dancer in the sky. The band is delighting themselves with their own sound, and without even trying to, I find myself moving in time to their jaunty tunes.

"Don't get carried away, sister," Sharon warns, during a pause in the music. "Just do what—"

She cuts off, turning abruptly toward the tent's entrance as if she's heard something, something I can't hear from up here. But the musicians have heard it and they put down their instruments and go out to see what's what.

Sharon listens a moment longer, then calls, "Victoria, come down."

"Why?" I ask, but I've already begun picking my way cautiously to the opposite end of the wire. She's not so small that I can't see the expression on her face. Something's wrong.

"Victoria," she says loudly when she sees what I'm doing. "Come down *now*."

"You mean . . ." I eye the net. I know it's safe but I don't want to do it. It is counterintuitive. It's scary.

"Victoria! Now. Trust the net."

I know better than to question her twice, so I fall. I just . . . fall, letting myself spill from the wire like a tear from the eye of God. When I hit the net, I become an animated version of a flailing Vitruvian Man, vaulted upward ten feet—my stomach leaps and drops at the same time, then I'm falling again, back into the net; it cradles me just as briefly, only to belch me upward once more into another shallower bounce. Finally, the net goes still and I scuttle to the edge to somersault off.

On the ground, I can hear what Sharon heard—running feet outside the tent, voices raised in authority, Oklahoma accents. It's barely eight o'clock in the morning. Something is *very* wrong.

Now the tent flap slaps inward; a column of light slices into the gloom and in it stands Cornelius, fastidiously put together even at this hour. His red coat is buttoned, his precious top hat sits upon his head like a crown—he is, even at sunrise, a force to be reckoned with. And when he speaks the single word he's come to tell us, I know why.

"Police."

TWENTY-ONE

~

CALLIE FOLLOWED QUINN UP the stairs into the carriage house.

Needless to say, the open house had ended early. A John Robinson if ever there was one.

All Mayor Baylor's concerns about the animals on the reserve posing a safety hazard to the citizens of Lake St. Julian had been summed up one in single public relations–crushing phrase, a phrase that had interrupted—and negated—Brad's flawless, heartfelt speech assuring his guests of their town's safety, because Callie had been unable to keep from screaming it at the top of her lungs:

The chimpanzee could actually kill you.

Quinn flopped onto the couch, kicking off her shoes. Callie went to her room, returned the Husky Pete's napkin to the corkboard, and stood in front of it, wondering if there could ever be a saying or a lesson to explain how something that had been planned with such good intentions could have gone so horribly wrong.

Her phone warbled and she grabbed for it. In all the commotion with Kristi, she'd almost forgotten about Jenna.

But it wasn't Jenna. It was Kip.

AT JENNA'S. PLEASE COME.

There was a brief hesitation, during which Callie quickly, instinctively untacked a business card from the bulletin board and slipped it into her pocket where the cocktail napkin had been. Then . . . *warble.*

Kip: HURRY.

Callie ran into the living room with the color draining from her face and showed her mother the phone screen. Quinn was on her feet in a flash, stepping back into her shoes.

Ten minutes later, they pulled up behind Kip's Jeep—and the two police cars and the ambulance that had gotten there before them. Callie sprinted up the walk, the seashells gnashing like teeth underfoot. When she pushed open the screen door, she saw Jenna, perched on the edge of the couch cushion, her body bent forward with her elbows resting on her thighs and her wrists dangling between her knees, gazing straight ahead with vacant eyes. Except for the fact that her hair was down and beautifully brushed, and she was wearing a cute little sundress with strappy sandals (one of which was missing its heel), Jenna could have been sitting on a bench in a dugout waiting for her turn at bat.

Kip was sitting in a wooden rocking chair watching Jenna watch . . . well, nothing. The room—all pale beach colors and beadboard and driftwood, something out of a breezy bed-and-breakfast—was a shambles. Books scattered, a broken vase, an overturned coffee table. From upstairs, Callie could hear voices—firm, calm, insistent:

"Mrs. Demming, can you hear me? Mrs. Demming, I'm here to help you. Can you move your head, ma'am? Can you hear me?"

Quinn rushed in and went directly to Jenna, catching her in a hug and smoothing her hair. "What happened?"

Jenna continued to stare and, like the ballplayer she seemed to be impersonating, let Kip field the question.

"Her mother was drinking all morning," Kip relayed. "Jenna kept trying to get her to stop. I guess because she wanted her to be able to come to the open house."

Jenna nodded. Then sighed, then nodded again.

"But when Mrs. D opened another bottle of vodka, Jenna got

super frustrated and kind of lost it and threw something across the room. Mrs. Demming freaked out and started trashing the place. Then she went upstairs—"

"Crawled," Jenna interjected dully. "She *crawled* upstairs. *With* the vodka."

"Yeah. Crawled." Kip rubbed his eyes. "Anyway, I guess she locked herself in the bedroom, and Jenna just decided to leave it alone for a while—"

"I did my hair. I never do my hair. I'm always too busy watching her to have time to do my hair." She looked at Quinn. "I have great fucking hair."

Quinn stroked Jenna's cheek and whispered something soothing as Kip went on. "She was leaving for the open house, but then she heard this, like, thump—"

"Thud. This *thud*."

"So she went upstairs and knocked on the door, but her mother didn't answer. So she tried to kick it down."

Jenna rolled her eyes. "Like that was gonna work."

But it did explain the heel.

"So she called 911, and they came and they broke down the door, and I guess Mrs. D had fallen out of bed, but something about the way she landed—"

"She broke her neck!" Jenna finished, her daze lifting, her anger burning hot. "She broke. Her fucking. Neck. *Her goddamn fucking drunk-ass neck!* Broke it."

Kip puffed out a long breath. "They *think* she broke it. They won't know until she gets to the hospital."

Quinn pressed a kiss to the top of Jenna's head, then went upstairs to talk to the EMTs.

Callie went to sit beside Jenna, placing a business card on the couch cushion between them.

Jenna looked at it. "And why exactly do I need the phone number of a deputy sheriff in Oklahoma?"

"Other side, Borderline."

"Ah." Jenna flipped it over.

Trust the net.

"Hm. Nice thought." Jenna cast a meaningful glance toward the stairs. "But you can't trust what you don't have."

"Why didn't you tell me it was this bad?"

When Jenna didn't answer, Kip said, "Why didn't you tell any of us?"

"I guess I thought you'd get the hint. I mean, it was kind of obvious, wasn't it?"

Kip sighed, then shrugged. "I don't know . . . I mean, maybe."

"That's why I stopped showing up at stuff." Jenna flexed her fingers as if she might make a fist, then let her hand fall back down to her thigh. "I got tired of making excuses for her when she'd pick me up wasted. Remember when she came stumbling into our seventh-grade choir concert smelling like tequila? Or that time she got loaded at the gumbo cook-off and everyone pretended it was perfectly normal for a fourteen-year-old to get behind the wheel of a car to drive her mother home?"

Kip squirmed. "Yeah, I remember," he said softly.

"The only thing I couldn't quit was work, but of course that came to a screeching halt last week when she showed up stinking drunk during my double shift and tried to steal a hundred bucks out of the cash register. Which, needless to say, was the real reason I got shit-canned."

"I guess we thought we were being respectful by giving you your space," said Kip, "but what we should have done was step up."

"Good times," grumbled Jenna, sliding the business card into her jeans pocket. Then with a jolt of realization, she turned to Callie. "How was the open house?"

Callie sighed. "Funny you should ask."

TWENTY-TWO

Oklahoma, 1965

CORNELIUS IS SHAKING HIS head. "Seems a few of our rowdier lads lingered in town last night and failed to mind their p's and q's. One of them paid a bit too much attention to the sheriff's wife."

Sharon rolls her eyes. "Lemme guess. Shaw."

Cornelius does not confirm or deny. "The unfortunate result of this indiscretion is that we now have a disgruntled law enforcement agent meddling in our business." His eyes flick to me, holding for the space of a heartbeat. "In particular, he would like to speak to any young ladies currently in my employ, and they will be expected to present proper identification for his consideration."

"But why?" I croak. "How could he know—"

"Mrs. Sheriff, who, I feel compelled to mention, was in fact a willing and enthusiastic participant in this ill-advised little dalliance, was coerced into giving a description of the lad, and noted that he'd been wearing a rather pristine Red Sox ball cap, from which her husband rightfully deduced that the young man had recently spent time in Boston." Again, his gaze grazes me. "It seems the sheriff has been reading the newspapers."

My legs buckle under me; I would have crumpled to the ground if Sharon hadn't caught me. She hauls me to an upright position.

"He doesn't know what you look like," she says, and I realize with a jolt that Cornelius must have shared the article in the *Globe* with her. I'm not angry, nor am I surprised that he would have; I told her as much myself that day by the elephant trailer, and we both know she'll take my secret to the grave. But I also know that if the sheriff discovers that Cornelius has been transporting an underage (not to mention missing) girl across state lines, the ramifications could be as devastating for him as they'll be for me.

"Naturally I've told the lawman that we will be happy to oblige him in this quest," Cornelius explains. "Which is why, in a few moments, he'll be going from car to car to examine each female performer's paperwork."

"Hell of a wake-up call," Sharon grumbles, looking around the empty tent. "Can we hide her in here?"

Cornelius shakes his head. "His deputy will be searching the grounds, and I suspect he will not ignore the Big Top. He's already started poking around the midway stalls."

"What about the menagerie?" I blurt. An idea, born of desperation and terror, has begun to bloom in my mind.

"He has instructions *not* to go near those cages without *me*."

Struggling to get my bearings, I glance from one rippling canvas wall to another. "The menagerie's . . . that way?" I point to the north-facing side of the tent.

Cornelius nods.

I tell him what I'm thinking. He agrees that it just might work.

Sharon kisses me hard on the forehead, then leaves through the front flap to return to the train car she shares with Genevieve, the tattooed lady. Cornelius follows her. I turn and sprint to the north wall. A moment later I see the Ringmaster's distinctive shadow splashed upon the canvas. He makes a quick motioning gesture with his arm. *The coast is clear.*

I crawl under the tent wall, scramble to my feet, and run full tilt to Rabelais's trailer.

The elephant looks pleasantly surprised to have company at such an early hour.

I creep in, scramble all the way to the back, and press myself into a shadowy corner where Rabelais's enormous form conceals me. As expected, Francie has not gotten around to mucking out the trailer yet, and I have never in my life been so happy to smell elephant manure.

Several minutes pass with me crouched in the back of the cage, occasionally murmuring reassuring things to my gigantic friend. He responds with soft rumbles and friendly chirps. He even flaps his ears, which, according to James, means that the elephant is relaxed.

Well, that makes one of us.

In the confined space, the motion of those oversize ears stirs up the stale air and magnifies the intensity of the stench.

"Keep flapping, Rabelais," I whisper.

Finally, I hear Cornelius's voice. He is guiding the sheriff's deputy to Rabelais's trailer, and I nearly burst out in nervous laughter because suddenly all I can picture is that scrawny, bumbling character from *The Andy Griffith Show*.

But this isn't Mayberry; this is East Dung Beetle.

And the sheriff's got a grudge.

When they reach the opening of the trailer, I peek around the gray girth that is my host, and see that this deputy is a far cry from Don Knotts—this is no comic sidekick, this is a burly lawman: a modern-day cowboy with a badge.

He immediately steps back, covering his mouth and nose with his hand.

"No need to be trepidatious. Rabelais is quite docile, I assure you."

The deputy gags. "It smells like *shit* in there."

"Well, of course." Cornelius chortles. "Did you imagine that an elephant could be housebroken?"

The deputy leans into the trailer a fraction of an inch, and I shrink deeper into the darkness. He gags more violently, as if he's about to hurl up whatever he had for breakfast. Despite my terror,

I roll my eyes. The mayor's prissy daughter in her Lilly Pulitzer and pearls did not protest this much.

"Anybody in there?" he shouts, his voice ricocheting off the trailer's metal walls. "Hey! *Hello?*"

The elephant, ever the professional, responds without missing a beat, just as he's been taught to—with an exuberant wave.

Wummppff.

Rabelais's trunk collides with the deputy's head; he staggers backward and lands on his ass a good six feet from the trailer.

I can just glimpse Cornelius, who politely—though none too urgently—offers the deputy a hand up.

"My good man, are you hurt?" he asks, knowing full well that Rabelais's signature move is all for show, and doesn't pack much of a wallop.

The deputy grumbles, swatting away the Ringmaster's hand.

"Had his handler been present he would never have done that," Cornelius informs him breezily. "Unfortunately, she's currently in her train car, being interrogated by your superior officer."

The deputy snorts.

"Now then, would you care to see if anyone might be hiding among the tigers? They aren't quite so friendly as the pachyderm, but they do smell slightly better."

The deputy mumbles something that from here sounds a lot like "No fuckin' way, you freaky circus bastard," and I am indignant on the Ringmaster's behalf. But Cornelius does not deign to address the insult; he simply leads the lawman away from the elephant trailer, leaving Rabelais and me alone, and safe.

But I don't dare move, not yet. I remain hidden behind the elephant for another hour at least, just to be sure the cuckolded sheriff and his olfactory-sensitive sidekick have given up and gone home, leaving the mystery of Catherine Hastings's whereabouts to remain unsolved.

When at last I remove myself from the trailer, I spy a small white rectangle on the ground. A business card.

HASKELL COUNTY SHERIFF'S DEPARTMENT
CARL HOLLIS LAMBERT
DEPUTY

It must have fallen out of the lawman's pocket; I take the card back to my car. Valerie, arranging her red curls into a loose braid, does not ask me where I've been, but I notice my cot has been hastily stripped of its linens. I strongly suspect this was done to make it appear as if she bunks alone.

So maybe she knows, and maybe she doesn't. I am certain of this much, though: neither of us will ever speak of it.

Trust the net.

I write this on Deputy Lambert's business card and place it in the jewelry box.

Then I head for the shower, anxious to wash the blessed odor of Rabelais's waste off me. But it isn't the smell that is making me feel sick to my stomach right now; it's knowing that if Oklahoma's answer to Barney Fife *had* found me in the elephant cage, there would have been hell to pay for Cornelius and his beloved circus. And not only would I have no hope of finding my independence in Austin, I would likely find myself being hauled back to a certain brick mansion in Brooksvale.

I am now more determined than ever to leave VanDrexel's.

The sooner the better.

TWENTY-THREE

~

ON MONDAY AFTERNOON, QUINN picked Callie up at school and they went to visit Ellen Demming in the hospital.

Ellen Demming, as it happened, was not in the mood for visitors. She was cranky and uncomfortable—turns out, administering painkillers to an alcoholic is a bit of a medical minefield and the doctors were still working out the kinks. And Ellen's attitude was not making things any easier for them.

The fact that she was going through withdrawal didn't help either.

Jenna looked exhausted and smaller than Callie remembered her when she peeked into the hospital room and saw her drowsing on the munchkin-sized couch across from the bed. When Quinn suggested a quick trip to the coffee shop across the street from the medical center, Jenna was more than amenable.

They took a booth in the back and ordered one slice of key lime pie with three forks.

"So I've been thinking," said Jenna without preamble, "about this whole chimpanzee thing. I think we need to draft a press release: part retraction, part public apology."

Quinn reached across the table to pat her hand. "Honey, you don't need to concern yourself with that. You've got plenty of other things on your plate right now."

"But I want to fix this. It's my fault."

"How is it your fault?" Callie asked. "You weren't even there."

"The open house was my idea. The only reason people were allowed in was because I suggested it, so we could convince everyone that the Sanctuary is safe. Which it is."

Quinn sighed and took a small taste of the pie. "It is safe. As safe as it can be. That was always our point. We've never denied that our residents were dangerous."

"Well, it's kind of a no-brainer. People know what animals are capable of."

"Yeah," said Callie, with a guilty sigh, "but it's probably better when *someone* doesn't scream out a reminder of their potentially deadly aggression in the middle of a catered event."

"Anyway, I don't think an apology is going to matter," Quinn said softly. "Brad's decided to close the Sanctuary."

Jenna's mouth dropped open and Callie whipped her head around to gape at her mother. "*What?*"

"If the cards weren't stacked against us before, they certainly are now. The irony is that Brad is so obsessive about safety. He's got alarms on all the enclosures, state-of-the art locking mechanisms on everything from DiCaprio's fence to the file cabinet in his office."

"I know," said Jenna. "I put that in my speech."

The one that no one got a chance to hear, thought Callie, cringing.

"The fact that the chimp could have hurt someone has to be balanced against the fact that Kristi, or anyone else for that matter, couldn't have gotten into that conservatory with a blowtorch," Jenna fumed.

"Of course not. But as we know, perception is reality," Quinn observed, "and the mayor has made a pretty convincing sound bite out of Callie's, shall we say, *poorly timed but not entirely incorrect* statement. I wouldn't be surprised if he's printing up bumper stickers as we speak."

Jenna's mouth twisted on a sigh. "Okay, so not to sound like a complete megalomaniac here, but if the Sanctuary closes . . . I'm out of a job, right?"

Quinn gave her a sad smile. "I'm afraid so, honey. But at least you'll be in good company."

Jenna shook her head. "That's a problem. Like, a major fucking problem. My mom's gonna need round-the-clock care for weeks, and after that, hell, let's face it, she's gonna have to check in somewhere to get sober. And that shit's expensive."

"I'm sure insurance will cover some of it," said Quinn.

"It would if we had some," Jenna grumbled. "And everything I've ever earned has been put away for college, but I guess that's about to be sacrificed to the gods of rehab. So, see ya around, higher education."

Callie felt awful for Jenna, she really did. But something her mother had said had been spinning around in her brain—*you'll be in good company*—and suddenly a tiny curlicue of possibility had begun to unfurl in her belly.

"Mom, if the Sanctuary closes, what happens next?"

Quinn toyed with the pie. "I guess we'll have to find other rescue facilities for the animals."

"No, I mean to us. We go back to VanDrexel's, right? We go back home."

Quinn's brow wrinkled. "Callie . . ."

"Where else would we go?" Her eyes were shining now. "You left the circus because you wanted to work at Mr. Marston's with Antony and Cleopatra and Gulliver and the others, but if there's no Sanctuary, why can't we just go back to VanDrexel's, so I can start traveling and performing again? Or we'll find a different circus, one that still has animal acts."

The scrape of Jenna's chair shooting back from the table cut Callie off. "Thanks for the pie."

"Where are you going?"

"Back to the hospital." Jenna was already halfway to the door.

"Wait." Callie jumped up and followed her. "What's wrong?"

"Nothing. I guess I just forgot how much you love your solo act. And in the spirit of going solo, maybe you should figure out a way to send out those circus applications for yourself. I've got my own job search to worry about now."

"You can't be serious. You're *mad*?"

"I'm not mad, I'm tired." Jenna scrubbed her hand over her face. "And I'm scared, because I don't have any idea how to do this. Some borderline genius, huh."

With her sad, ragged ponytail whipping behind her, Jenna stormed out the door.

TWENTY-FOUR

Texas, 1965

THREE WEEKS HAVE PASSED since my near miss in East Dung Beetle. Since then, VanDrexel's has played to small audiences in small towns throughout Oklahoma and the northern part of Texas, and though Sharon has been spending much of her free time with Vadim, she sets aside an hour every day to coach me on the wire.

I have become quite proficient at walking the sky. Knowing that in mere days I will no longer have an outlet for this budding talent brings on waves of grief and regret I can't even begin to describe.

Today the cast played a matinee to a packed house in Houston. Tomorrow the train will carry the show westward to Austin, but tonight we're staying put so Cornelius can throw a farewell party for Valerie. She will be leaving from Austin the day after tomorrow to meet up with her cousin further west in El Paso; from there they'll travel on together to the coast.

At the send-off bash, Hasty Pudding is inconsolable; she is only able to speak audibly when reprimanding Gus for drinking too much alcohol or devouring more than his share of the jumbo shrimp Hank has included in the party spread.

But there is nothing like a circus party. This is where the clowns who spend their lives amusing strangers can burn off some of the laughter they've saved for themselves. Tonight, the music and the merriment are not for public consumption. Tonight, the circus is a command performance by invitation only. Friendship here is of a most unique caliber; born of our common uncommon experience, it envelops us under softly glowing lanterns that twin-kle brightly in every color the circus can dream up.

Valerie snaps pictures like crazy. She can't wait to go, and she can't bear it either.

I know just how she feels.

Austin is the place where I will move on.

If you've found it, then it's meant to be. The one rule I have not tucked into my jewelry box. The one rule I'm choosing to break.

Cornelius stays at the party only long enough to make a toast in Valerie's honor, which of course ends with a heartfelt "See you down the road" that is echoed by all in attendance. I raise my glass to Val, but imagine the promise is for me.

Then, because he is mostly made of magic, the Ringmaster dis-appears, perhaps to perpetuate the illusion that he is a little left of human, or perhaps simply to let his beloved employees cut loose and party freely in his absence.

"Gus, please! Remember your gout!" Hasty scolds, and another fresh burst of tears begins.

James and I dance close, like we did at Husky Pete's. I snuggle against him and commit his heartbeat to memory. He ducks away briefly to smoke a joint with some of the roustabouts. Forget It—also known as Shaw—is among them and I wonder if James would be so willing to smoke with him if he knew that the last few times Boo's performed, Shaw's been in the rafters aiming a rifle at the lion's head.

I try not to be mad about that. Boo, for all his gentleness and dignity, is at heart a thing that's wild. As is James, who returns from the shadows, smiling in slow motion with his eyes at half-mast.

"Hi," I say, as he sweeps me into his arms.

"Yes, yes I am."

When I kiss him, I can taste the earthiness of the pot on his breath, and promise myself I'll remember it. He takes my chin on his thumb like he did that first time we kissed and looks at me with sincere but bleary eyes. "I love you, Victoria."

I can't stop the sob that escapes me, and he looks so alarmed that I have to laugh.

Then Duncan is shouting, "It's Madison Time," and suddenly we're all in a big strong line, doing the popular party dance with all the silly moves. Sharon slides into place beside me and we laugh at each other's mistakes. The Madison becomes the Alley Cat, and then the Hully Gully, a complex dance to which only Valerie and the other dancers do justice.

Finally, when Gus is good and drunk, and Hasty Pudding is all cried out, the celebration comes to a close. I hug Valerie so hard she gasps.

"Good luck," I manage in a strangled voice. "I'll miss you."

"It's for the best," she assures me, and when she whispers, "See you down the road," *I* know that *she* knows I'm not long for this circus, and never was. I press a kiss to the dancer's cheek, then take James by the hand and escort him back to his room. I will spend the night with him, though based on his present state—which is to say *altered*—I don't expect much in the way of romance.

Perhaps that, too, is for the best.

My belongings are packed in the Woolworth's bag most of them came in. My mother's brooch will come with me, but the jewelry box is too cumbersome for the sneaky getaway I'm planning. I've arranged to ride ahead to Austin with Rick, the advance man, spinning some vague yarn about visiting old family friends who live there.

But I won't return to the train. I'll sell the brooch and use the cash to find an apartment. Given my lack of documentation, I'm sure it won't be in a particularly reputable building, but at least it will be a start. Tomorrow I'll look for a job, though I doubt anyone in the city of Austin, Texas, is looking to hire a former debutante turned amateur tightrope walker.

I thought I might leave a letter for James, but after many false starts discovered that there really wasn't anything I could say that would make any of this all right.

So I will vanish from his life, just as I vanished from my father's—without a word. The difference, of course, is that this time I wish I didn't have to go.

We put ourselves to bed. James musters enough energy for one goodnight kiss, then crashes off to sleep while I cry softly into the pillow beside him.

The motor of Rick's battered Chevrolet is already sputtering when I slip into the front seat at twenty minutes to five the next morning.

"You're late," he snarls.

"I know, I'm sorry . . ." My nerves are so frazzled that I actually had to stop twice to upchuck during my short walk from the train to the Chevy.

I set the bulging Woolworth's bag on the seat between us. He lifts an eyebrow.

"Oh . . ." I give a casual toss of my head. "Just some circus souvenirs for my friends in Austin."

Rick nods and throws the car in gear, and we ride the next three and a half hours in silence. Fine with me; I'm sure if I tried to speak, I'd end up weeping instead.

So I aim my eyes at the rose gold of the horizon, clutch my mother's brooch, and tell myself that whatever I find in Austin, while not necessarily meant to be, will have to be enough.

Rick drops me at a corner I pretend to be familiar with. "They live just down the block," I lie, climbing out of the car.

"Little early to be payin' social calls, ain't it?" he asks.

I smile brightly. "It is, isn't it? I guess I'll have some breakfast first, maybe do a little shopping. But thanks for the ride and I'll see you later, at the fairgrounds."

I wait for him to turn the corner, then start down Congress

Avenue. The capitol building looms importantly, catching the rays of the already scathing Texas sun.

I grab a copy of the Austin *Daily Texan* at the first newsstand I pass, then hunker down on a stool in a coffee shop to search the real estate rentals, circling all the one-bedroom apartment listings. Back in Brooksvale, I had a bedroom larger than any studio apartment all to myself. But in the train car, I got used to Valerie humming herself to sleep.

The elderly waitress behind the counter—Lula, according to her plastic nametag—brings me a cup of coffee before I even ask for one. I guess this is my cue to quickly scan the menu.

"What can I get ya this mornin'?" she asks, her accent as thick as the coffee.

I order a Swiss-and-mushroom omelet with homefries. As she scribbles my choice on her check pad, I summon the nerve to ask, "Are you hiring by any chance?"

The moment is such a far cry from the night I sat in Cornelius's paneled office and made a similar inquiry. "Find her something to be good at," he'd told Duncan, and it occurs to me now what a generous thing that was. He could have said, "Find a position that needs to be filled," but instead, his goal was to find a way for *me* to be fulfilled, a way for me to succeed.

And although I never did get to walk the wire for a crowd, I doubt there is anything in Austin I'll ever be as good at as that.

"No openings at the moment," Lula informs me, "but you can check Crandall's Doughnut Den. They're always lookin' for help."

"Thanks." I'm hoping my hours spent apprenticing for Hank in the pie car will count as applicable food-service experience.

My breakfast arrives in record time, but I find I can only stomach a few bites. I'm still a little queasy.

"Excuse me."

Lula turns away from the ketchups she's marrying. "Somethin' wrong with yer omelet, hon?"

"No, it's delicious. I was just wondering if there's somewhere nearby where I might hock some jewelry."

She looks at me funny; I guess I don't come off as a jewelry-hocking type of girl. Or maybe she doesn't have any idea what I'm talking about. Luckily, the fry cook is a bit more worldly.

"Lone Star Pawn," he tells me, his face framed by the kitchen pass-through window, glowing red from the heat lamps. "Three blocks down."

"Thanks."

"If you get to McMartin's Music Shop you've gone too far. Hit the buzzer, ask for Stan. Tell him Corby sentcha, so you don't get screwed." Then he slides a steaming plate across the metal shelf and bellows, "Steak and eggs, short stack on the side!"

I finish my coffee, leave a generous tip, and push out into the growing Texas heat. The city is awake now, and I lose myself for three blocks in a sea of suits and Stetsons.

At Lone Star Pawn, I press the button and am immediately buzzed into a room crowded with radios, TV sets, power tools, fringed leather jackets, and tarnished silver tea sets. A balding man in a short-sleeved dress shirt stands behind a glass jewelry case filled with watches, bracelets, necklaces.

"Are you Stan?"

He nods.

"Corby sent me."

He smiles with half his mouth. "You buyin' or sellin'?"

"Selling." It hurts to say the word. My fingers grip the brooch.

"And what are you looking to unload?"

I step up to the counter and lay the jeweled pin on the glass top. Stan looks at it, does a double take, then turns it over and looks some more. There is a loupe on a chain around his neck; he presses it to his eye, then he lets it fall, jerking his head up to look at me with his bushy eyebrows crunched low. "This is Cartier." Not a question. Stan knows his stuff.

I nod.

"Platinum. The diamonds are exceptional, and that ruby's damn impressive."

"It was my mother's. She died."

He mumbles his condolences—a reflex. I'm sure 95 percent of the baubles in his case came with a dead-mother story attached. Stan does not give any indication that he believes me, or even cares.

"I'll need a minute to make some calculations," he says, trying not to tip his hand, but it's clear that items of such value rarely find their way to Lone Star Pawn.

He hands me the brooch, then ducks through a dark curtain into a back room, his inner sanctum. I stare at the pin gleaming in my palm, refracting the streaks of Texas sunlight that pierce the blue letters painted on the window. I can still see my mother's hand placing it in mine, and I remember the prisms it threw off in a world where she still existed. Tears well up in my eyes, blurring the jumble of electric guitars and mantel clocks and engagement rings . . . so many engagement rings. I wipe my eyes, but more tears bubble up. Which is why I don't immediately recognize the man passing by the large front window of Lone Star Pawn.

Until I spot the overalls.

"Vince?" I lean closer to the window. He looks troubled, upset, gripping his trusty fedora as he looks up and down the busy street.

He sees me in the store at the precise second that Stan breezes back through the curtain.

"Miss?"

Simultaneously, Vince is outside speaking my name. I don't hear him of course, but I see his lips forming *Victoria*, and there is no mistaking the look of relief on his face. It's me he's looking for. My stomach flips and I almost vomit again.

Did Valerie tell? Or perhaps something's happened at the circus.

I turn to Stan. The pawnbroker inclines his head and holds up what can only be described as an enormous fistful of bills.

"I'll be right back," I tell him, then rush out through the door he is kind enough to buzz open for me.

"There you are! I been lookin' all over Austin for you."

"How did you know I was here?"

"Genevieve heard you askin' Rick for a ride last night. Somethin' about visitin' friends in the city."

"Vince, what is it? Is it James? Cornelius?" Another horrible thought hits me. "Boo?"

"It's Sharon."

A yelp of dread escapes me, but he quickly holds up his hands, like he's on the wrong end of a stickup. "She's fine. Not sick, not hurt, just . . . gone."

I gape at him. He might just as well have said she sprouted fins and swam off into the Gulf of Mexico. "Are you sure?"

His response is to produce an envelope from the back pocket of his overalls and hand it to me. "She left this," he explains. "Cornelius found it on your pillow, when he went to ask you if you had any idea where she might've got to."

I take the envelope, half expecting it to burn my fingertips, and see that my name is written across the front in Sharon's handwriting. "What does it say?"

"Well, hell, Victoria, I don't know. It's addressed to you."

This stuns me. Even in a moment of urgency, Cornelius respected my privacy enough to refrain from reading my letter, opting to send Vince looking for me instead.

It is humbling to know that a person could be that . . . decent.

I have to tuck the Woolworth's bag under my arm and slip the brooch into my pocket in order to open the envelope, which I do with trembling fingers. I read quickly, silently. Halfway through I'm crying; thankfully they are tears of joy.

"She isn't gone for good," I tell Vince, my voice shrill with relief.

"Hallelujah," he huffs, rubbing his brow. "So where the hell is she?"

I can't help the giggle that escapes me. "She's with Vadim. They're on their way to Niagara Falls! They've eloped! They ran off last night after Val's party."

So this was what she was trying to make me understand that night at Husky Pete's.

"Son of a bitch," he murmurs, more in awe than in anger. Then: "When are they coming back?"

I read a little further.

"They are comin' back, aren't they?"

"Well, yes . . . and no. They're taking some time for a honeymoon first."

Vince ponders this briefly, then shrugs. "Okay. I guess we can't blame her for that. How long?"

I hesitate, knowing he isn't going to like the answer. "They'll be back at the start of next season."

"Aw, hell."

I see his point. Sharon's happy news has left him, the gaffer, with a significant problem. He has no tightrope walker, not only for tonight's performance, but all the way through to next spring.

A sudden flash of anger streaks through me.

How could Sharon be so selfish, so unreliable, as to leave Cornelius without a tightrope walker?

The answer is, she couldn't. And she didn't. At least as far as she knew, since she had no idea I was planning to skip out in Austin.

My eyes go again to the bottom of the page, where before, I'd only skimmed over her signature, ignoring the closing entirely.

I read it, my heart growing heavier with each syllable.

Your turn to walk the sky, sister. Love, Sharon.

Except it wasn't. Because I had already left VanDrexel's for Austin. Indeed, I was having this conversation with Vince *in* Austin. The decision had not only been made but executed. I was going on alone in the Lone Star State. No more entanglements, no more heart-stopping moments like this. No one to worry about, or answer to, or learn from. No one to overhear you asking for rides, no one to respect or be respected by. Or love.

Vince lets out a heavy sigh. "I should be getting back," he grumbles, adjusting his fedora. "Enjoy your visit, Victoria. I'll see ya back at the fairgrounds."

No, you won't. "Goodbye, Vince. I'm glad you'll be able to tell Cornelius Sharon's all right."

"So'm I," he says, raising his arm high to hail a cab, "but I sure ain't lookin' forward to tellin' him he's gonna have to make do without a wire walker for the foreseeable future."

Folding the letter, I glance back through the Lone Star Pawn shop window, where Stan is still holding that ridiculous pile of cash. He gives me an expectant look.

I shake my head. Transaction complete.

"Vince. Wait."

As I climb into the taxi, I realize two things: One is that this is the first time since Vince and I met in New Jersey that he hasn't called me First of May.

The second is that while freedom may be something, home is everything.

The rest of the day is a whirlwind. Sharon left her costumes behind for me. Myrtle helps me select the one that best suits my coloring—a dazzling sapphire-blue satin with white sequined trim. I spend at least an hour in the wardrobe car, having it fitted to my figure. I turn this way and that in front of her mirror as she hitches it up and cinches it in, adjusting the neckline ever so slightly.

Then I meet with the band and tell them that instead of using Sharon's lilting music box number, I'd like to try something a little . . . different. "How familiar are you with current music?" I ask.

The trombone player, Gary, smiles. "We're a lot hipper than we look," he says. "What is it you'd like us play?"

I write down a short list of titles. "Try McMartin's downtown, if you need the sheet music. Oh . . ." I turn to Marcus, the drummer, smiling. "And feel free to keep that drumroll."

Marcus laughs and Gary says he can shoot into Austin, pick up what they need, and still be back in plenty of time to play the Spec into the tent.

I spend some time practicing on the wire above the net, just to be certain that what I'm planning isn't going to look silly, or worse, kill me. When I've put together what I believe is a solidly entertaining routine, I climb down the ladder and go in search of Cornelius.

I don't find him in his office, so I try the menagerie, and sure enough he's there, standing beside Baraboo's wagon, arguing in hushed tones with James. I halt a few yards off to let them finish their conversation. When James thunders away, it is all I can do to keep from going after him. Instead, I join Cornelius, who is stroking the lion's head through the bars.

Boo is very still, very thin, wheezing in the heat. It's clear he's far worse than he was in Chicago.

"Mr. VanDrexel?"

Cornelius turns away from the lion, and again I am struck by how meticulous he always looks in his Ringmaster's uniform. The nap of his velvet coat is smooth, his trousers are unwrinkled, and his top hat is as black as midnight, without a speck of dust or lint to mar the silken sheen.

"Greetings, Victoria."

"I just wanted you to know that I'm going to do my very best for you tonight." *Because I owe you that. Because I love you and your son, and your circus.*

He smiles, but there is sadness in it. "I have every confidence that you will shine, my dear. I only regret that the same cannot be said for our fabulous feline friend."

"I saw you speaking to James. Did you suggest—" I can't bring myself to say the words *put down*, but I don't have to. He knows what I mean.

"I did. Sadly, the boy is still too blinded by his love for the animal."

"But he's suffering."

"They both are. James is relying a tad too heavily on the old adage 'where there's life, there's hope.' He wants to believe Boo can get well. If he weren't so afraid of losing him, I know he would be the first to want to end his misery. So I will try again tomorrow, but for now, all I can do is attempt to provide a bit of comfort." Cornelius pulls a silver flask from his pocket and pours an amber-colored puddle onto the floor of the wagon, which Boo slowly laps up. The Ringmaster helps himself to a hearty swig.

"Will that help him, do you think?"

Cornelius shrugs. "Who can say? But as I have no other solace to offer this poor, noble king of beasts, I choose to believe it will." He takes my arm in his and leads me away from the lion. "And now, Victoria, regardless of . . . well, everything . . . you must go and prepare for your debut. You know what we say in the circus."

"The show must go on," I recite, a disciple steeped in faith.

"The eleventh commandment," he says loftily. "The words we live by." He smiles again and this time I see only fondness there. "I wish you the best tonight. Know that I will be watching and cheering you on."

I climb the ladder into the shadows where gravity has less authority. My wire is rigged to span the center ring.

James and Gideon have just completed their performance with Clemmy, Scruff, and the tiger prince in the ring to the right of the grandstand. They exit to a riot of applause. James returns immediately and tucks himself off to the side to watch me, unseen by the fans who would surely be distracted by having one of the dashing VanDrexel boys in their midst.

Cornelius's deep, melodic voice rings through the tent. "And now, my friends, prepare to be enchanted . . . entranced . . . enthralled! Lift your eyes to the skies and welcome the dainty and death-defying, beautiful but brave, sassiest sweetheart ever to walk the wire . . . our own . . . *Victoria!*"

The spotlight flares and I feel it light me up from inside, as if I've somehow become incandescent. The band strikes up—a drumroll!—and as I also requested, the next few notes belong to Sharon. I asked them to play the intro to her program hoping that it will be the next best thing to having her here to watch me.

I step out onto the tightrope, kicking one leg up behind me, then the other, a little prancing march that takes me to the midpoint of the wire. I sense the net stretched out beneath me, rendering me fearless. Then I flick my wrist—a signal to Marcus to change tempo. The band switches to the first of the songs I requested . . . "The Wah-Watusi," the song James and I (more or less) danced to at Husky Pete's. As played by a circus band, it sounds much different than it did on the jukebox, but when the teenagers in the crowd recognize the song and the moves, they cheer and holler, and some even leap up and begin dancing in their seats along with me.

When the band segues into Petula Clark's "Downtown" I slide into the slightly sexy, kittenish motions of the Frug, and again, the young spectators applaud and join in.

Finally, the band slows into a moody version of "Ticket to Ride." For this, I soften into an airborne ballerina (or is *air born* more accurate?—since truly, I feel as though my life is starting fresh right here, right now). My every step is lithe upon the wire, exactly the way Sharon performed her routine that first night I saw her back in Brooksvale.

When the music stops, I retreat to my ledge and pose in the glow of the spotlight.

Cheers float up to the wire like bubbles in a glass of champagne. James is whistling through his teeth, beaming, and Cornelius, his face filled with fatherly pride, removes his iconic hat and bows his head to me in a show of respect that has me wanting to skip back out onto that wire and do it all over again.

Which I will. Tomorrow night. And the night after that. And every night and weekend afternoon for the rest of my life.

I know that I could not leave VanDrexel's now if I tried. As long as the circus is willing to protect me, I will stay on that train and I will perform in the sky.

I will be part of this unique and powerful family, and in that, I will know more freedom than I could have ever hoped to experience on my own. The freedom to shine, and the freedom to fall.

And always, I will trust the net.

TWENTY-FIVE

~

"WHY *CAN'T* WE GO back to VanDrexel's?"

"Because," said Quinn, stomping up the carriage house stairs in front of Callie. "It's not practical."

"So what *is* practical, Mom?" Callie persisted, stalking her mother to the kitchen. "Staying here without a job?"

"I'll find a job."

"Okay, you find a job. I'm going back to the circus."

"You can't go back to the circus" was Quinn's infuriatingly calm reply as she went to the kitchen sink to fill the teakettle. "End of story."

End of story? Callie didn't think so, not while she still had some tantrum left to throw. "You're so selfish!"

"Maybe so, but I'm also your mother, and you need my permission, which I am not prepared to give."

"Then I'll get permission from Marcello."

"No, you won't." Quinn said this with such utter conviction that Callie actually gasped out loud.

"You spoke to him!"

"I did. He called me when he got your letter."

Traitor! "You told him not to let me come live with him in Italy!"

"I told him I didn't think it was a good idea and he agreed. I told him I'd break the news to you myself, but he offered to be the bad cop and write you back, since there was no point in having you hate me, when you could hate him from five thousand miles away."

"I have an idea. How about I hate both of you?"

"That's certainly your choice."

"The only one I'm allowed to make, apparently. You never even asked me if I wanted to come here. You just decided for me."

"Well, if you refer to the *Official Parenting Handbook*, you'll see right there in the job description that that was absolutely and undeniably my right."

"What about my rights? The circus was my life, and you didn't care. The circus was—"

"In trouble, Callie, that's what the circus was."

This brought Callie up short. "What are you talking about? VanDrexel's is in trouble?"

"Not VanDrexel's specifically." Quinn sighed. "Not yet anyway. But times change, opinions change, and over the last few years, I've had to watch a lot of people walk away from the only life they'd ever known. I heard an awful lot of 'See you down the road's." She took two mugs from the cabinet, then dug around in the canister for tea bags. "It's a very different perspective, Callie, watching the circus from ground level, as opposed to up there on that wire."

Quinn poured the hot water, took the cups to the living area, and sat down on the sofa. "Come and have a cup of tea."

"I don't want any tea. I want to go back to the circus. And if it can't be VanDrexel's then I'll find another one!"

"Callie—"

"Jenna's going to help me find a job. And if you and Marcello won't give me permission, I'll run away."

"Callie—"

"I'll run away and join the circus," she exploded, hearing the threat in her voice. "People have been known to do that, you know. It's called following a dream. You came here to follow yours, but you dragged me away from mine! And now your dream no longer exists and you still won't let me do what I love."

"*Callie!* Please . . . will you just shut up and drink the tea?"

Glowering, Callie dropped onto the couch and took a sip.

"Do you know why Jenna got so upset back there at the coffee shop?"

"I dunno, because she's psycho?"

Quinn shot her daughter a look over the rim of her mug. "Try again."

"Because she was worried about her mother. Although I'm not sure why, since she's basically hijacked mine, and you two have been ganging up on me ever since."

"If you call two people trying to help you see what's best for you when you can't see it for yourself 'ganging up,' then okay, I suppose that's what we were doing. And you're right—Jenna was upset about Ellen, but she was also upset about the incident at the Sanctuary, and she was devastated to hear that she was about to lose her job. Her head was spinning and her heart was breaking. She felt lost."

"Gee, Mom, I'm tempted to go with a cuttingly sarcastic, 'Been there, done that,' except I'm way too wrapped up in my own little world to even know if the cool kids are using that comeback anymore. But on the outside chance that it's still a thing, here goes . . . Fucking been there, fucking done that!"

"All the more reason for a little empathy to kick in when you saw that it was happening to your friend—the girl who's been so determined to help you and make you feel welcome here. But no, you just climbed up on your wire and went into your walk, and suddenly it became all about you and your circus."

Callie felt as if she'd been unjustly slapped. "Jenna knows how I feel about what I do. She knows what the tightrope means to me."

"As do I. But you know what part of that you've never explained to me?"

Callie waited.

"Why."

"Why what?"

"Why you took it all so deeply to heart."

"Said the woman who spent two nights sleeping in Cleopatra's cage when she was in labor."

"That was different. That was about making a connection, filling a need. I took my job to heart but you took it much, much further. You put so much pressure on yourself to be the best that you couldn't embrace anything else. So . . . I'm asking you. Why?"

Callie was about to say she didn't know, but that would have been a lie. She turned away.

"If you don't want to say it out loud for my benefit, maybe you need to say it for your own."

Callie pressed her lips together. She shifted on the sofa cushions. The last thing she wanted to do was give her mother the satisfaction of an explanation.

But the words came out anyway.

"When I first started working with Gram, I didn't take it seriously at all," she began reluctantly. "I was always good—Gram said I was a natural. But during those first few lessons, I was always—I dunno, goofing around, getting distracted, wanting to learn those silly hand-clapping games the Bertières were always playing."

"Try not to beat yourself up about it, Cal," said Quinn, biting back a grin. "You were six."

"But one day, Gram was acting . . . different. Like, she was sad or something. Really sad."

"Let me guess. September 23?"

"Maybe." Callie thought about it. "Yes, actually, it was. I remember because we had just started the new school year. I wasn't focused, so I kept making mistakes and laughing about it, and finally Gram got so frustrated she turned around and walked out of the tent. It freaked me out."

"I'm sure it did," said Quinn stroking Callie's hand. "That wasn't like Gram."

"It wasn't. So I ran after her, grabbed the back of her leotard, and she sort of, like, spun around—like a move on the tightrope. She looked at me really serious, like maybe she was about to start crying or something, and she said, 'Calliope, do you know why this circus is called VanDrexel's?' I remember shaking my head, and then she said . . ." Callie swallowed hard because she could still hear Gram's voice as plainly as she had heard it that day. "She said, 'We're called VanDrexel's, my darling, because the very last thing your grandfather did before he left this circus forever was to fight for that name. *His* name. Which became *my* name. And now it's yours, and you must remember that every single time you step onto that wire you're taking our name, that thing of enchantment, out there into the spotlight with you. That is your true center of gravity. But if you can't handle the responsibility, the privilege of that legacy, well, then I think perhaps we should reconsider whether or not you're meant to walk the wire.'"

"Wow," breathed Quinn.

"I know," Callie agreed. "So even though my act was a solo act, it was never just me out there. It was me and Grandpa James, and the name he fought so hard to keep. If I fell, he fell. So I decided I wouldn't fall. Ever. Let the Bertières play all the games they wanted; they could, because they were Bertières. But I was a VanDrexel. And I had to live up to my name."

"And you did," Quinn assured her. "In every possible way, Callie. You did."

They sat quietly, letting the words settle softly into the atmosphere like dust kicked up by prancing horses.

When Quinn spoke again, her voice was wistful. "She never told me about my father fighting for the VanDrexel name. She never told me a lot of things. But why didn't you?"

"Because you were always so busy with the animals."

"Well, the animals needed me. You didn't." Another long stretch of quiet. Then: "Callie, you know I never expect or even want you to stop loving the circus. Like Gram used to say, it's in our blood. It was in my father's and your father's, and every time I hear a tiger chuff or an elephant trumpet, I feel it thrumming away in mine. God, I missed them when they came to live here. And let me tell you, Cal, when you're watching your mother die, but you just can't make yourself get past missing a goddamn elephant, well, that's pretty much the definition of a guilt trip."

It was Callie's turn to stroke her mother's hand. She'd never stopped to wonder how it felt for Quinn when she lost the animals she'd loved her whole life. Or maybe she'd just been too selfish to care. But she cared now. And more than that, it was something Quinn and Callie had in common.

"The circus is who we are, Callie. But here's what you were too young to understand that day Gram said what she said, and what you never had a chance to learn later because you were too busy trying not to fall. You can't just love a legacy. You can't let one *thing*—one talent, one person, one particular way of life—stop you from loving other things too. The world has more than three rings, Callie."

"I don't do that . . ." Callie reached for her tea, then put it down, knowing even the smallest sip wouldn't get past the knot that was suddenly forming in her throat. "I don't not love other things. I loved Gram!" She hadn't meant to shout it; she hadn't expected the gasp that followed it. "I still love her, and I miss her so much."

"I know, baby." Quinn used the side of her thumb to wipe the tear that came rolling down Callie's cheek. "She loved you too."

"And I love Uncle Gideon, and Marcello—I mean, I guess I don't really know them all that well, but I *love* them. And just because I could never remember which Bertière was which—"

Quinn chuckled. "I've got news for you, Cal . . . *Nobody* could."

When Callie laughed, it cracked into a sob, and everything that followed came out in rush. "I even kind of loved them too, because . . . I don't know . . . because we shared a circus. And I know

I never told you this before, but sometimes I would go watch them rehearse on the trapeze, because it reminded me of Marcello, and I'd always be so happy when they'd make their catches, I was happy *for them* because no matter how crazy the stunt, they always had somebody to catch them . . . but all I had was a net, and I guess that was fine, the net is good, but it's not a sister, right? It's not a friend.

"And Jenna . . ." Callie gave a loud sniffle. "Jenna . . . oh God, she's so pushy, Mom, and she knows everything and she's such a profoundly borderline pain in my ass! But in some stupid way, I feel like even though she's not a Bertière, she would catch me, right? Don't you think Jenna would catch me?"

"I think she would. I think she has."

"I know, right?" Callie dragged her hand down her face because the next words still felt spiky. But she needed to say them . . . wanted to say them, so she did, and they came out in a rush with the tears clinging to them, and slightly bruised by the spite and the anger that had kept her from saying them for so long. "And I *do* love you, Mom. I do. And I'm sorry I've been impossible. I'm really sorry . . ."

She wasn't sure when she'd come to be leaning against her mother's chest, or when Quinn's arms had gone around her.

"I love you too, my darling girl."

"I just don't know if I'm ever going to be all that good at walking on the ground."

Quinn stroked Callie's hair and placed a kiss to the crown of her head. "Well, here's a little secret, kiddo—that's pretty much how everyone down here feels most of the time. But we keep walking anyway. We just keep moving forward. And if we're lucky, we find some people who don't mind stumbling around with us, and somehow that makes it a little easier to stay on our feet." Another kiss, another smile; Quinn's eyes were soft, lit with that VanDrexel spark. "Well now . . . I think we've taken a perfectly good metaphor and worked it way beyond its pay grade, haven't we?"

Callie pressed her face into her mother's neck and nodded hard, laughing, crying . . . wiping away the tears, then letting them start fresh again.

Tomorrow she would find a way to explain this all to Jenna.

Then again, being Jenna, she probably already understood. So maybe all Callie would have to do was say she was sorry.

And possibly shoot a text to the Bertières to ask about Beatrice and Liang.

Or was it Bianca? Never mind, she'd figure it out.

When Callie finally felt ready to unwrap herself from her mother's arms, she went to her room, and flicked her fingers over and under the ruffle of scraps tacked to the board. When she found the one she was looking for, she took it as a kind of confirmation, a whisper from the past that as long as there were mothers, there would be daughters who occasionally needed to cry—hard—on their shoulders.

They call them sob stories for a reason.

As always, Gram was right.

TWENTY-SIX

Texas, 1965

AS HASTY PREDICTED BETWEEN crying jags, an excess of bourbon and shellfish at Valerie's party has caused Gus's gout to flare up. His right foot is now ghastly to behold, swollen and purple and, if his wincing is any indication, quite painful.

Needless to say, he won't be driving his daughter to meet her cousin in El Paso this afternoon, so the task falls to Shaw, who is one of very few human beings Gus will allow behind the wheel of his old truck. Shaw will make the nine-hour drive, spend the night in El Paso, and be back late in the day tomorrow, in plenty of time for the takedown.

"Have a care with that clutch," the mechanic tells the sharpshooter. Then he wraps his arms around his little girl and whispers a litany of blessings in her ear, while Hasty strokes Valerie's long red curls. Finally Gus lets her go, though it's clear he'd have preferred to hold her that way forever.

We all wave as Valerie and the roustabout head out in Gus's truck, billows of dust rising and swirling in their wake.

As Gus hobbles away, his shoulders stooped with sadness, I stop him.

"She'll be all right, Gus. She's a good girl."

He nods, his face twisted by his manly attempt to ward off tears. Then he pulls me into a hug that is all strong arms and broad shoulders, and filled with the warmth of a man who has loved and raised a child. I know this is what remains of the hug he hadn't finished giving to Valerie, but I'll take it anyway.

238

Just before showtime, Myrtle surprises me with a leotard she's made using pieces cut from four of Sharon's favorite costumes— pink satin, blue chiffon, lilac tulle, and silver spangles, which she has somehow managed to blend together beautifully. It is a coat of many colors, and the fit is flawless. She's cut and sewn it on the bias to provide more stretch, and I am immediately imagining a whole repertoire of highly acrobatic stunts and movements.

James jokingly christens Myrtle's masterpiece Frankenstein, but he can't take his eyes off me when I put it on.

That night, my routine delights our second Austin audience as much as, perhaps even more than, it entertained the first. Afterward, as James and I walk the midway under a sky alive with Texas stars, several fans stop us for our autographs; some even ask to have their photos taken with us.

He walks me to my room, where we giddily push the two cots together, and proceed to utilize every single inch of them. James tells me a hundred times that he loves me, and it is better than a thousand spotlights and a lifetime of applause.

It is an entirely perfect and wonderful night.

And then it isn't.

Sometime around three o'clock I roll over and find emptiness. I sit up fast, with a sinking feeling that pulls my heart into my belly.

There is a noise, a mournful noise, like wind howling in a storm: wind that is afraid of the storm it's a part of. I listen and it comes again but this time I know what to call it:

A roar.

It is eerily soft, a roar that begins as a roar, but ends as a whimper. Baraboo.

I leap from the bed and run in my baby dolls for the menagerie, my bare heels skidding to a halt at the lion's cage. Standing beside it is Gideon, shirtless, with blue jeans pulled over his pajama bottoms. Cornelius has thrown on a burgundy-colored robe.

James is in boxer shorts and nothing else, unless you count the golden fur coat he's huddling beside. He's spooning himself against Boo—his arms are wrapped around the cat's big body, and his face is hidden in that regal mane.

The lion's breath is coming as fast and as sharp and as shallow as if he's just run miles to triumph in the hunt—and perhaps in his failing mind, in his swiftly receding hold on whatever constitutes reality for a lion, he has. Suddenly, I just want to imagine him imagining himself strutting against the hot wind across the grassy expanse of some African savanna under a sky dripping moonlight.

"What can we do?" I ask, hoping I've whispered but knowing I've screamed.

At the sound of my hysteria, Boo opens his eyes. The depth of the hurt I see there makes me want to gather him into my embrace like Gus gathered me into his and take away his pain. I reach into the cage to stroke James's back with one hand, and Baraboo's paw with the other and as I do, my anguish wanes to something quieter: simply grief.

"James," Cornelius begins, but his voice trips over the tears in his throat. "Son. It's time we let our noble friend find his peace."

James shakes his head. "It's not time yet," he whispers, but I can hear the defeat in his voice.

"Where's Shaw?" I ask.

Gideon's voice is dull and gravelly. "El Paso."

Right. I'd forgotten. A king is in agony, and we have sent the man with the rifle on an errand.

As the tears spill down my cheeks, a windswept echo comes rippling into my thoughts. It is a zephyr of a voice that has put an end to misery once before.

My mother's voice. *Go, Catherine*, it says.

And I obey, rushing to the roustabout's car, where I bang on the door. No one answers, so I barge in, only to find Shaw's roommate, Derrick, having a tumble with some willingly nameless woman from town.

He sits up and gives me a look that is more curious than startled.

"The rifle," I bark. "Where does he keep it?"

"Behind there." Derrick motions with his tousled head to a shabby footlocker shoved against the wall near Shaw's empty cot. "It's not loaded. Ammo's in the trunk." He hesitates. "Is it Boo?"

I nod, yanking the weapon from its hiding place. Then I throw myself at the trunk, fling it open, and fumble among old work boots and girly magazines until I am grasping a cardboard box of bullets. I tear into it, and because my hands are shaking, most of the cartridges spill out onto the floor. They sound like hail. They sound like death.

"Load it for me," I command shrilly.

Derrick springs out of bed to do what I've asked. Then he hands me the rifle. "Tell him g'bye for me, huh?"

I nod again, heading for the door. "And Derrick . . ."

"Huh?"

"That better not be the sheriff's fucking *wife*."

I leap out into the night and sprint back across the grounds. When Gideon sees me toting the rifle, he looks surprised and then not surprised at all. He opens the cage for me. It isn't locked. The lion is no longer a predator. The lion is no longer a lion. He is nothing but pain and softness and a big cat's memories of a million astounding shows performed before a million astounded children.

I don't know when the crowd began to gather, but everyone is there. Myrtle is crying and Evangeline is crying and Gus and Hasty Pudding are holding each other and weeping almost as hard as they wept this morning when Valerie left. The roustabouts who bothered to put on hats when they came scrambling from sleep take them off now in a show of respect.

I step up into the cage to deliver the rifle.

"Victoria . . ." Cornelius's voice, as always, is musical; tonight it is a dirge. "Victoria, my girl, be careful."

With enormous effort Boo lifts his head.

James doesn't.

I offer Boo a smile, as if a pleasing countenance could mask the fact that I'm holding a weapon. "Hey there, you beautiful boy," I sing. "Hey there, you star of the circus."

It's anyone's guess which of the two I'm addressing. Both, I suppose. But James has gone deaf and Boo is in no mood for compliments. He knows exactly why I've come. His topaz eyes are pleading with me to hurry. And in them, I see a distant reflection—my mother, sitting on the porch in Brooksvale, a jewelled brooch glinting in her hand.

I'm dying, my love, my darling girl. We both know it.

"James?"

He doesn't answer, just gives the slightest shake of his head against Baraboo's fur. I take a deep breath and try again, offering him the rifle. "James, please . . . you have to."

Again he shakes his head, and this time his whole body shakes with it as he draws himself up on his knees, burrowing his face deeper into the lion's mane. The soft sound of his sobs wrecks me. It wrecks Boo, too. A hollow whine escapes him.

"*James!*" I say more sternly.

He utters two words into Boo's fur. "I can't."

"You have to. James . . . you *have* to."

"I know I do. I know it. I know I have to . . ." His voice is broken, his heart is broken, and he looks at me with swollen eyes. "But I *can't*. Victoria, I can't do it." The crack in his voice gives way to a sob as he presses himself and all his uselessness into the lion's frail rib cage. Boo lets him, because Boo will wait. He will wait until James is ready. And all I can do is stand there, forgetting how to breathe, forgetting how to think, holding the rifle that has become like a paralyzed limb.

When I feel movement behind me, I realize Gideon has climbed into the cage. He walks past me like a ghost, then bends down and kisses the lion on his forehead, between and just above his eyes.

Aim for the brain. Instantaneous. Humane.

Then he takes hold of his shivering brother, his arms encircling James's midsection. He helps him stand, and as James stumbles out, his hands continue to reach for the cat, even when Cornelius guides him down the steps. Together, father and brother entrust James to the two burliest roustabouts, and then Gideon returns to the cage. He holds out his hand for the rifle and I surrender it to him. As I lift it into his grasp, it no longer feels heavy. It seems to have lost all substance. In this moment and this moment only, it has ceased to be a thing of violence and has transformed into a weightless instrument of mercy.

I exit the cage in a fog and join the roustabouts who continue to support James.

"Take him away from here," Cornelius instructs. "He needn't see this . . . He shouldn't see . . ."

Like angels singing Hamlet to his rest, they usher the lion tamer away from the cage, and I follow, with my hand reaching out for James, with James's hands reaching out for Boo.

James spares one last look over his shoulder. "Goodbye, buddy," he whispers, his voice a hoarse rasp. "Goodbye, Boo."

As we move further into the darkness, I hear Cornelius's voice: "Long live the king."

A moment later, a single gunshot rings through the night.

I don't know what becomes of the lion's body; I don't think I want to know.

I don't know what's become of James either. The roustabouts carried him into his car. When they were gone, I tried to curl next to him on the bed, but he rolled away and pressed himself against the wall where an intricate map of Spain spanned half the length of his room.

It was as though he wished he could be there, or anywhere, instead of here.

So I went back to my own car, and fell asleep just as the sun was rising.

~

That night, VanDrexel's Family Circus pays tribute to a fallen friend.

Gideon performs with the tiger triplets in a ring scattered with rose petals while the band plays "The Lion Sleeps Tonight" at half tempo, and it sounds like a lullaby mixed with a hymn. The notes chiming from the xylophone and the glockenspiel sound like happy tears and fond farewells.

Cornelius skips the show—for the first time since he became Ringmaster, I'm told—to sit with James. Together they mourn Boo, making good use of that silver flask.

Before the crew dismantles the rings, I go in and collect every last rose petal from the dusty floor. Then I go to Shaw's car, knowing it will be empty since both he and Derrick have work to do before the jump to Arkansas.

The ammunition box sits on the lid of the trunk, empty; the gold-toned cartridges still lie scattered and shining on the floor. I tear off one of the box's end flaps, a yellow-and-red rectangle of thin cardboard.

Back in my room, the marker hovers above the piece of the ammo box, as I try to settle on one of the many lessons I learned last night from Boo. In the end, I choose to leave this scrap blank, to remind myself that there are some things that can't be, and perhaps need not be, put into words.

I place this in the jewelry box, climb into my double cot alone, and cry myself to sleep.

~

Arkansas, 1965

Our next stop is just outside Little Rock. We do three shows in two days and James stays in his car for all of them.

After the second show, I knock on his door.

"James?"

He doesn't answer right away. Then: "I'm okay."

"Can I come in?"

Another flash of silence, a fault line between us.

"James?"

"Just . . . I need a little more time, okay?" He is speaking from the other side of the door but it feels like he's sending smoke signals from the moon. "Can you just give me a little more time?"

"Sure. Of course." I swallow hard. "How much time?"

I wait, hoping for an answer, for another word through the door, another wisp of smoke.

But no word comes, so I turn and walk away.

~

Pennsylvania, 1965

In the Keystone State, I emerge as a star of the circus beyond any measure of doubt.

The resounding ovation bestowed upon me by the Allentown crowd fills the Big Top and shows no sign of stopping. For this reason I become the first ever VanDrexel's performer in the circus's illustrious history to return to the ring for an encore.

The next day, new posters are printed up in full color, featuring the "Vibrant Victoria" posed on the wire wearing a multicolored leotard fashioned from four hand-me-down costumes from a friend. Cornelius's off-the-cuff epithet—"dainty and death-defying, brave but beautiful"—is printed in a bold arc across the top.

I knock on James's door to show him.

This time he opens it. I hand him the rolled-up poster.

"Look!" I say, beaming at him. "I'm wearing Frankenstein."

He unrolls the glossy sheet, eyes the photo. He looks thin, pale. I doubt he's even seeing the poster at all.

I throw my arms around his neck. He lets me kiss his cheeks, his hair. Then he pulls back and I see the tightness around his mouth, the dark circles under his eyes.

I let go and he steps back into the car, gently closing the door.

I hate the thought of sleeping without him again tonight; I've discovered that waking up next to the boy you love is something you grow used to very quickly. The urgency I felt to devour him back in Oklahoma, back in Texas, was nothing compared to the need I'm feeling now, the need to not lose him.

But somewhere deep in the pit of my stomach, I'm starting to fear that I may already have.

~

Connecticut, 1965

In Bridgeport, before Vince and his crew even start laying out the tent poles, Cornelius suggests that he, the boys, and I go downtown together to walk in the footsteps of the "Prince of Humbugs." We'll stroll around town, he says, and perhaps even visit the building that was once called the Barnum Institute of Science and History and was constructed under the auspices of Mr. Phineas Taylor Barnum himself.

Gideon and I are happy to indulge the Ringmaster. Gus will drive and Hasty will come too, as will Myrtle, making ours a slightly motley and boisterous band of true believers, setting out on a short pilgrimage to one of the closest things the American circus has to a holy land.

After much prodding from Cornelius, James agrees to join us. He walks several steps behind the group as we make our way to the edge of the fairgrounds where Gus's pickup waits. Determined to keep the mood of this outing light, I run for the passenger door, crying out, "Shotgun!"

As soon as the phrase leaves my lips, I want to die, just drop dead right where I'm standing. Gideon freezes in his tracks. Myrtle and Hasty keep walking, pretending they didn't hear. Cornelius throws his shoulders back and waits.

I'm staring at James, whose face has gone pale. But then, that sweet, sweet mouth of his curls up ever so slightly and he laughs. Thank God, he laughs.

And there it is. The fog has lifted, the spell is broken. Quite by accident, I've wrestled his grief from him and turned it into something else, something bearable:

A memory.

As I climb into the pickup's front seat Cornelius leans close to me and whispers, "Well done, my girl. The show must go on. And now, it shall."

We enjoy our afternoon in the Park City, and when we arrive at the red-toned Byzantine building at 820 Main Street, we find that it is undergoing a remodel of sorts.

It is going to be reimagined into a museum where the legacy of the man who brought Earth its Greatest Show will be forever honored.

Again . . . *Memory.*

On the ride home, Myrtle recounts in somber tones the horrific Hartford circus fire of 1944. James and Gideon know the story, but this is the first I've ever heard of it, which is surprising because it occurred only two decades ago and remains one of the worst fire disasters in U.S. history. But despite that, or perhaps because of it, the circus goes on, because joy trumps tragedy every time. Loss is absorbed and stored in the heart, and the lights come up and the show goes on.

Myrtle finishes the story just as we pull back onto the lot, where the Big Top has bloomed in our absence. The circus has taken shape like some hardy perennial plant, some evergreen blossoming thing supported by the strongest and deepest of roots, bearing flowers that are as resilient as they are beautiful.

Which, I suppose, is exactly what the circus is.

That night, James joins Gideon and the tigers in the ring. After his act, just before mine, he slips into the tent—I know he's there without even looking down. This walk is for him, for James, and when it's over I am so eager to get to him that I don't even take the ladder, I simply drop from the wire and into the net. There is a shriek from the audience that spins into one great cheer when they realize the fall was on purpose.

Later, James and I shake Hank out of a sound sleep and badger and beg until we've talked him into rustling up a feast of cheeseburgers and french fries and leftover lamb stew and butterscotch pudding with whipped cream. I gobble it all down, putting away twice as much as James, which he finds in equal parts astonishing and adorable.

"I can't help it," I say, poking out my lower lip in a pout. "Applause just makes me feel . . ." I choose my word carefully and deliver it with a wink. "*Insatiable.*"

"Well, in that case . . ." James leans back in the booth, and with a silky half smile toying at the corner of his mouth, he begins a slow, steady clap. Applause.

We race back to my room and fall into bed, laughing and joking suggestively about "encores" and "standing ovations," which turn out not to be jokes at all.

The next morning I sleep in.

James is gone when I wake up, a good thing since last night's after-hours smorgasbord has me running to the bathroom to vomit.

~

New York, 1965

In Poughkeepsie, I have trouble zipping Frankenstein all the way up. It seems those late-night pie-car binges that have become our custom have finally caught up with me. I notice, while leaning close to my vanity mirror to apply the silver-blue eye shadow Sharon chose for me at Woolworth's, that my face looks fuller. And my breasts . . . well, let's just say Evangeline's yellow baton twirling dress wouldn't stand a chance.

I muse that it's love that's making me plump—the love of James, Cornelius, of everyone in this colorful talented family I was meant to be a part of. Before VanDrexel's, I was undernourished in that regard but now I'm feasting on helping after helping of kindness and camaraderie every single day. The roundness becomes me, slight as it is.

There is only one small dark cloud hanging over me and it's this:

In three weeks, we return to Boston.

The fine citizens of Albany turn out in droves for VanDrexel's Family Circus. Cornelius credits the posters of me wearing Frankenstein because from what he's heard they've come almost exclusively to see Victoria, the prettiest tightrope walker in the business.

I don't know if that's necessarily true, but on the chance that it is, I plan to reward them all with something new I began teaching myself back in Arkansas: a backward somersault while lying on the wire.

The clowns are in particularly good form, as are the jugglers and the trapeze aerialists, who spin and flip like sequined hurricanes across the tent.

When Cornelius announces me, the band plays my usual drumroll, and I pose on my ledge to raucous applause. Then the hush . . . there is always that hush, and it is in that hush that the magic begins.

With the whispers of the awed spectators swirling beneath me, like the rush of water at the base of Niagara Falls, I lower myself to a reclining position so that the wire is pressed against my backbone, like a shiver running up and down my spine. I curl one leg up to my chest, then use the strength of my legs and hips to roll backward into a somersault.

The world begins to swirl. Suddenly the Big Top ceiling is where the floor should be, and the bleachers seem to be leaping back and forth across my wire like it's some child-giant's jump rope. For a second, I think I'm falling.

But I'm not falling; I'm safe on the wire. Dizzy. That's all, just dizzy.

I rise from the crouch the somersault has left me in and invoke the power of my center of gravity—knees bent, arms out. The spectators are pleased, and this pleases me.

But I do nothing more. The crowd seems satisfied, so I call my own John Robinson, skipping the final three stunts of my routine and exiting the spotlight.

I've never been dizzy in the sky. Then again, I've never done a backward roll under the lights before, so maybe that's what my equilibrium is objecting to.

Or maybe . . .

As I climb down the ladder to shouts and whistles and thunderous applause, the dizziness subsides, only to be replaced by a flood of wonderment, panic, euphoria, terror, and joy.

I'm not dizzy. And I'm not plump.

I'm pregnant.

TWENTY-SEVEN

~

BAYLOR WAS A LONG way from VanDrexel in the alphabet, which meant that Callie was going to be late for homeroom.

Gliding into room 103 as though she were walking across a Big Top, she planted herself purposefully in front of Kristi's desk. Jacob, seated at the desk next to her, let out a low whistle. "Hot girl on a mission. This oughta be good."

"What do you want?" Kristi asked, refusing to look up from her Instagram feed, where Porthos had gotten more likes in the last twenty-four hours than Kristi herself had earned over the entire course of her social media history.

"I want you to give your father a message for me," Callie said.

"I'm not his secretary. She's the one who sits at the desk outside his office—which happens to be the biggest one in city hall. Even a circus freak can't miss it."

Callie grinned. "Tell your father the Sanctuary is important. The animals are important. They need to be taken care of, and studied, and protected. The fact that we can recognize this is what makes us human."

Kristi smirked. "Sure you don't want to hit pause till your violin player gets here? Sappy speeches like this are always so much better with a soundtrack."

"It may be sappy, but it's true."

"Fine. Anything else?"

"Yeah. Unfortunately, what I said about the chimp being able to kill someone was also true. But here's what I didn't get to say. That

251

particular ape, d'Artagnan, is a frightened creature, who, prior to being rescued by Mr. Marston, lived in a cage roughly the size of your Gucci backpack, where he was starved, neglected, and beaten every day of his life."

Jake's eyes went wide. "Beaten? Damn, that's fucked up."

Callie was vaguely aware that a crowd had gathered outside room 103, which meant that word of the Kristi versus Callie confrontation had spread like wildfire. Not a problem; Calliope VanDrexel was used to keeping her cool in front of an audience.

"My mother's been working with d'Artagnan every day, because that's what she's trained her whole life to do. But that kind of trauma's not the sort of thing that goes away overnight. So you see, Kristi, the reason we triple locked the gate, and refused to allow you or anyone else inside the conservatory, was because after a lifetime of horrific abuse, that sweet, innocent chimp, *my chimp*, just wasn't quite ready to put his trust in strangers, or to be gawped at by a crowd that still wasn't sure they wanted him as a neighbor. And he sure as hell wasn't ready to pose for a selfie."

"Don't you get that everything you just said basically proves exactly what my father's said all along," Kristi sneered. "The Sanctuary is dangerous."

"Actually—" It was Jenna, shouldering in through the knot of people clogging the doorway. "What she said proves that the Sanctuary is *safe*. Or didn't you hear the part about the locks on the gate, and the Instagram junkies not being allowed in?"

"Exactly," said Callie. "The Sanctuary is as safe as anything of its kind can possibly be. Not one hundred percent, because nothing ever is."

"And just to be clear," said Jenna, "we all respect your father for wanting to protect our town. Unless of course his motives for evicting the animals weren't entirely about safety and were actually about paving the way for that five-star resort that fell through. The one he surely would have been given the option to invest in, if the deal had been made."

Kristi glared.

"If the mayor wants to do away with everything in this town that doesn't come with an iron-clad guarantee of total safety," Callie went on calmly, "he's going to have a very long list. Starting with the croquet league—"

"Just ask Zach," said Jenna.

"And shop class," Jake added. "I almost broke my thumb three different times building Ponce de León's stupid boat."

"And all the liquor stores," Jenna added meaningfully. "And the gator gumbo cook-off, or have we forgotten about the Food Poisoning Debacle of 2012?"

"And the Surfing Conquistador Competition." *From the doorway. Kip.*

Kristi rolled her eyes, but this time she did not push back. Instead she just tossed her hair and said, "I'll give my father the message."

Then the homeroom teacher was shoving his way through the crowd and into the room. "Get to class, people," he commanded. "Bell's about to ring."

"Nicely done, Calliope," said Jenna, as they squeezed out with the spectators into the hall. "But you do realize that if it works you may have just saved your mother's job. Which means you probably won't be going back to VanDrexel's anytime soon."

"It really wasn't *her* job I was thinking about." Taking out her phone, Callie found one of the videos she'd searched for the night before, attached the link, and hit send. "I mean, it would be a shame if somebody like you couldn't afford to go to college."

Jenna ignored the dinging of her phone to fake a pissy look. "Somebody like me?"

"You know . . . preposterously gifted."

"Profoundly gifted, wiseass. But you know what I've always wondered? *After* something *pre*posterous happens, is that considered *post*posterous?"

"I think you're both pretty preposterous," said Kip.

"I've been called worse," Callie noted, attaching another link, causing Jenna's phone to ding again.

"Are you texting me right now?"

"Yes. And for the record, I think what would be truly preposterous would be you sleeping on that hospital couch another night. You're staying with us. I already cleared it with my mom, who's clearing it with your mom as we speak."

Jenna's phone pinged again. "I think you mean as we text."

"Whatever. You're moving in with us."

Jenna smiled, tapping on the link to the first video, and tilting the phone so Kip could watch too. It was a clip of a trapeze artist spinning through the air and being caught by his partner . . . only to slip from his grasp and drop into the net.

"Oooh," said Kip, "somebody didn't get paid that day."

Jenna swiped, and a second video appeared. She tapped the play arrow and another troupe of aerialists swung into action, two of them launching themselves across the Big Top, somersaulting toward their partners who were hanging from the trapeze bars by their knees; the catchers reached for the flyers' outstretched arms, but both missed the grab by mere inches. The tumblers fell out of the sky, again to land bouncing in the net.

"Interesting." Jenna looked up from the screen to quirk a brow at Callie. "'Trapeze artists failing miserably.' What are you trying to tell me?"

Callie just smiled and said nothing.

To her very pleasant surprise, Kip leaned over and brushed a kiss on her cheek just as the bell rang. Then he followed Jenna, who was still staring at her phone, perplexed, into room 105.

Callie began the long walk to room 127. On the way, her phone tingled.

SOMETHING TO DO WITH FRIENDSHIP??

YEP.

AND IN THIS SCENARIO I AM A TRAPEZE
ARTIST?

CORRECT.

AND I'M FALLING?

CORRECT.

SO THAT MAKES YOU THE ONE FAILING
TO CATCH ME?!

GUESS AGAIN.

As Callie slipped into Mr. Kurtz's homeroom, there was a brief
delay during which the borderline genius struggled to decipher the
meaning of the videos.

OKAY . . .

SO THERE'S THIS TRAPEZE ACT.
AND I'M THE FALLER, BUT YOU'RE NOT
THE CATCHER.

😳

DOESN'T MAKE SENSE!!!
THERE'S NOTHING ELSE YOU CAN BE.

ISN'T THERE?

OKAY. 😖

IF YOU'RE NOT THE FALLER AND YOU'RE
NOT THE CATCHER, WHO THE F#@%
ARE YOU?

Slipping into her seat in the back row of room 127, Callie
grinned and thumbed her reply:

I'M THE NET.

TWENTY-EIGHT

New York, 1965

I GO BACK TO my car to sit with this a bit, just me, by myself.

And of course, my baby.

I perch on the vanity stool with my hands on my belly, which is still mostly taut, but I can't stop myself from caressing it anyway. I think back to the night when James talked circus to me after we danced the Watusi at Husky Pete's. He wrote that he loved me on a cocktail napkin.

That was the night. *That was the night.*

I'm pregnant and in any other world, in Brooksvale certainly, this would be catastrophic news. I am sixteen, unwed, and I am carrying the child of my seventeen-year-old boyfriend. In school, at my father's country club, in deb circles—in all of those places I would be considered the worst kind of tramp. I would be shunned.

But this is the circus.

And here . . . it will all be different. This baby, this child of the lion tamer and the wire walker, is already a tiny miracle, made of miracles. He . . . or *she*—my God . . . *she!* The image of a soft, small girl with James's cupid's-bow lips and green eyes and my dark hair has my heart melting in my chest. *She* will have a father who can teach the deadliest of beasts to be gentle, and who runs toward adventure at every opportunity. She . . . or *he*—oh, how darling my and James's son would be! Funny, and sweet and smart. And brave . . . brave, because he'll have a mother who survived a tyrant's fists and found the courage to make the circus her home.

I change out of my costume, brush my hair, and put on the nicest of my hand-me-down blouses. Then I unlock the drawer of my jewelry box, take out my mother's brooch, and pin it just below the collar.

Outside, the midway is all bells and barkers and laughing teen-age girls and children awake long past their bedtimes. I smell sizzling funnel cakes and roasting peanuts. It is that first night all over again; everything feels new and dusted with magic.

I find James coming out of Cornelius's office car.

"Hi." I press myself into his arms.

"I was just coming to find you." He kisses the top of my head.

"I was coming to find you! I have something wonderful to tell—" I pause at the sight of two men wearing business suits coming out of the office after him. They are carrying briefcases and look-ing . . . victorious. "Who are they?"

He pushes me away gently, holding me at arm's length. "My father's sold the circus."

I blink up at him. "He . . . what? James, is this another Baby Bongo joke? Because—"

"Not a joke." His face is tight with anger, maybe even shock. "We all knew the money was tight, but Cornelius and Gideon never let on how bad it really was. Not even to me." He gives a dark chuckle. "Especially not to me. I guess because they knew I would never have let them sell."

I frown down at my Keds, thinking back to all the times I'd seen Cornelius toting his ledger around, looking through the pages with a pained expression. "Maybe they just didn't want to upset you. You were so upset about Boo."

"Or maybe they just thought what they've always thought—that the only thing I was good for was squiring brainless mayors' daughters around. The point is, we were going broke and I barely had a clue."

"But what about Allentown? And Poughkeepsie? We've been playing to packed houses for weeks. And here, in Albany . . . we've been selling scads of tickets. Loads of them."

James shakes his head. "Wasn't enough. The only good news is that the corporation that bought us out made Cornelius a very fair offer and they agreed to keep him on as Ringmaster. He can stay as long as he wants. Same goes for everyone else, every clown, every acrobat, every roustabout."

I open my mouth but realize I have nothing to say. All I can picture is that old handbill in Cornelius's office. *VanDrexel's Family Circus: Three Rings of Fantastical Fun.* What would Oskar say, and Lukasz? I think of the little boy who set up the rings, believing they were infinite.

"Oh . . ." James drags his hand through his hair and sighs. "And we get to keep our name."

A kind of enchantment.

"How?"

"I fought for it. You should have seen Gideon, looking daggers at me, trying to get me to shut my mouth. But I said if we couldn't keep VanDrexel's on the marquee, Cornelius wouldn't sign and there wouldn't be a deal. The corporate vultures weren't crazy about it, but I stood my ground until they agreed."

My fingertips go to my abdomen as I picture the moment— James in his VanDrexel's T-shirt challenging those men in their expensive suits, fighting for his name, for his father's legacy, with Gideon glowering all the while, wanting him gone.

"Cornelius must have been proud of you," I say, my voice wobbly.

"Yeah." He smiles, but it's bittersweet. "I think that's why he's letting me go."

"Go?" My breath catches in my throat.

"He's letting me go overseas. To Europe." James grasps my hands and brings them to his lips to kiss. "I think he finally saw that

I've got something to contribute besides my damned charm. He wants me to go do what I've been talking about all these years . . . visit the European shows to study with the masters. He's giving Gid and me each a third of the buyout money. We would have inherited it anyway, and now I can afford to make the trip."

"The trip?" I echo, dully, stupidly.

"To Rome, Madrid, Nice."

Even though I have only the flash of the midway lights by which to gauge his expression, I can see that the hurt and anger are already subsiding and his eyes are twinkling.

"Everywhere there's a circus, that's where I'll be."

"That sounds . . . very exciting."

He brushes a wisp of hair out of my eyes. "I'll only be gone for a couple of months," he whispers, sensing my change of mood. "Three at the most. And God, Victoria, I'm gonna miss you so much, but—"

"I know," I whisper back. And I *do* know. I felt the same way in Austin, when I decided to come back to this dream I didn't even know I had. It was less a choice than it was a need, and his need, his dream, is to go off and collect the dust of those European circuses onto the soles of his buffalo sandals, and bring it back here to mingle magically with the soil of every small town and city VanDrexel's has the privilege to play. My dream was to stay; his is to go, and if the tightrope has taught me anything, it's that the world is always a study in balance.

"What's wrong?" he asks.

I swallow hard. "It's just, well, what if the thing Cornelius has always been afraid of is true and you *are* like your mother? What if you decide not to come back?"

"That won't happen," he whispers into my hair. "I swear it. You know why?"

"Why?"

"Because you're here."

With your unborn child growing inside me, I think, and it takes incredible effort not to say it out loud. Instead, I wrap my arms around his waist and pull him close while I still can.

"My father has connections with every decent circus on the continent, so he'll make all the introductions. Victoria, I'll be working with the best Europe has to offer. It's amazing, right?"

I nod against his chest. It's not quite as amazing as *my* news of course, which would change everything were I to blurt it out right now.

After all, he deserves to know.

Doesn't he?

As much as Europe means to him, all I have to do is tell him I'm pregnant, and he'll stay. Because James VanDrexel, who huddled beside a dying lion, would not miss one second of becoming a father. He simply wouldn't go. Not for three months, not for three hours. He'd stay with me, with *us,* the us we're on our way to being.

"James, are you sure this is a good idea?"

He looks at me as if I've lost my mind. "You're kidding, right?"

I manage a smile. "I'm sorry. I know this is what you want."

What you need. He's just lost his circus, the circus he was born into; I imagine it's like losing a family member, a hundred family members. And there are still nights when he cries out in his sleep, calling for his lion. Watching Cornelius sign those papers must have been like hearing that gunshot ring out all over again.

So if Europe is what he wants, I won't deny him. It's time for James to become James. Just as Catherine—who would have been terrified to see him go—became Victoria . . . who, perhaps more than anyone, understands the power of freedom.

And of dreams.

But none of that stops me from feeling crushed at the thought of seeing him go. The tears well up behind my eyes, but I don't let them fall.

"So what were you going to tell me?"

I shake myself out of my reverie. "Hmm?"

"What you were going to tell me?" His chin is resting on the top of my head, his fingers are caressing the small of my back.

Stay.

No.

Go.

"Before I told you about the sale," he reminds me. "You said you had something important—"

"Wonderful," I murmur. "I said wonderful."

"Even better. So what is it?"

My throat aches with the words I can't say: *A promise infused with fate. A baby; our baby.* Instead, I brush my fingers over my still-quiet belly on their way up to cup the brooch at my collar. "I was . . . I was just going to tell you that . . . um, well, I found this pin I'd thought I'd lost. Val found it, actually, when she was packing, and I'm just . . . I'm just so glad to have it back."

"Okay." He cocks an eyebrow. Maybe he doesn't believe me, but he doesn't pursue it. I almost wish he would.

Looking down at the ground, I ask, "When are you leaving?"

"Tomorrow," he says, pressing a kiss to my forehead. "It'll be easiest to just fly out from New York City."

"Sure, of course, since it's just a few hours' drive to Idlewild from here."

He laughs, pushing a wisp of hair behind my ear. "It's JFK now. They changed it, remember?"

"Oh. Right." I shake my head. "I forgot."

Leaning my cheek into his chest, I listen to his heart. I wonder if he feels how madly mine is racing, imagining him *en France*, chasing down all those *fantaisistes* and *dompteurs* and *funambules*.

"I want you to enjoy every minute of this adventure," I tell him.

He is sweet enough not to say, "I will." Instead he whispers, "I'll miss you."

And the secret remains a secret. For now. My pregnancy will become apparent soon enough, and although James will be taming lions in Siena, or Toledo, or Prague when it does, I can take comfort in the fact that I will be here at VanDrexel's (still VanDrexel's, always VanDrexel's, thanks to James) with the family I've chosen for myself.

Or perhaps they've chosen me.

I suppose, like all good and lasting things, it's been a little of both.

And when James does come home, we'll be another kind of family. A family within a family, but a family of our own.

And it will be wonderful.

The morning after Cornelius signs away the circus, James goes down to the Western Union office in Albany to wire Hadrien Archambeau, *Monsieur Loyal* of a small but accomplished circus, presently situated in Toulouse but planning an early autumn jump to Paris.

Gideon, with his eyes unreadable, sees to the task of purchasing his brother's airline ticket. Cornelius, groggy from a difficult night spent with his trusty flask but looking as immaculately suave as ever, wraps his son in his arms, blesses him softly, and wishes him well. Then he retreats to his office and pretends to be busy.

I put all my faith in my center of gravity and offer to help the father of my unborn child pack for his journey. He reminds me repeatedly that he will miss me like crazy, but he is also excited. So excited. He is standing on the precipice of his dream, and the happiness that spills over from his heart finds its way to mine. I will be seeing him soon enough—and then I'll tell him everything, and we'll start again, except this time, we'll already be in love.

"Three months" is how he says goodbye through the open window of the taxicab that will deliver him from the Big Top in Albany to the airport in Queens.

And then he is gone and I am rushing back to my car to prepare for the night's performance. James is gone, but still the calliope sings and whistles and sighs in his wake, and the barker in his straw hat cries out what my friend Sharon once described as the most seductive words in the English language:

"Step right up . . . *the circus is in town!*"

TWENTY-NINE

~

BRAD MARSTON WAS NOTHING if not a gracious host. When he heard that Quinn and Callie would be entertaining the Sanctuary ambassador as their houseguest for the foreseeable future, he purchased a second queen bed with a wicker headboard, paid extra for one-day delivery, and had it set up in Callie's room.

"What is it with Florida people and wicker?" Callie mused, helping Jenna with the fitted sheet.

"It goes great with the gator gumbo," Jenna replied with a perfectly straight face.

"Which I still have no desire to taste. Although, think about this: if I'd ordered takeout from Gumbo Hut that night instead of Benigno's Pizza, you never would've had the chance to force your way into the Sanctuary—and consequently my life—and we wouldn't be here right now."

Jenna paused in making the bed. "Yeah. About that. There's something I feel like I should tell you."

"Lemme guess: you've got great hair?"

Jenna took the folded flat sheet Quinn had left on the dresser and shook it out. "Seriously, Calliope. I need you to know that there were actually two reasons I was so anxious for us to be friends."

"Okay."

"One is that it was pretty obvious the day I delivered the pizza that you had landed in unfamiliar territory. And I guess because I already had so much experience with taking care of people, thanks to the fact that I am what we in the business refer to as the child of an alcoholic, I just sort of defaulted into compassionate caregiver mode and decided to take you under my wing."

"Show me the ropes," said Callie, wriggling one of the new bed pillows into its case.

"Plus you looked like you could be a fun person to hang with, and of course, you had your own lion. So there was that."

"There was that," Callie echoed, handing over the other pillowcase.

"But it wasn't all a completely selfless gesture on my part." Jenna paused, smushing the pillow into place. "See, I'd kind of become a solo act myself."

"What do you mean?"

"Well, I quit hanging out with my friends, and I stopped inviting people over because the house always smelled of either booze or barf. And since everybody felt like they had to walk on eggshells when I was around, it made me a total buzzkill."

When Callie quirked an eyebrow, Jenna laughed.

"Okay, given the context I suppose that was an entirely insensitive metaphor. The point is, I just couldn't take the way they were always looking at me with these worried looks, these concerned faces."

"Wow. Friends who cared. That hadda suck."

"It didn't suck. But it was like, to them, I wasn't just Jenna anymore—I was Jenna with the alcoholic mother. But then you showed up and you didn't know any of that shit and I guess I saw my opportunity to just be Jenna Demming again. Didn't work, of course, since I'm now the child of an alcoholic who is living in your garage apartment."

"Carriage house," said Callie.

In response, Jenna flung the pillow at Callie's head.

As she ducked out of the projectile's path, Callie's elbow bumped into Victoria's empty jewelry box, knocking it to the floor where it landed open, on its side. There was a metallic clink as a miniature key fell out from the satiny depths of the chest.

Callie and Jenna looked at each other, then simultaneously dove for the key.

"How did we miss this?" said Jenna, plucking it from the floor.

"I guess it was buried in all that ruching," said Callie, righting the box.

Jenna offered her the key, then, just as quickly, yanked her hand back.

"I swear, Jenna, if you say 'psych' right now—"

"What am I, nine? I wasn't going to say 'psych.' It's just, before we open this ugly little blue vinyl drawer, I have one more tiny little confession."

Picking up her phone from the bed, Jenna tickled the touch-screen until she'd opened a website. A beautiful website.

Callie's website. The homepage featured several stunning photos, all from Victoria's album, most of them taken when Callie was mid-trick on the tightrope, but there were some of her with Victoria, and even one candid of Callie with Quinn. There was also a shot of her wearing her first costume, the purple-and-pink ruffled nightmare.

"I can take that one down if you want," Jenna offered.

"Don't you dare" was Callie's reply. "But you told me you never got around to making this."

"I lied," said Jenna, her voice catching.

"Why?"

"You have to ask?"

No. She didn't. A month ago, perhaps she would have. But now Callie understood what it meant not only to have a friend, but to need one. As difficult and prickly as Callie had been since the day they met, Jenna still didn't want her to go.

"Just remember," said Jenna, "I'm gonna want front-row tickets whenever your circus comes to town."

"Of course," said Callie. She hadn't meant it to come out in a whisper, but it did.

Clearing her throat, Jenna pointed to the site's navigation bar—which she'd somehow managed to make resemble an actual tightrope. "Okay, so here's the link to your videos, and this"—Jenna tapped her finger on an email icon—"is where you get your mail."

"Mail? I have mail?"

"Yeah, Meg Ryan, you've got mail."

"But how is that possible?"

"Callie, don't you know me by now? I was hired—or, more accurately, indentured—to do a job. So I did it. I've been sending queries and resumes to every circus in the western hemisphere."

"But you were so busy with the open house. And your mom."

"What can I say, I'm a hell of a multitasker. And look." Jenna opened the first email in Callie's inbox. "These guys are definitely interested in meeting you." She tapped again. "And so are these guys, and so is this French circus—can you say *oh là là*—and this show, which I think could be a good fit for you, except it's out of Washington State, so I hope you don't mind the rain." She shrugged. "You told me you were a star. Obviously, you were right."

Callie stared at the phone she was clutching. It was like she was holding every dream she'd ever had in the palm of her hand. "That's a lot of job offers," she said.

"Sure is. So I guess after we open this ugly little blue drawer you're going to want to start going through them, huh?"

"Not necessarily." Callie grinned and tossed the phone back onto the bed. "I'm no expert but I'm thinking a quick Delete All should take care of it."

"You mean—" Jenna swallowed hard and brushed a tear from her cheek. "Oh. Okay. Cool."

"Now gimme that key."

With her heart racing, Callie slipped it into the lock. Taking hold of the glass knob, she slid the drawer open and blinked at what she saw inside.

A brooch, encrusted with diamonds, rubies, sapphires, pearls.

"Holy shit," Jenna murmured.

But there was something else. An envelope, slightly yellow, but smooth, unwrinkled.

Unopened.

Callie removed it and read the inscription on the front. Then she smiled at Jenna, who smiled too.

"Hey, Mom? Can you come in here a sec?"

Quinn brushed into the doorway, an expectant look on her face. "Need more pillows?"

Shaking her head, Callie held up the envelope so that her mother could read the name written across the front in Victoria's elegant handwriting. *To Quinn.*

Quinn's hand flew upward to cover her mouth, but a breathy "Oh!" escaped anyway, and her eyes welled with tears as Callie slipped the letter into her mother's hand.

When Quinn opened it, a goldish slip of paper—a telegram—that had been tucked in along with a letter slipped out and fell to the floor.

Callie picked it up, not in the least bit surprised to find that Victoria had written yet another lesson in marker across the back of it: *The Show Must Go On.*

She placed this in her mother's hand, kissed her gently on the cheek, and asked softly, "Shall I go and put the kettle on?"

"Yes," Quinn whispered, her eyes fixed on the telegram. "Go, Calliope."

THIRTY

Massachusetts, 1965

THE TRAIN ROLLS INTO Boston during the pre-daylight hours of a Tuesday morning.

I am wide awake, peeking through my window as the roustabouts disembark. They fan out in waves of denim and muscle to start and finish in mere hours what it took God six whole days to create—an entire world.

As I watch my circus spring to life, Rabelais trumpets as though to summon the sun, and it obeys him. I can picture the way the suburban Boston light will be falling across the kitchen table at the house I grew up in.

Six months I've been gone.

Six months ago, Cornelius and I struck our silent bargain. *Everything will eventually come full circle.*

If the Ringmaster has any concerns about me being back in the hometown from which I fled, he has not expressed them to me. Then again, he's been preoccupied with transitioning the circus from something old and personal to something new and corporate, and of course, his heart is heavy with missing James.

We all miss James. Scruff and Prince Edward and Clementine feel his absence as acutely as they feel Boo's. I've talked myself into believing that the child inside me misses him too, and the fact that I can't tell anyone about it—not before I tell James—has begun to take its toll.

I need to share this with someone. Sharing is a kind of safety net, after all, and I'm in an emotional freefall.

Luckily, there happens to be a safety net nearby.

At nine o'clock, as though everything is perfectly normal, I go have breakfast in the pie car with Duncan.

"Any word from James?" he asks me, slathering a piece of rye toast with marmalade.

"He sent one postcard from Toulouse," I report. "And a letter came just yesterday, from Paris."

"How's the show?"

"The show is exceptional. One of the best, he says. But he's not getting on well with the cat trainers. He caught one of them beating a lioness and . . . well, let's just say he and James had words."

Duncan somehow manages to frown and laugh at the same time. "That sounds like James. No question he'd get rough with a guy over that. I mean, Christ, what kind of bastard beats an animal?"

He's quiet for a minute, and as I sip my orange juice, I wonder if he remembers that this is where we met six months ago, same town, same fairgrounds, same table in fact.

"One time," says Duncan, sipping his coffee, "when the boys were real young—Gideon was about ten, so James couldn't have been more than seven—there was a group of teenage boys came to the midway just to cause trouble. Started out harmless, stealing candy, hassling the barkers, just being disruptive and crass." He pauses to take a bite of toast. "And then they got to the menagerie."

The spoonful of oatmeal I'm about to put in my mouth stops midflight. I don't think I like where this is going.

"At the time, we had an old camel, Virgil, funniest-lookin' thing you'd ever wanna see, but sweet. And we all loved him, but I'm sure I don't have to tell you who loved him most."

"James."

Duncan nods. "So these rowdy punks come upon old Virgil in his pen, and they start shoutin' nasty things at him, laughin' and calling him an 'ugly-ass bastard'—pardon my French. Then one of the punks scoops up a rock and just chucks it at poor old Virgil, *smack*! Right between those big, gentle eyes."

My stomach clenches, turns to ice.

"The next punk picks up another rock and hurls it at the camel's chest. And if you've never witnessed a camel crying out in pain, I'm here to tell you, it's a sound you don't ever want to hear. It's a sound that'll break your heart."

Around us, the pie car has gone quiet. The silverware has ceased clinking; all conversation has ground to a halt. Everyone wants to hear the story, even though they don't. Not me, or Evangeline or little Arthur, who are all hearing it for the first time, or Hank or Gus or Vince the gaffer, who were there when it happened.

But it's a story of our circus, so we have to know. And Duncan goes on:

"The punks were gettin' a real kick out of Virgil's pain, and when Cornelius hears tell of it he comes running, strutting like nobody's business, ready to throw their sorry asses right out of his circus. But then, outta nowhere, comes this little human *missile*, this seven-year-old rocket, hurling himself at the punk who cast the first stone."

"James," I say again.

"The punk goes down, and James throws himself on top of him, pummeling him, fist after fist, punch after punch, this little pipsqueak just pounding away on a guy three times his size. And for a minute, the guy doesn't fight back—I figure he was in shock, and who wouldn't be, by the sight of that little bitta nothin' sitting on his chest, sluggin' him in the face like a miniature Jake LaMotta. We were all stunned. Me, Cornelius, Vince." He turns to Vince for validation. "Remember, Vince? Remember how we all just stood there, stunned?"

Vince gives a slow nod and says, "I remember."

"But the shock didn't last long and the next thing we knew the guy had pulled out a switchblade. He pulled a *switchblade* on a seven-year-old kid! Course, I didn't see it right off, neither did Cornelius.

But Gideon saw it . . . *Gideon!*—ten years old, jumps in to pull his brother away, at the very same second the punk lashes out with the knife, catching Gideon in his forearm, and suddenly there's blood everywhere."

"Blood," Hank repeats dully. "Everywhere."

I remember the scar on Gideon's arm . . . the one I noticed the day he opened the door to the wardrobe car for me.

"By this point, the roustabouts had been sent for and they all come a-runnin', grabbin' hold of every last one of those punks, and haulin' 'em off the grounds to . . . well, truth be told, I don't really know where our guys took them rowdy little sons a bitches, or what they did to 'em. But whatever it was, they sure as hell had it comin'."

"Sure as hell had it comin'," Vince echoes.

And Hank agrees. "Had it comin'."

"Anyhow." Duncan leans back against the booth and lifts his coffee cup for another sip. "All's I'm sayin' is that this French lion tamer son of a bitch just better think twice before he goes beatin' on some poor lion again. At least while James VanDrexel's around."

I take a taxi to the lovely affluent neighborhood that is technically still my neighborhood, though I have not set foot here in six months. It is a back-to-school morning that makes me think of new shoes and freshly sharpened pencils. The day is clear with a fall crispness that people typically call exhilarating, but to me, today, it just feels cold. The houses are quiet because the women are out doing Tuesday morning things . . . hair appointments, charity work, tennis lessons, bridge.

The men, of course, are at work.

In a million years I never would have thought I would do what I am about to do. But she is so close. Too close. And I am missing the boy I love, and there is no one else I can tell my wondrous secret to.

Just speaking the words to her will make up for not having said them to James.

I will go to the cemetery on Brooksvale Avenue to give my mother this last gift of letting her be the first to know that I am safe, and happy, and carrying James's child.

It's a risk, of course. Brooksvale is a small, gossipy place and if anyone were to catch sight of me . . .

But I've become very good at taking risks—when they're for the right reasons.

The cabbie drops me on the corner, where the tidy, picturesque little cemetery sits. It is as exclusive as the rest of this town; only the remains of the well-to-do are welcome.

I am wearing the sunglasses I bought at Woolworth's, and I've wrapped the pretty, faux-silk kerchief à la Grace Kelly over my hair to prevent the neighbors—or more likely, their domestics—from recognizing me. As I make my way toward the filigree iron gate, I see the Gleasons' maid, Clothilde, shaking a bath mat over the side of the front porch. Twilly, the Mancusos' gardener, is raking the first drizzle of leaves into a pile. We have not had a domestic in our house since the abrupt departure of my jitterbugging namesake nearly ten years ago.

As I unlatch the gate and slip onto hallowed ground, I hear the Murphy family's screen door creak open. Lucy, the housekeeper, comes thumping down the kitchen steps with a basket of laundry for the line. She doesn't see me; she's preoccupied with making sure the sheets don't drag in the grass.

I make my way along the winding path, reading the blue-blooded names etched into the tombstones until I find my mother's. The stone is lovely, the engraving impeccable: *Meredith Quinn Hastings. Devoted Wife and Mother. 1932–1965.*

As epitaphs go, it falls horribly short. They left out *Victim, Captive, Hero.*

Lowering my scarf, I push the cheap sunglasses upward into my hair.

"Hello, Mom," I say, surprised to hear that my voice is clear, as clear as the fall sky billowing overhead. "You were right about the circus." A tiny explosion of joy rises up from my heart when I add, "I'm pregnant."

I reach out to run my fingertip along the smooth stone of her memorial, which is warm from the sun, and suddenly I'm talking a mile a minute—about Sharon and Cornelius and poor Boo, asking if perhaps the lion is there with her in heaven, then feeling silly about it, then not silly at all. I describe how it feels to dance on a wire stories above an astonished crowd, and I tell her how the world looks rushing past outside the window of a speeding train.

My stomach swirls when I tell her about James, things I think I might have been embarrassed to tell her when she was alive, but which I need to tell her now—like what a sweet and gentle kisser he is, and how his muscles feel against me when we're sleeping. I choke up when I tell her how much I miss him, now that he is away. "In Paris!" I cry out. "Remember how much we loved Paris?" And then I'm laughing and crying at the same time, recalling a zillion little things I'd thought I'd forgotten about that trip—the handsome waiter who brought her a rose every morning with her café au lait, infuriating the other society ladies in our hotel; my first bottle of Chanel N°5, which she secretly bought for me even after my father forbade it, and which I spilled in my suitcase when I was trying to hide it from him. More memories present themselves, memories of our mad dash to Maine where we ate nothing but lobster for three days straight, and the first cotillion dress I tried on, which made me look as if I'd been swallowed by a wedding cake, and the second one, which made us both weep for how beautiful it was and how beautiful I looked in it, and because we knew that the sleeves would hide any bruises I might incur in the days leading up to the coming-out ball.

When a wind rustles through the trees lining the outer edge of the cemetery, I tell myself she's laughing and crying, too.

Mothers and daughters.

I am so engrossed in my reminiscing that I don't immediately notice the noise.

It's not a big noise, not a circus type of noise, just the small ordinary sound of footsteps on a stone walk.

I glance over my shoulder, instinctively re-donning my scarf and sunglasses. A disheveled figure is shambling in my direction. I peer at him, this elderly, grieving widower, through the green-black plastic of the lenses, and I feel a tug of sympathy. But it doesn't last.

No, it can't be.

This is impossible. It's a Tuesday for God's sake, a business day, and he is a businessman.

I can't breathe. Just seeing him has me on the verge of suffocating. I know I should run before he spots me, but he is on the only path to the exit. I could skitter my escape through the maze of tombstones, but even with the terror prickling at the back of my neck, I just can't bring myself to tread on the grass, knowing what—who— lies beneath it.

He draws steadily closer, his eyes fixed on the brick pavers of the walkway. I, on the other hand, am struck motionless, like one of the life-size granite angels adorning some of the more extravagant gravestones.

When my father finally looks up, his mouth immediately drops open and his brows arc upward. It is a cartoon expression, yet perfectly appropriate to this most uncomical of moments. For a long time, he just stares at me, confused. Disoriented. It is as if he is asking himself, *What in the world is Catherine doing here in the cemetery on the one Tuesday morning of my life that I've decided not to go to work?*

I, too, am trying to process the situation. A few months ago I hid in a trailer full of elephant shit just to keep from being dragged back to this man, and now here I am standing mere yards away from him while he blinks at me across my mother's final resting place, as if I'm part of some nightmare he can't stop having.

Then a thought floats into my mind as clearly as an autumn leaf: *The minute he snaps out of his daze, he's going to kill me.*

I spring onto the path, my white Keds scuffing the paving stones as I bolt past him. Had he been slightly less bewildered, he probably would have stretched out his leg to trip me, just as he's done a hundred—a *thousand*—times before. But he doesn't, and I run, heading for the iron gate.

"Stop, Catherine!"

My heart slams on the sound of my father's voice, because for once it is not a shout or a growl; rather it's a rasp, a croak. A plea.

"Catherine, please . . . *stop*."

Unwillingly, I stumble to a halt. Part of me knows I should keep running, but I have never heard weakness in his voice before, and I am both shocked and intrigued by it. I turn back slowly, and see that his eyes are less steely than I remember. His skin is paler and his shoulders are not his shoulders at all. They are hunched, so deeply hunched, as though his center of gravity has abandoned him.

Suddenly I can think only of the child curled inside me, whose tiny heart, just by beating, connects me to James, to the circus, to everything I love. It is as if my baby is reminding me of something James said on the night we became its parents.

When in the lion's cage . . .

Show.

No.

Fear.

So I stand straighter and meet his gaze. "What do you want?"

He opens his mouth. He closes it. He turns up his hands and shakes his head. "I just . . ." He sighs heavily, as though he's expelling his entire soul into the cool September air. "Catherine, I'm just so . . ." He shakes his head and lowers his face into his hands.

I back up a step on the chance that this is some cruel trick. "You're just so *what*?" I demand.

And when his shoulders begin to shake, I sway on my feet. *He's crying*.

My father is crying. I swear I can feel the earth tilting further on its axis.

As I gape at him, it slowly begins to register how loosely his suit hangs on him, as though he's borrowed it from someone taller, stronger. His hair, which was always perfectly combed and oiled, is in desperate need of a trim.

With a jolt I realize that the man I thought my father was— the man *he* thought he was—no longer exists because he *can't* exist without my mother. As dark and powerful a presence as he was in our home, it was always her job to ensure that he'd shine brightly outside of it. It was she who oversaw his wardrobe, who kept tabs on his grooming. Even when the illness was nearly all that there was of her, my mother still managed to curate his precious Davis Hastings–ness by choosing the right barber, the best shoe polish, the appropriate lapels. And before that, it was she who orchestrated their enviable social life, cultivating a stunning circle of friends to host at lavish sit-down dinners or smart cocktail parties where she would deftly, un-failingly find ways to steer the conversation toward topics on which he could speak with the most confidence and authority. Not because she took any pleasure in helping him feel important, but because if she didn't, she would be made to pay.

As a child, I would creep out of bed and watch these parties from the stairs, peering over the handrail in my pink flannel night-gown. Perhaps, on some level that was distinctly female, I understood that Meredith Quinn Hastings was the best thing a woman in her world could be—a proper wife, the woman behind the man ... when she wasn't the woman cowering at the feet of the man, that is.

And *that* was why he hated her. Because *he* knew that *she* knew how very much he needed her. And I suppose, by extension, it was why he hated *me* as well: because he feared one day I would know it too.

Well, *this* is that day! This day, when I've unintentionally ambushed him in a quiet cemetery on a Tuesday morning, only to catch him with his suit wrinkled and his shoes unpolished. No tie clip, no haircut. Not even his trademark pocket square.

Nothing.

For all his physical might, for all his money, status, and power, that is exactly what he's always been—nothing. Without *us* to be bigger than, meaner than, in charge of, he's shrunk down to something even less than nothing. We left him alone with that bottomless hatred and all that need, but no one to use it on—no faces to slap, no spirits to trounce—and in the wake of losing whatever it was about hurting us that he loved so much, he cannot even bring himself to visit the barbershop.

We've won, I think. *By dying, by leaving . . . we've won.*

Sadly, I can't imagine a more hollow victory.

"I'm so—" He grips his face with his hands and wails, "*Sorry.*" The word comes wet and muffled through the spaces between his fingers. He is speaking in a foreign tongue—a language of apology and tears that does not come naturally to him. I almost don't understand it at first. And when I do, I feel sick to my stomach. I could gag on his remorse, his contrition. In truth, I don't actually believe he means it. And even if he did, he couldn't possibly be sorry *enough*.

"Forgive me, Catherine," he pleads.

I glare at him so long that the shadows thrown by the gravestones actually shift. Then I hear myself say this: "I forgive you."

He looks up from his hands. I hate that my eyes are his eyes. Worse, I hate that my mother isn't here to witness this moment.

Or maybe she is.

"I forgive you," I repeat. "But not for you. And not for me. I'm neither strong enough nor good nor merciful enough for that." I bend a smirk at him. "I suppose, in that regard, I take after you."

He flinches, and I know the insult has hit its mark.

"But I can forgive you for *her*," I tell him. "That's the best I can do."

"So . . . you'll come home." Not a question.

Never.

"Catherine?"

I shake my head, rejecting the name as well as the request. "I've found a new home, where I have a family—a real family—who will do whatever it takes to protect me." I pause to unravel my scarf, freeing my hair, which glints in the sunshine. "On the chance that anyone should try to come between us," I add pointedly.

I can tell by the way he crumples deeper into his slouch that he knows exactly what I mean. Automatically, his trembling fingers move to his breast pocket in search of the silk handkerchief that isn't there. Despite my indifference, it's hard to watch.

So I turn to leave, but on a hunch, I turn back. "When you realized I was gone, after that newspaper article, exactly how long and how hard did you look for me?"

His answer is the scarlet flush of shame that colors his pale cheeks.

It would be funny if it weren't so completely appalling; I spent the last six months hiding from someone who wasn't even trying to find me. I take a deep breath, walk toward him, and lean close. To anyone who happens to be watching, I imagine I look like an ordinary daughter giving her ordinary father a kiss goodbye.

But there is no kiss, no embrace, no sense of connection at all, just a useful piece of information, delivered in a whisper, partially out of respect to my mother's sense of what the world told her was her duty, but mostly out of good old-fashioned pity.

"She kept the pocket squares in the top drawer of the dressing room armoire."

If he remembers me for anything, I hope it will be for that.

And then I do something that would have been unthinkably reckless when I lived under his roof.

I turn my back on him, on the wild animal that was once my father, and I walk away.

And for the first time, I am not afraid.

The cab drops me at the fairgrounds.

As I make my way across the grass, I sense a strangeness, a quiet that is quieter even than Brooksvale, but it's a darker kind of quiet.

The roustabouts move slowly, which is something they never do, and their heads are bent. There are dancers huddled in a small knot; there are tears—the dancers are crying. Clowns in half makeup and incomplete costumes stand around with their arms at their sides. No juggling clubs, no unicycles, no laughter.

"What's wrong?" I ask Hopscotch. Her white face paint is streaked with tears and the effect gives me gooseflesh. She is holding Arthur, who is weeping soundlessly in her arms. "What happened?"

She can't speak, or won't speak—she just shakes her head at me.

The Ringmaster. Where is the Ringmaster? My chest goes hollow and electric, pulsing with waves of panic. I walk on, and grab hold of Rick, who is pale and mopping his face with a handkerchief.

"Is he all right? Is Cornelius all right?"

Rick, too, merely shakes his head.

Cornelius. Oh, God. Cornelius . . .

I run for the Big Top, and see a small crowd at the entrance. Vince is there, and Hank. Myrtle is doubled over at the waist, sobbing, and Duncan looks small and lost and angry. Gideon is there, crouched beside a folding chair that someone has pulled up . . . for Cornelius.

Cornelius is sitting in the chair, and at first I am relieved that he is here, but as I get closer I can see that something is very wrong.

Has he had a bad spell of some sort, a heart attack, maybe? He is slumped in the chair with his chin on his chest. I can't suppress the flash of an image, a recent one: my father slumped on the cemetery path, beaten. And while I shudder to compare that father to this one, there is no way to deny that Cornelius looks beaten, too. His face is not ruddy with excitement, with magic. And his velvet coat is uneven, bunched up on one shoulder and sliding off the other. His tie has been loosened.

And his hat . . .

His *hat*!

Is on the ground. In the dirt.

As if the silky emptiness of it was suddenly too heavy for his head to hold, so there it lies, abandoned in the dust.

Gideon looks up and sees me standing there.

My eyes ask, *What is it? A stroke? Another animal lost to a bullet?* It can't be money. Cornelius solved the problem of the money.

So it isn't money.

It's worse. Much worse. Unfixable, whatever it is.

The baby inside me says, *Mama, be strong*, and I open my hand to accept the thing that Gideon is now holding out to me. It is an oddly sized piece of paper, not quite square, and it is a yellowish golden color, the color of lions.

Across the upper margin are the words WESTERN UNION TELEGRAM, and it's dated September 23, 1965.

And as I read the message printed on it, something inside me— *everything* inside me—shatters.

THIRTY-ONE

~

CALLIE HAD A FLEETING moment of cold feet right before selling the brooch. It was a family heirloom, after all. But like the lesson Victoria had written on the cotton candy cone, this pin had a job to do.

She knew from the letter that Meredith's whole purpose for giving it to *Catherine* (Catherine! she still couldn't quite wrap her mind around that) over half a century ago was to fund a new life for her daughter, and Callie decided that such a generous impulse should not go unrealized a moment longer. She would use her great-grandmother's gift of the Cartier brooch to do the most possible and most immediate good.

Along with her letter to her daughter, Victoria had enclosed a telegram—the telegram announcing James VanDrexel's tragic and untimely death. On the back, she'd written what everyone who's ever been associated with the circus has long considered its most important rule: *The Show Must Go On.*

What Callie realized the night her mother read Gram's letter aloud to her and Jenna, pausing to weep, stopping to laugh, her eyes twinkling as only a VanDrexel's could, was that the rule itself was unfinished, incomplete. There was more to the lesson, and it had nothing to do with not disappointing the spectators who paid for their tickets and came for the show. That was the business part; what Callie now understood was the life lesson part, and it was this:

The show must go on, even when it's not the show you expected to be in.

And it doesn't just go on for one night, it goes on for infinity, like the rings on the floor of the Big Top. The show gets passed down from those who lived it to those who are living it, to the ones yet to live it, with all its surprises, and changes, the catches made high above the crowd and the falls into the safety of a waiting net.

The show must go on whatever the show turns out to be. And it does.

So Victoria's little Cartier masterpiece would go up for auction, and while most of the money would be put in trust for Callie, a portion of the proceeds would be spent on the best alcohol rehabilitation program they could find, where Jenna's mother would be allowed to stay for as long as she needed in order to find her way home.

Because home is everything.

And finally, a small amount of the cash would go toward covering the cost of two airplane tickets. To Boston.

Callie knew that people often left instructions about where they would like their ashes to be scattered. Victoria had left no such directions, and to be honest, Callie wasn't ready to part with the Victoria-ness she believed was still in some way present in the powdery contents of that pretty pewter urn. Indeed, she might never be ready.

But she had the notes . . . the lessons, written in her grandmother's distinctive penmanship, written from her heart. For Callie there was no doubt that a glimmer of Victoria's essence could be found in every one of those mismatched, inexplicable scraps.

So on the day before she and Quinn were scheduled to fly to Boston, Callie removed all the notes from the corkboard one by one, taking the time to read each sentiment again, contemplating how it was that Victoria had come to write *this* rule on *this* scrap, and trying to guess in what order the lessons had brought themselves into her life. Of course, these were things she'd never really know for sure, but there was something deeply warm and wishful in the wondering.

When nothing remained on the bulletin board but the black-and-white candid of Victoria and James holding hands beside the lion's cage, Callie gathered up the notes, placed them in a shallow tin pail, and set them aflame.

As she sat in the driveway of the carriage house watching them curl up and turn to char, somewhere not far off, the mighty DiCaprio chose that moment to offer up a roar. It filled the gathering twilight and seemed to shake the stars.

In the pail the fire went small, then cool. And what remained were the ashes she would take with her to Boston.

Finding the Brooksvale fairgrounds was a bit of a challenge, since most of the field to which Catherine Hastings had run on that spring evening in 1965 had been developed or paved over decades ago. A small grassy park was all that was left to bear witness to the magnificent fact that twice, a long time ago, the circus had indeed come to town.

Quinn and Callie found a place to set up the portable tightrope they'd brought from home, and when the line was taut and ready, Callie mounted the wire. Onlookers whispered, but she didn't care; she was used to whispers like that.

In each hand she held a fistful of ash, and in her heart she carried the words she'd heard Victoria say a thousand times—*Shoulders back, Calliope! Center of gravity! Keep moving forward . . . always moving forward . . .*

Gliding to the midpoint of the wire, Callie slowly stretched her arms outward and unfurled her fingers. Feeling the nearness of the sky, the ashes began to stir against her palms. With her breath in her throat, Callie flung up her hands to release the words and wisdom of a life hard-earned:

When in doubt . . . show no fear . . . come full circle . . . those who know . . .

Beneath Callie's feet, the wire felt friendly and alive; above her head the cinders caught the breeze, powdering the air with Victoria's memories, which swirled and drifted until they disappeared. For all the gifts her grandmother had given her, Callie knew that this was the most precious, and the most permanent thing that she could give in return:

A place where a girl named Catherine could always remain safely above dangerous ground, where lessons are taught and lessons are learned and somewhere along the way, they are elevated from lesson to legacy.

The air above Brooksvale took in the ashes, and made them a part of itself, just as Cornelius and his circus had taken in a frightened girl, and made her feel safe and worthwhile—just as any sanctuary of any kind will always seek to protect those who need it most.

Step right up . . .

Prepare to be enchanted.

And always, keep moving forward.

Because this is how you make your mark on the circus. This is how you make your mark on the world.

This is how you walk the sky.

EPILOGUE

My Dearest Quinn Emily Sharon VanDrexel,

If you've found this, it is meant to be. If you, my darling girl, daughter of the circus, star of my life, have discovered this letter, then it is meant to be that you should know.

I am writing to you just moments following your birth on this, your opening night, in the midst of my debut performance as your mother.

What I am about to record are the things I have decided not to tell you about how you came to be born into VanDrexel's Family Circus. These are the parts of the story—my story—that are so painful, so complex, or simply carved out of places so deep inside of me, it would be impossible for me to tell them to you out loud.

But if you've found this, then it's meant to be.

First, about your name. Your grandfather Cornelius always said that a name should be a kind of enchantment, and I am confident that you will grow into yours, live up to it, and come to cherish it for the blessing that it is.

You are here, you exist, because of the grace of three women:

A woman called Sharon, who never got to Hollywood, but found a place where she could walk the sky.

A girl named Emily, who was one hell of a liar.

And my mother, Meredith Quinn, who, on the day the circus came to Brooksvale, found the strength to send me away with a priceless brooch

286

clutched in my trembling fist. (Since you have opened the drawer, you know that I was never forced to sell it as she intended, so it is yours now, to do with as you wish.)

I've named you after all of them, in the hope that a bit of the magic I took from each will forever sparkle inside of you, along with the magic you've inherited just by being of VanDrexel stock. Cornelius was both a conjurer and a saint, a teller of tales and a finder of those who were lost. He was a showman, a Ringmaster, and the only day of his life that he did not throw off sparks was the day his son—your father—was taken from us.

My life spun forth from what can only be called a whimsical cliché. I ran away to join the circus! But it did not begin as some glittering dream, or happy ambition. It began as an escape. I will never tell you because I do not want you to feel sorry for me. I only want you to look at me and see the luckiest woman who has ever lived. But before I was lucky, before my name was Victoria, I was Catherine Hastings of Brooksvale, Mass.

My father was Davis Winston Hastings, a man of so-called success and refinement, who was never more delighted than when he was feeling the force of his hand crashing against my face.

My mother was, in every way, his opposite and his superior. She was smart, she was kind, and in the end, she was fearless. Meredith Quinn was forced by the mores of her time to submit to her husband's arrogance. He hit her, I believe, harder and more frequently than he hit me, and I know that was how she wanted it. Because if his fists were landing on her, they were not landing on me. If his barbs and insults were slicing into her, then that was one moment in which I would not be made to feel worthless, less-than, despised. I am sorry to tell you that she never asked for help. I think she feared that it would have only made things worse, and she was probably right.

So she sent me to the circus.

And at the circus, I fell in love. With many things, actually. The *giggling-angel sound of the calliope, the quiet majesty of the animals, the miracle of learning to walk across a wire in the sky. But more than any of that, more than all of that, there was James.*

James VanDrexel, who called himself the younger, braver, more interesting son of the Ringmaster, who knew that a lion could be taught but not tamed, who dreamed of traveling far across the sea, so he could return home again better than he was when he left.

I did not join the circus ever intending to stay. I did not join to meet elephants, or to sew buttons, or even to walk the tightrope like a star. But then, I discovered that among clowns and dancers, sharp-shooters and lion tamers, I could be funny and brave. I could be someone I truly liked, and I could have a home. Because home is not a place. Home is the people who take care of you when you need it, and even when you don't.

I never did tell James the truth about my past. I think perhaps I was ashamed of the life I'd lived before I came home to the circus. I didn't want him ever to equate his Victoria with someone else's Catherine, a girl whose own father could hold her in such low esteem. This, I believe, is something all creatures who've been abused must feel. After being hit enough times, you come to think of yourself as worthy of nothing except being hit.

You already know (because this is something I will tell you when you are old enough to understand) that your father died in an incident overseas, but the whole truth is that he was killed in an altercation with a man who'd been brutally beating a lion. As the story was later told to me by the <u>Monsieur Loyal</u> *whose misfortune it had been to watch the tragedy unfold, James had witnessed a French lion tamer punishing a lioness by attacking her with a metal rod. He immediately intervened, warning the abuser that if such violence were repeated, he would sorely regret it. The man did not heed the warning, and when your father saw him again days later punishing the cat in the same manner, he threw himself into the cage to put himself between the man and the lion. But the man did not back down; instead he turned his metal rod on James, and began beating him as relentlessly as he had beaten the cat.*

When it was over, my beloved, heroic James lay dead in the lion's cage.

And I confess that it was all my fault.

You see, your father was only there because I chose to keep the news of you a secret from him. He never knew, not even for the space of a heartbeat, that you were there, waiting to be his, waiting to be ours. If only I had told him about you, I'm sure he would be alive today, gathering you into his arms. But he's not.

And for that, Quinn, I am more sorry than I can ever say.

We learned that we lost James in a telegram, which I have enclosed here. On the back of it is written something I've heard repeated again and again since the day I arrived at the circus, but did not fully understand until the day we heard of James's death. It was the last time I would ever write down one of my lessons. I suppose I thought that in losing James I'd learned everything there was to know, and in the worst possible way.

But then, one day . . . this day, Quinn . . . there is you. Small and sweet and perfect, resting now in my arms, but how fitting it seems that up until this moment, the place in my body where I carried you is the place where all true balance begins and ends—my center of gravity. For nine months you nestled there, and the anticipation of you is what kept me on my feet. Once, on a breezy day, in a rumbling truck, I heard a friend utter a phrase in a way that made me think it contained the answer to every question in the cosmos. "Mothers and daughters," she said, and it was as though she were sure it was the most powerful prayer in the whole wide world. And today, because of you, I understand that she was right.

The night we learned that your father was dead, I walked the wire. Before I climbed the ladder, I asked your grandpa Cornelius to introduce me for the first time as Victoria VanDrexel. And as the crowd looked on and cheered, I felt my heart take comfort. Then I went back to my train car and wrote down the greatest truth I would ever know: The show must go on. And so it does, and so it will.

Of all the many wishes I have for you, the greatest is that when the time is right for you to choose your dream, you will go after it with everything you are. As I look at you now, with your tiny fingers fluttering gracefully, I can clearly picture your father's hands, reaching out to stroke a trembling lion, to pat a charismatic camel, to feed a charming elephant, and I wonder if perhaps you have already inherited his great love and respect for animals, his noble instinct to protect and to appreciate these mysterious, innocent creatures. If that turns out to be the case, well, I will be more proud than I can say.

But for now, little one, I welcome you to your home in the circus, my darling, my coconspirator, my child.

Your loving mother,
Victoria